The Stell^rs

Jeffrey Aronson

Published by Jeffrey Aronson, 2024.

The Stell^rs
ISBN: 979-8-218-98107-5
Copyright © 2023 by Jeffrey Aronson
Registration Number TXu 2-388-650
Effective Date of Registration: August 23, 2023
Registration Decision Date: October 5, 2023
Thestellarsbook@gmail.com
Thestellarsbook.com The Stell^rs website available in the Fall

This book is a work of fiction. Any references to future historical events, people, or real places, including the aliens are products of the imagination of the author, but then again...

THE STELL^RS

First edition. August 5, 2024.

ISBN: 979-8218981075

Written by Jeffrey Aronson.

Table of Contents

A bit of background on the Stell^rs

The Stell^rs have been closely watching the Earth from the far side of the moon for thousands of years. To their utter amazement, the humans have not yet destroyed themselves or their planet since dropping the first atomic bomb in 1945. And now it's a race against the clock to stop that from happening.

The Stell^rs are extraterrestrials that reside on different habitable planets across the Milky Way and Andromeda galaxies. While they are an incredibly diverse community, they coexist in peaceful harmony. Their central home planet is Xanthe.

These Stell^r civilizations are two million years more advanced than humans on Earth. Through quantum advancements in genetics, biotech, nanobots, regenerative medicine, AI, disease management, mindfulness, and nutrition, their average lifespan is 1200 years. By the age of one thousand, 85% of their body parts have been replaced with replicas.

Their long lifespan allows the Stell^rs to explore the cosmos and expand their benevolent ways with other civilizations that are ready and open to accepting them. They do not colonize worlds or introduce themselves to civilizations that are not willing partners or equipped to be part of the greater Stell^r community of planets.

The number one rule is no planet can be invited to join the Stell^r community if they are at war between their own people. Especially if they are a threat to each other with weapons of mass destruction. Currently on Earth, it's estimated there are over 13,000 nuclear weapons spread across nine countries.

However, after thousands of years, the Stell^rs are about to break their most important rule. They have no choice but to introduce themselves to the humans.

But why now? Strap in, as we travel through the galaxies to places near and far, to find out in this once in a lifetime adventure.

Dedication

The telling of this story is largely due to the inspiration of two men in 1962. One was my wonderful loving father, and the other was my soon-to-be childhood hero, John H. Glenn, Jr.

A significant memorable happening took place at 11:03 UTC on February 20, 1962. That event was the launching of the Mercury-Atlas 6 (MA-6) spacecraft piloted by astronaut John Glenn who strapped into his seat atop the enormous Atlas LV-3B rocket. He would be the first human to orbit the Earth three times. He may have also been the first human to witness unexplained objects floating around his capsule. He transmitted verbatim to mission control: "I am in a big mass of some very small particles, they're brilliantly lit up like they're luminescent. I never saw anything like it. They round a little: they're coming by the capsule and they look like little stars. A whole shower of them coming by. They swirl around the capsule and go in front of the window and they're all brilliantly lighted."

After Glenn's historic 4-hour 55 minute 3 orbits were completed, he touched down in the North Atlantic Ocean at 19:43:02 UTC.

It was one of my earliest childhood memories. Not long after the sun came up that day, my dad woke me up and said, "Son, today is going to be a great day that you will always remember." How right he was!

Thanks to my father, on that special morning 62 years ago, I officially became a child astronaut. My thoughts were consumed with everything outer space, the planets, the galaxies and my first thought-provoking question was now swirling around in my young head: are we really alone in the universe?

And that answer would be a resounding no, we are certainly not alone in the vastness of the cosmos. As Carl Sagan once said- "The universe is a pretty big place. If it's just for us, seems like an awful waste of space."

I believe that one day in the near future, we will have that answer. It will change everything forever.

Jeff Aronson

March 27, 2024

Prologue

Over New Mexico

July 1947

Their shuttle craft surveilled New Mexico for three days, checking on military installations. Commander Roseaelyn and her copilot, Fralix, were concerned specifically about the further expansion of the US nuclear program. Only two years earlier, on July 16, 1945, the first test had occurred in Los Alamos, about a hundred miles north of Albuquerque, which they were flying above at that very moment.

She remembered the reverberations on the moon base from that explosion, the alarms that had shrieked and screamed. People had *felt it,* as if a vast chasm had been torn open in the universe.

What do you think, Commander? Should we continue south? We haven't seen much so far around here that indicates proliferation.

Let's be sure and head over to Roswell, Las Cruces, and Carlsbad.

He nodded, made a couple of instrument adjustments, then let a part of himself meld with their vehicle, as she did. They had perfected the meld long ago when they realized they didn't need spoken words. Not many Stell^rs did. But when piloting a spacecraft, spoken words were sometimes needed between most pilots and copilots. Yet, she and Fralix were the exception in that regard. It was part of why they were always paired on these missions.

This was their fifth surveillance together of Earth. In the past, they surveyed other planets around this solar system. The Council had made it a priority to search for viability across the cosmos. However, ever since the Los Alamos event, they had been focusing a great deal around the American southwest. And before that, closer to Xanthe, in their own Andromeda Galaxy, searching for exoplanets to ensure its collective survival in the future. Rosaelyn's essential nature was that of an optimist, but that tear in the universe two years

5

ago had daunted her optimism about the survival of Earth. Now that the power of that atomic explosion had been witnessed, what was to prevent the proliferation of nuclear weapons and eventual Armageddon?

You're fretting, Fralix remarked.

Just trying to remain optimistic.

I understand. But maybe all that optimism is overrated. For centuries now, we've been sending those giant battle cruisers to within striking distance of the massive field of monster asteroids on a deadly glidepath heading towards Xanthe. We've vaporized a bunch of them, and now there are countless numbers of smaller boulders headed toward us. I mean, those fragments of boulders will obliterate our home planet by 2056. And we'll still be alive. I have a tough time being optimistic. I'm fine living on the far side of the moon for now.

She wasn't. The moon was cold and inhospitable. Earth was a beautiful planet, but the population was hostile and prone to violence, and now it was armed with nuclear weapons. Who knew what would happen next now that these primitive people had unleashed the power of the atom?

When they were over a military base in Roswell, their ship suddenly began to lose altitude for no reason that she could determine. She snapped out of the meld, anxiously scanned the instrument panel, and realized there had been a catastrophic malfunction in the craft. It plunged downward through clouds, sunlight, and she leaped up and pulled on a special crash suit.

Fralix hadn't moved.

"The suit!" she screamed. "Fralix, c'mon, put on the suit!"

The sound of her shouts shocked her as deeply as Fralix's paralysis, his inability to snap out of the meld. Once Rosaelyn was suited up, she grabbed his shoulders, struggling to pull him free. But now she would see the land below clearly, rushing towards them, and then instinctively threw herself into the pilot's seat and secured herself for the inevitable.

Minutes before impact, Rosaelyn removed a device, a part of her suit that sent continuous signals back to the moon base. She crushed it. If she had any chance of survival, it would need to look like she'd died in the crash. The Stell^rs wouldn't take the chance on their technology being reversed engineered and would destroy the craft if they were sure they'd perished.

When she looked up again, the Earth was nearly close enough to smell, to touch— that infinite desert, the heat, the strange white sands. She forced herself to lose consciousness seconds before impact, but the telepathic part of her still experienced it and felt the severe injuries to her physical body. She knew that Fralix had died on impact. Then even that part of her sank into darkness.

When Rosaelyn came to, she was in a military hospital. Her injuries were bad but not life-threatening because of her crash suit, and yet she might have died because of their rudimentary medical devices. So she had to telepathically instruct the two physicians what to do for her with the primitive medical instruments they had.

As they followed her instructions, she could hear them talking. "Mark, we're operating on an alien! Look at the bluish skin, its face!"

"I, uh, saw the craft. So did you. Not one of ours... And her eyes were large and oval shaped. Dan, how the hell are we doing what we're doing?"

"She's...guiding us... I hear her voice in my head. The bleeding has stopped. I...I don't know how, but it has."

"Does she have a heart? A pulse? Blood pressure? I'm not sure."

Dan brought his fingers to the side of her thin neck.

"Okay, a heartbeat. Slow, very slow, but present."

Now he fastened a cuff to her arm and took her blood pressure.

"Okay, pressure appears good. It's..."

Doesn't matter, she told him. *I'm still bleeding internally. You need to cut me open on the right side, near where your appendix is, and cauterize my bleeding intestine.*

"She's telling me...that..." Dan stuttered as he removed the cuff.

"I hear her, too."

"Since she's still conscious, she must be able to feel pain, right?" Dan asked.

I'm not conscious as you know it. I won't feel pain. Just hurry up or I'll bleed out.

And in those moments when one of them made an incision, she visualized the spacecraft the Stell^rs on the moon base had dispatched; the ship now circled the remains of her crashed shuttle. They believed that neither she nor Fralix had survived, that nothing could have survived it, and they had fired a pulse beam that vaporized the remnants of her destroyed transport. Along with the remains of her good friend Fralix.

I'm now it, she thought.

"Jesus, look at the blood," Mark exclaimed. "We gotta act fast. And she's saying that she's *it*. What the hell does that mean?"

She felt Dan's hands against her intestines, his hands in the pools of blood. *Hurry, please. I don't know how much longer I can hold on.*

"You hear that?" Mark exclaimed. "We gotta move fast. Hold that intestine steady. Or whatever the heck it is. Okay, good, that's good... I see it!" Mark shouted. "Hold it steady, Dan. I can get it. Steady..."

For an instant, she felt the unbearably intense heat, felt the bleeding stop, and knew she would survive. Then Rosaelyn sank into a darkness so thick and pervasive that she lost track of everything.

Part One

Discovery

"The real voyage of discovery consists not in seeking new landscapes, but in having new eyes."
— Marcel Proust

Chapter 1

A New President

August 2029

President James Mitchum sat at his desk in the Oval Office, going through computer files during the congressional hearings on UAPs that were held six years ago in August 2023.

His Golden Retriever, Nomad, was stretched out in a patch of sunlight that streamed through the windows. Now and then he sighed heavily, as if he were dreaming. Jim, as he was known by his friends, leaned over and drew his fingers through Nomad's reddish fur.

In the last seven months—Mitchum's first year as president—everyone in the White House had grown to love Nomad and always had treats readily available. Maybe too available. Whenever a visitor arrived, Nomad checked them out. If his tail failed to wag, if he didn't offer his belly to be scratched, if he emitted a low growl, it meant the individual wasn't trustworthy. That had happened when Alexander Zhukov, current leader of Russia, had visited a month or so after Mitchum's inauguration, and Nomad had taken one look at him and bared his teeth. Zhukov paled and requested that the dog be removed.

Mitchum turned back to the files on the UAPs and searched for more definitive information. But there was nothing. It incensed him that so little information about any of this had been released. He punched out the extension for his chief of staff, Steve Whitley.

"Hey Jim," Whitley said. "What's up?"

"Can you stop by my office when you get a chance?"

"Be there in five."

When Whitley entered the office, Nomad immediately woke up and trotted over to him, tail whipping back and forth. "My favorite dog," Whitley said, stroking him, then reached into his jacket pocket and brought out a treat. "Sit, Nomad."

Nomad sat.

"Good boy." Whitley handed him the treat, then settled in one of the chairs in front of Mitchum's desk.

Whitley, in his early fifties, had been involved in politics for nearly two decades. He knew the ins and outs of it all so well that Mitchum's question didn't faze him.

"What do you know about Area 51, Steve?"

"Pretty much just what I heard in those congressional hearings and on *X-Files*." He smiled at that last part. "My daughter loved that show when she was a kid, so Judy and I saw every episode. Why?"

"I want to know what's being kept at Area 51 in Nevada. All of it."

Whitley frowned. "Does this go back to your time on the International Space Station and what you saw?"

"Yes." In 2002, when he was 31, he'd been one of four astronauts on the ISS and had seen a UFO—triangular with a transparent dome on the top—while conducting an experiment in the lab. The iPhone hadn't been invented yet, and he'd used his clunky old cell phone to snap photos, which hadn't shown much of anything. By the time he'd scrambled to find a better camera, the unusual spacecraft had sped off.

"You sure you want to go there?"

No, he wasn't sure. He had been president for just seven months. Suppose all the lore and conspiracy theories were right? Suppose the DOD or some other agency has been keeping an alien in Area 51 for all these years? Did he really need to know that? And if the answer was yes, what kind of reality would that open up?

"Yes, I'm sure. I made inquiries to the Pentagon during my first term as senator and was completely ignored. I ran my campaign on the issue of transparency. And for decades, our government hasn't been transparent at all about Roswell, UFOs, any of it. Those congressional hearings six years ago were a joke." What was really going on in our cosmic backyard?

"Do you remember who you contacted at Defense when you were in the Senate?"

"Nope."

"It may not even be the Pentagon that knows," Whitley said. "But I'll talk to General Dirkson and see what I can find out."

"It's not just about finding out, Steve. I'd like to go there myself, as soon as possible, and have a look around. The fewer people who know the better."

Whitley looked somewhat rattled now. "I can arrange for Air Force One. How about the VP?"

"I'll call her and let her know." He wanted Helen Hargraves on this trip. He trusted her more than anyone, with the exception of Laurie, his lovely wife. She deserved to know whatever he found out. "Minimum of secret service, then you, me, Helen, and the pilot. And no Air Force One. The Gulfstream G700 would be ideal. It can hold nineteen and fly .85 mach."

"I hear the pilot and astronaut speaking here."

Mitchum grinned. "Yeah, well, still love that part of my life. This trip must be kept top secret. No press. No attention."

"You know about Janet Airlines, Jim?"

"Should I?"

"Yes. According to rumors and lore, the letters stand for Joint Air Network for Employee Transportation, or Just Another Non-Existent Terminal. They have a fleet of six Boeing 737s that fly out of Las Vegas to Area 51. One of our vetted ex-military pilots flies for them part-time. I know him. I'll see what he can do and recommends. We'd have to fly under cover at night, directly into Area 51."

"Thanks, Steve."

Whitley pushed to his feet and started toward the door but paused before he reached it and turned. "Question. Suppose there are aliens there. What then?"

"Beats me. I just want to *know*, Steve."

"Yeah, I'm with you. Me, too."

As soon as Whitley had left, Mitchum texted Helen. *You in the WH?*

With my espresso. You want a cup?

Definitely.

Bring Nomad. I got some new treats.

Mitchum pocketed his phone, whistled for Nomad. "C'mon, boy, let's go see Helen."

Nomad immediately got to his feet, tail wagging, and hurried to the door. He turned, making sure that Mitchum was behind him, and led the way down the hall to Helen's office. Nomad trotted in with a bark, announcing their arrival, and Helen quickly stood.

She was tall, probably 5'10" in her bare feet, and her thick blonde hair fell around her face as she leaned down to hug Nomad.

He licked her face, then wiggled free, barked, and sat down, tail thumping the floor.

"He knows you've got treats, Helen."

She reached into a jar of treats on her desk and slipped one out. "Some sort of concoction of dried pork or beef on a stick," she said. Nomad barked, and she laughed and handed it to him. Nomad took the treat gently, then settled on the floor next to her desk, working away at it. Mitchum noticed how immaculate Helen's desk was, just a large screen Apple computer, a yellow legal pad, and a pen.

"What's on your mind, Jim? Or are you just providing my Nomad fix?" She hooked her blond hair behind her ears, slipped on her blue rim glasses, and picked up the pen. "Ready to take notes."

"No notes. What do you know about Area 51?"

She grinned and leaned forward, those Aegean blue eyes fixed on him. "What're we onto, Mulder?"

"Well, Scully, it's like this. I want to know if all the lore is true. Are we keeping an alien there? Or *aliens*?"

She drew back with a laugh. "You must've watched *Independence Day* again."

"Yup. Laurie and I watched it the other night. I love that scene where Bill Pullman as the prez first enters the room that holds the UFO, and the wacko guy with the wild white hair tells him how exciting the last few days have been since the UFOs showed up on the planet. I doubt if the real place looks quite like the movie version, but I'd like to know for sure."

"Mulder, you've got that tone in your voice."

"Steve's going to arrange transport. Minimum of secret service, then the three of us and the pilots."

She sat back, momentarily pensive. "Are you sure about having POTUS and the VP on the same flight? I can meet you there and take a separate flight."

"Ok, but I'd like Nomad to join us. He can make friends with anyone. And as we learned with Zhukov, the dog reads character very well." Nomad raised his head, looked at each of them, aware that they were discussing him. Then he turned back to the treat to finish it. "Okay, six humans and one dog in two Gulfstreams."

"Great," she said. "When do we leave?"

"We have to wait to hear from Steve."

She rubbed her hands together. "Oh wow, I can't wait. Clothing for two days just in case?"

"Good plan."

"Keep me on speed text."

"You're there as Scully."

"My heroine!"

+++

At dusk, he still hadn't heard anything from Whitley, so he and Nomad went upstairs to his private residence. His wife, Laurie, was in the kitchen with their chef, who was instructing her in how to cook some complicated dish that smelled great. Laurie, a statuesque 5'11", wore a full apron, her dark hair was fixed at the back of her head. At 54, she was four years younger than he was and looked just as lovely as she had when they'd met at NYU. She'd been a freshman at the time, he was a senior, and he'd fallen in love with her on their first date. They were married four years later.

After graduation, he'd enlisted in the US Air Force and enrolled to become a fighter pilot. They'd moved to Vance Air Force Base in Oklahoma for his training, a vastly different place than Queens, and had relocated to various bases around the country so he could complete his training. He became an F-22 Raptor pilot, and after several years had enrolled in NASA's astronaut training program and excelled. He piloted several successful missions to the ISS, and after twenty years of service had returned home and run for a recently vacated Senate seat for New York. His experience as a pilot and an astronaut swept him into office in a landslide.

Five years later, he was nominated by his party for the presidency. On January 20, 2029, he was sworn in as the 48th President of the United States. Now, more than half way into his first year in office, he was ready to finally uncover the truth about Area 51.

Nomad bounded into the kitchen to greet Laurie and Carmen, the chef who had been with them since he was in the Senate. Carmen tossed him a plump chunk of what looked like chicken. "*No ha comido,*" she said.

He hasn't eaten.

She handed Laurie a large spoon and poured some dry food into Nomad's bowl. "We've got to cut down on the treats he has been getting," Mitchum said. "He has gained eight more pounds in the past year!"

"We?" Laurie drolled. "C'mon, he's with you nearly all day, so *you* need to make sure those treats are cut back." Laurie stirred whatever was in the pot. "You're going to love this,

Jim." She raised the spoon from the pot, sipped at the edge of it, then held the spoon out for Mitchum to sip from the other side.

He did. She was right. He loved whatever this was. Some sort of Cuban dish, he guessed. Carmen was like family, but she'd never had dinner with them. He and Laurie needed their time alone, especially this evening.

Once Carmen had fixed Nomad's dinner bowl, she took him outside for a walk and to do his business. "You look preoccupied," Laurie remarked, dishing up the concoction on the stove. "What's going on?"

"Area 51."

She looked at him, her eyes on fire. "Like we've talked about?"

"Yes. Steve is trying to put things together."

"Too many questions would be asked if I left with you. Just promise me that if you see an alien, I get to go with you two at some point in the future."

"Deal," he said, and kissed her hello.

+++

At 2:11 a.m., he got a text from Whitley. *I'm on the way to pick up you and Nomad. Be there in a few minutes.*

I'll be ready.

For situations like this, he used a burner phone with Whitley, Laurie, Helen, and Ken, the Secret Service agent who usually accompanied him on these oddball trips. He asked Ken to meet him at the foot of the stairs to the private residence. He occasionally used the burner phone with his daughter, too, but Emily had asked him to keep it at a minimum. *Every time one of those holographic messages comes through, Dad, I get worried.* So he didn't hologram her about this.

She was in her junior year at Smith, living in an apartment in Northampton, Mass. for the summer while she took a graduate school course in her passion—creative writing. Hell, if it turned out that the lore about Area 51 was true, maybe Emily would write the book on it. That was the kind of bizarre twist his life often took.

He woke Laurie and told her Whitley was on the way. "I'll message so keep the phone handy."

She patted her pillow. "Under here." She kissed him. "Stay safe, Jim."

"Nomad is coming, too."

"Perfect." Then her head dropped to the pillow.

He hurried out into the kitchen to get food and treats for Nomad for the flight to Nevada. He contacted Ken and asked him to meet him at the back stairs from the residence to the rear lot behind the White House.

When he stepped outside, the cool air bit at his cheeks. Nomad paced back and forth.

"Mr. President?"

He glanced around. "Hey, Ken. Sorry about the late hour."

"No problem, sir. Where're we off to?"

"Uh, Area 51."

He was a good-looking man in his mid-30s, well-built, and rarely seemed surprised by anything. But now his eyes widened. "For *real,* sir?"

"Yes."

"Awesome."

The 2 black SUV's pulled up, and Whitley hopped out and opened the passenger doors of the first vehicle, front and back. Nomad jumped inside and settled next to Jim and his secret service detail along with Todd, another young man in his mid to late 30s. Helen then got in the second vehicle with Whitley, who announced that we are taking 2 Gulfstreams. They fly about 700 miles an hour, so the trip should take a bit over three hours. A lot quicker and more comfortable than the Janet 737."

"Okay for Nomad to be on board?" Mitchum asked the driver.

"Yes. There's a small grassy area in the back."

A grassy area. Mitchum tried to imagine that and nearly laughed out loud.

"Does anyone know we're coming?" Helen asked Whitley.

"Nope." Whitley shook his head. "All of this is under the radar. Way under."

+++

They drove to Joint Base Andrews where the very private specially retrofitted Gulfstreams waited for them.

The SUV's pulled in between a van and the two aircraft, they all promptly exited the vehicles. The pilots strode toward them from the pair of sleek jets. "Air Force Colonel Russ Morgan. Pleased as hell to be tapped for this." He vigorously shook Mitchum's hand, then Helen's. "Such a pleasure. I voted for you. After the craziness of the last seven or eight years, it's wonderful to know that someone sane is in charge of the country."

"Thank you for your vote. I appreciate it." *I hope I'm still sane after this trip.*

"Do any of the employees you fly into Area 51 ever talk about their work?" Helen asked. "About what they see in there?"

"They're mostly aeronautical engineers working on the next generation of aircraft designs. Top secret stuff. I'm not allowed in. I drop the employees off, pick them up and take them back to Las Vegas." He gestured at the stairs and opened door. "Let's get things underway." He stroked Nomad's head. "You're one handsome dude."

Mitchum removed the dog's leash, and Nomad bounded up the stairs with Mitchum and the others behind him. Mitchum looked at Helen as she proceeded to Gulfstream II. "See you soon in the desert," he called.

A slender black woman greeted the President at the door with bottles of cold water and introduced herself. "Hi, I'm Lieutenant Vicki Harris, Colonel Morgan's copilot. Make yourself at home."

The interior was spacious enough for them to stretch out. Nomad got his own row of seats, and Mitchum gave him a chewy to keep him occupied during takeoff. The plane, of course, was technologically well connected. In front of each seat was a screen and a charger for devices. Since it was barely three in the morning, Vicki handed out pillows and blankets and asked if he or Whitley wanted a bite to eat or coffee. "I'll be serving breakfast in 90 minutes or so." She set a bowl of water in the aisle next to Nomad's row, and Mitchum got out a bowl and poured in some dry food. He set it next to the bowl of water.

He reached over the top of the seats and stroked the dog's head. "I think you're pretty well set for a while, big guy."

Nomad raised his head and drew his warm, moist tongue over the back of Mitchum's hand, then turned back to the chewy.

As the two Gulfstreams started moving along the runway, Mitchum's burner phone dinged with messages. Two of them, from Laurie:

How's Nomad doing on a plane?

When do you think you'll be back?

He snapped a photo of the dog and sent it to her. *He made himself right at home. It's just three hours in this Gulfstream. So probably later tonight or early tomorrow a.m.*

People will ask where you are.

I left instructions for Barb to say that Helen and I are on a sensitive diplomatic mission.

Barbara was the White House Press Secretary. Like Whitley, she had plenty of political experience and knew how to deal with pushy members of the press. She also knew the purpose of this flight. He had messaged her.

Taxiing. Will hm later.

Already got an inquiry from journalist who saw Steve's black SUV leaving from the WH. Told him the cover story. I'm sure there will be other inquiries now. Let me know if you find you know what!

Will do.

He shrugged off his jacket, plugged the phone into a portable charger and slipped it into his shirt pocket, then plugged the official phone into the seat charger. He reclined his seat, fluffed up his pillow, drew the blanket over himself, and promptly fell asleep.

At some point, Nomad woke him up the same way he sometimes did in the White House, with a whine and a lick that meant he had to go outside. "No yard here, Nomad." He got up and walked him to the back of the plane, just beyond the bathrooms, where the fake grass was laid out. As Nomad sniffed around, Lt. Vicki Harris joined them.

"You need anything, Mr. President?"

"No, I'm good, thanks, Vicki. Where are we now?"

"An hour closer. I'll be bringing breakfast around in a few minutes."

Nomad did his business in the plot of grass, and a fan embedded somewhere underneath it whipped on and dried the area. "Interesting addition, that fan."

She nodded.

"C'mon, guy, I need to get some more sleep. Or get ready for a really early breakfast."

Nomad led the way back to their seats.

.

.

Chapter 2

Stell^r Commander Rosaelyn

Commander Rosaelyn, now known simply as Rose, sat in the library of Area 51, studying the designs spread out across the table. Liam Powers, one of the aeronautical engineers, had left them with her yesterday. *I just need to know if this design is viable, Rose, for an exceptional spaceship that can reach the moon in under 24 hours.*

It wasn't just viable, it was brilliant. On the computer she used in here, she jotted some suggestions that would make the trip of 240,000 miles smoother, more comfortable, and more protected. These engineers had come a long way since she'd started working with a group of them in 1948, at Harry Truman's urging.

She'd never met Truman, but he'd been aware of her existence. In 1955, Ike was the first President who had come to Area 51—initially just to *see* her, but then he changed his mind and wanted to talk with her. He asked about the injuries she'd sustained in the crash in 1947 at Roswell, and wanted to know when they had moved her here and where were her people from.

Rose answered all his questions, then he asked her what she *wanted,* what she *needed,* and she liked him for asking, which no one ever had. She'd told him she'd love to use the facility library, to help with more aeronautical designs, to eat different food, to have living quarters that were larger and more comfortable, and that she would like to take a walk outside. She hadn't been outside in nearly eight Earth years.

He'd been appalled by that and because he was such a gentleman, he'd offered her his arm. *A stroll in the sunlight, Rose?*

To leave her private quarters, they'd headed through a pair of enormous vault-like doors, then strolled down a long corridor where several security people stared at them, and finally, they were outside.

Rose inhaled the desert air, the smell of the heat against the sand. Eight long years. She had almost wept with joy.

In the end, Ike had been responsible for her being moved to larger, more comfortable quarters, for her being able to use the library as often as she'd liked and being allowed outside for brief periods. More engineers had begun to consult her about their designs, with questions that begged for answers. Rose had liked and admired Ike.

The library doors suddenly flew open, and Liam Powers hurried in, his cheeks flushed. He had a strong odor around him—of excitement and maybe a dash of dread. "Two planes just landed. Two G700's! Rumors are rampant. You should probably get back to your quarters."

"Why? Is it someone hostile?"

"We don't know. The..." His phone rang. He glanced quickly at the screen. "You won't believe this Rose. It's the President, VP, and Chief of Staff. No one knew he was headed here; they didn't have any warning. The guards outside are, like, my G-d, we gotta let him in, he's POTUS..." He paused and glanced up.

Now she felt his panic.

It's okay, Liam. She spoke to him telepathically, and he immediately calmed down. *I'll be fine here in the library. And your design is brilliant. But I've got a few suggestions for improvements when we have a chance to talk.*

His face drained of color. He wrenched back. "Wow, I heard...your voice in my head. How'd you... do that, Rose?"

"It's how my people communicate most of the time. If it's okay with you, I'd like to stay right here. I don't feel like hiding somewhere in this cavernous place, Liam. The last president who came here was JFK. He believed he was going to see some weird thing with huge eyes and gray skin. He wasn't expecting a woman with bluish skin who was six and a half feet tall."

Liam looked at her for a long moment, then laughed. "Wow, JFK. What year was that Rose?"

"October 1962, in the middle of the Cuban Missile Crisis. When he realized we could communicate, he asked me what the hell he should do. So I gave him my opinion."

Powers ran his fingers back through his chocolate brown hair. "By the stars," he breathed, and hurried over to where she sat. "So how can I improve this design, Rose?"

He pulled up a chair and she started talking about the specifics. His phone kept dinging, and he broke in with mini reports on where the president's party was now in Area 51. "Look." He brought up a video someone had sent of the presidential group.

She recognized three of the humans from TV—the President, VP, and Steve Whitley. She guessed the other two men were secret service. And with them was a creature she knew about but had seen only on television and the Internet. A dog. Golden Retriever. Then the group was at the open library doors, and she and Liam stared at them, and they stared back, and the dog barked and trotted in.

The Golden came right over to Rose, sat down, and lifted his right paw. Rose took it in her hand. "Good to meet you...."

"Nomad," said Whitley. "His name is Nomad."

"Well, my pleasure, Nomad." And telepathically she whispered, *Thank you for befriending me.*

She knew that even if he didn't understand the words, he certainly understood the sentiment. He barked, plopped to the floor, and rolled onto his back, offering his belly for a rub. She smiled and obliged him, then introduced herself to the President, Helen Hargraves, Whitley, and the other two men. "And this brilliant man with me is Liam Powers, one of your amazing aeronautical engineers."

Flustered, Powers shook hands with all of them and then leaned in close to Nomad. "You may be the most beautiful dog I've ever laid eyes on."

Nomad barked—in agreement? Rose wondered. Then Nomad offered Liam a paw, too. That raised paw was his seal of approval.

"You mind if we join you both?" Mitchum asked.

"Please," Rose said, gesturing at the table, the empty chairs.

The Mitchum party claimed chairs. Powers found a bowl somewhere, filled it with water, and set it in front of Nomad. Then he sat at the opposite end of the table, flanked on either side by Secret Service men.

"Rose, this is just truly unbelievable. There are no words to express the countless thoughts running through my head at this historic moment. It changes everything. I have so many questions I'm not sure where to begin," Mitchum said.

Whitley leaned forward. "Well, I do. Where are you from? What planet? What star system? Why'd you come here?" Mitchum gave his Chief of Staff a stern look to take it easy.

Mitchum noticed how Whitley's eyes locked with hers for a long, intense moment as something passed between them. Then he heard Rose's voice in his own head. *I'll handle his question.* It stunned him to realize she was telepathic.

"To answer your question, Mr. Whitley, in 1945, this country, your country, tested a nuclear bomb. We felt it on our moon base. It tore open a chasm in the universe. So two years later, my copilot and I were sent from the far side of the moon, where Xanthe had a home base, to find out if you humans had more weapons like that. Our shuttle craft malfunctioned over Roswell, and we crashed. My copilot was killed, I was seriously injured. I was moved here to Area 51 after I healed." Whitley was still in shock knowing that Rose entered his mind.

Mitchum next vocalized, "How far is Xanthe from Earth?"

"Ten light years."

"And all this time your people have had a hidden base on the far side of the moon?" Helen asked.

"Since the early part of the twentieth century."

"She has been helping our engineers with designs for the next generation of space vehicles," Powers said. "And the next generation of stealth aircraft. She helped design the VB-21 Raider."

"An absolutely incredible aircraft," Mitchum said.

"Have you flown in it, Mr. President?"

"Not yet."

"You'll love it," Rose said. "Ever since Ike gave me access to the library here, I've been reading everything and studying human history and culture."

"Ike," Mitchum repeated. "Eisenhower?"

She nodded. "You're only the third president who has come here."

"JFK was here," Powers exclaimed.

"What was he like?" Helen asked.

"A terrific man. It was during the Cuban Missile Crisis. He was under a lot of stress. He asked my advice about it, and I gave it. He followed my advice and war was avoided."

"Impressive," Mitchum said.

She sensed that Mitchum possessed the precognitive vision of JFK, the moral compass of Ike. But there was something else about him that struck her as rare in humans—the guiding force in his life wasn't religion or self-interest. For him, that force lay in doing what was *right*.

+++

Mitchum's questions multiplied almost too quickly for him to keep straight. "Were you shocked when he was assassinated?"

She folded her long, bluish fingers together on the top of the table and leaned forward. Except for the color of her skin and her rather large head, she didn't look like any alien image Mitchum had ever seen of the so-called Grays and other descriptions in science fiction folklore. Her face was young, exceptionally pretty, with high cheekbones and large almond-shaped eyes. Her mouth was small, but her smile was comforting. Her dark hair fell in graceful waves along the side of her face, but he was fairly certain it was a wig.

He felt shocked, humbled, jubilant, and then royally pissed off that Rose has lived in Area 51 for 78 years and that the place. The location was an urban legend, the fodder of books, podcasts, and conspiracy theories.

He was six-two, but she must have been at least four inches taller. She towered over the rest of them even when everyone was seated.

"Shocked?" she repeated. "No. Saddened. There was an aura of death around him, and I warned him to be careful."

"So you're psychic?" Helen asked.

We Stell^rs prefer to communicate like this.

"I already experienced your telepathy," Mitchum said.

Whitley acknowledged the same. The others all looked shocked.

"Wow," Helen exclaimed.

"A lot easier than talking," Powers said.

"That was...indescribable," Whitley murmured.

Ken seemed worried. "Are we supposed to be privy to all this, Mr. President?"

"Yes, it's fine."

"That's good," Rose said, "Because if your answer had been no, he and Todd would have to leave the room. My telepathic net is for anyone in this room. People are more accepting these days than they were 50 years ago. If it's okay with all of you, telepathy is the easiest way to me to provide you with my history."

"Then by all means continue," Mitchum said.

Nomad raised his head and looked at them. Rose glanced at him. "Your dog is very perceptive, Mr. President. He could hear me as well as you four did."

"You got that, Nomad?" He stroked the dog's head. "So please tell us all about your home planet, your people, all of it."

So she did.

She began by showing them images of her home planet, Andromeda, and some of her elders, who had lived out the full lifetime of most Stell^rs, 1,200 years. She showed them images of her family's move to Xanthe and how early Stell^r explorers first arrived on Earth during the Paleolithic era some 35,000 to 40,000 years ago. If they'd been cruising around Earth tens of thousands of years ago, Mitchum understood just how advanced their technology was.

At the time, they'd observed the beings on Earth by hovering at an altitude high enough in the atmosphere so they couldn't be seen. Even 35,000 years ago, their crafts didn't need to replenish supplies or anything else and could travel one light year—a trillion miles—in a single Earth year. The Stell^rs were also exploring other galaxies for livable exoplanets to ensure Xanthe's collective survival well into the future.

She also showed them images of Zorgons, a hostile species of bipedal reptiles and the greatest threat to the Stell^rs as their interstellar capabilities further developed.

In terms of their long lives, Rose communicated that when a Stell^r reached 1,000, nearly 85 percent of their body parts had been replaced. Mitchum suddenly broke the telepathic connection and spoke aloud. "How old are you, Rose?"

The others also snapped out of the telepathic connection.

"I was wondering the same thing," Powers said. "I mean, you don't look a day over 30."

Rose's smile struck Mitchum as enigmatic. "I was born in the Earth year 1892."

"*What?*" Whitley balked. "You're *137?*"

"Incredible!" Helen exclaimed. "That number represents the fine structure constant. It gauges the strength of the electromagnetic force, and this force governs how charged elementary particles like electrons interact with light's photons. It determines how stars burn, how chemistry happens, and even whether atoms exist all. Physicists now refer to it as the DNA of light."

Mitchum smiled and remembered that his brilliant VP held a graduate degree in physics.

"The number on our craft was 137," Rose said. "So now I'm going to think of this year as my year of light!"

"Now tell us more about yourself," Whitley said. "Your planet, culture, everything."

And for the next several hours, she filled their heads with images that told them a great deal about her life and background and the Stell^rs and their history. And when Mitchum felt like he and the others were on information overload, he disengaged from that telepathic connection and so did everyone else.

"I need a break," Powers said. "Anyone like some water? Coffee? Snacks? Anything?"

Mitchum also got to his feet. "Water and coffee for me. Anyone else?"

Whitley pushed his chair back and stood. Nomad was already up, tail wagging. "I need to walk around. So does Nomad. Rose, can you and Liam give us a tour?"

"I'm supposed to be escorted every time I leave the library. I'm not allowed to wander around."

"You'll be with the President." Mitchum said. "Who's going to object to that?"

She grinned. "No one!"

Helen got up, too, and so did Ken and Todd, and they all headed to the door, the dog leading the way. "I'd love to see your quarters," Helen said.

Mitchum nodded. "Me, too. I hope it's comfortable enough. Can you walk around outside? What can I do to make your stay here more productive for you?"

"I'd love to be able to get outside more frequently. In 78 years, I think I've proven I'm not a flight risk."

"You should be able to walk around wherever and whenever you want," Helen said. "Jim and I will make sure it happens."

"In fact, let's take a walk outside now, " Mitchum said. "Nomad could use a bathroom break."

The dog, hearing his name, glanced back at Mitchum, and barked.

Helen laughed. "That makes it official."

"This way," Powers said, and turned right up a long, wide corridor.

+++

The soldiers in this corridor watched them as they moved along with Liam and Nomad in the lead, and of course no one stopped them. Or her. No one said anything. But they saluted Mitchum, and he saluted in return. Rose liked the freedom of walking toward the outside door without interruption, challenge, or questions.

"Let's stop by your quarters on the way back in," Mitchum suggested, and pushed open the door to the outside.

It wasn't the surrounding desert, but a spacious patio area with grass, various cacti, a fountain, some benches, and a couple of tables. A 10-foot-high brick wall enclosed all of it, and it looked like it had electrified wiring on top of it. That part, Rose thought, was a bit much. The slant of the sun spoke of midafternoon, and although the air was chilly, the sunlight felt good.

Nomad hurried off to the grass and they all settled at one of the tables. "Sometimes I sit out here studying the designs that Liam and his team bring me," Rose said. "The air smells so good."

"Different than Xanthe?" Helen asked.

"Yes and no."

She showed them telepathic images of Xanthe's hillsides and oceans, its cities and houses and wooded areas. Then she showed them images she'd seen of the field of asteroids headed toward Xanthe that would obliterate her beloved home planet in 2056. "Even back in 1947, we were sending our giant battle cruisers to within striking distance of these planet-killing meteors and vaporized many of them. But there were still millions of smaller boulders on a deadly collision course to Xanthe. Maybe in the years I've been here, they've managed to destroy it. But I kind of doubt it."

"What's the population of Xanthe?" Mitchum asked.

"Now, it's probably 100 million Stell^rs."

She didn't mention that even back in the 1940s Plan B was to find suitable exoplanets where Xanthe's 100 million inhabitants could be relocated. During the years they'd been looking, they'd found only two suitable planets close enough to evacuate the entire populace. One planet twenty light years from Xanthe was uninhabited and the other planet was Earth.

Over 80 years ago, the Council leader of Xanthe, Epsilon, had declared Earth an ideal spot for the Stell^rs, with everything they could possibly need. However, the population might be hostile and prone to extreme violence. And that was before nuclear weapons. But because of any close proximity to early Neanderthals, they had unexpectedly and sadly wiped them out. Epsilon had made it explicitly clear they would need special space suits to protect humanity from the same fate. If Rose had some way of communicating with Epsilon, she could tell him that in 80 years, not a single human had died from her presence among them.

She debated mentioning all this to Mitchum and the others but decided not to since she didn't have any idea what had transpired on Xanthe since she'd left. Maybe they'd decimated the massive field of asteroids and didn't have to leave Xanthe. That would be the best development, but she doubted that had happened. By now, in 2029, the search would be intense for a place that could sustain the population of Xanthe and be close enough to reach before 2056.

What she really needed, she thought, wasn't just more sunlight and fresh air, but news about her home planet and news from Epsilon who believed she was dead. Then again, if she were Mitchum, she would want to know about the possibilities.

So, as Americans were fond of saying, it was a catch-22. Rose had learned American lingo from reading books and watching movies.

Before Mitchum's group left an hour later as evening set in, he drew her aside. "Rose, I'd like to invite you to stay with us at the White House, where you'll be much more comfortable. I'd also like to figure out a way to introduce you to the rest of the world without causing panic."

"I'd love that, thank you." She chuckled. "It would sure blow major holes in all the conspiracy theories. But there's something else you should know." *Here it comes,* she thought, and rushed on. "Even as far back as 1947, we knew that a field of massive asteroids was going to obliterate our planet by 2056. Unless the Stell^rs have figured out a way to eliminate that threat, they're going to need another planet to settle on. And this is the closest habitable planet. It takes ten years to travel to Earth from Xanthe. I suspect the Stell^r Leadership Council is making plans now, so you may hear from Epsilon, the Council leader, soon."

Mitchum's frown threw his handsome face into a chaos of worry lines. "They're going to move *100 million people* here?"

"I don't know what their current plans are. I haven't been in touch with any of them since my lunar shuttle craft crashed. Like I said, if they've eliminated the asteroid threat, then none of that will be necessary. But I feel it's only fair to inform you of all that."

"I appreciate it, Rose. I need to make some security preparations to move you to DC and that will take a bit of time. Meanwhile, decide what you would like to take with you."

"I don't have much. A few clothes, a couple of books from the library, eBooks on my device."

"Helen and Laurie, my wife, will love taking you shopping."

"Out in public?"

"At first I suspect it be through Amazon with a smile."

"I've been on that site. They don't deliver to Area 51."

Mitchum laughed. "Laurie and Helen will make sure you get whatever you need."

She extended her hand. He clasped it. Thank you so much, President Mitchum."

"Jim."

"You're rare for a human being, you know. I sense you aren't driven by money or power but by doing what's right. You have the moral compass that Ike had and the precognitive vision of JFK."

Mitchum's expression shifted. She could tell he was moved by her words. Then he did something no other human had ever done—he put his arms around her and hugged her. She was nearly half a foot taller and for her, it was like hugging a growing Stell^r child.

When he stepped back, he said, "I'm going to talk to Liam and make sure he watches after you until we can move you to the White House."

"He's a good man. He will."

Rose accompanied them back to the library, where Mitchum spoke for a few minutes privately with Liam. Nothing more was mentioned about visiting her quarters. Mitchum snapped several photos with his phone of the group and Rose with Nomad. Then

Helen and even Whitley hugged her goodbye, and they all shook hands with Liam. Even Nomad came over to say good-bye with a lick and a raised paw.

When they all left, Rose was sorry to see them go. She felt a pang of her long-time companion, loneliness.

Chapter 3

Jim & Rose

Exhaustion nibbled away at Mitchum, but he couldn't sleep. Every time he shut his eyes, he saw the images Rose had transmitted telepathically. Or he heard her quiet voice there at the end of their visit to the patio. *"Even as far back as 1947, we knew that a field of massive asteroids was going to obliterate our planet by 2056. Unless the Stell^rs have figured out a way to eliminate that threat, they're going to need another planet to settle on."*

Those words haunted him and so did the implications.

So often in his political career, there had been synchronous timing connected to events, decisions, people. Was his insistence on making this trip to Area 51, meeting Rose, and learning about her life, planet, and people part of some new synchronous timing event? *Are aliens finally going to make themselves known here? When will they arrive?*

Just the thought stunned him. That seismic earth-shattering revelation would irrevocably change everything forever. The people of Earth would have their ultimate answer. *Yes, life exists elsewhere. And their technology is millions of years ahead of ours.* And from the images Rose had transmitted to them, the Stell^rs were a peaceful race. *And there are 100 million of them!*

Considering how long Xanthe and the Stell^rs had been around, that number seemed small. Yet, with a lifespan of 1200 years, it made perfect sense. He wondered about this field of massive asteroids that she'd mentioned. If she'd known about it in 1947, how long had it been around? Where was it now? With Xanthe ten light years from Earth, could human scientists know anything about this?

He unplugged his phone from the charger, went online and Googled the Webb telescope, the most powerful ever invented. The query took him to NASA's website, where he read, "Webb studies every phase in the history of our Universe, ranging from the first luminous glows after the Big Bang, to the formation of solar systems capable of supporting life on planets like Earth, to the evolution of our own Solar System. "

...capable of supporting life on planets like Earth...

The images Rose had shown them of Xanthe certainly suggested it could support life, and Rose herself was a testament to that. Had the Webb telescope detected any fields of planet-killing asteroids like what Rose had described? He knew the Webb had observed the Crab Nebula, a supernova remnant 6,500 light years away in the constellation Taurus. By comparison, Xanthe was only ten light years from Earth. A close neighbor in the infinite vastness of space.

Mitchum knew the head of NASA well. That was why he nominated him for the position. When he was in the Senate, he'd reached out to Paul Spenser and asked how much NASA needed to get the Webb telescope up and running. They'd met several times in DC for dinner. Spenser had come over to his and Laurie's place in DC for a get-together, and he was a dog person. Several times, they had met at a local dog park, when Spenser had a German Shepherd and he and Laurie had had a black Lab. He'd come to understand that Spenser's passion was like his own—find life elsewhere in the cosmos. So in the Senate, Mitchum had gone to bat for additional funding—and it had come through.

So he holograph messaged (hm'd) Spenser on his private phone.

Paul, I know it's late, and I apologize. When you get a chance, can you check to see fields of massive asteroids Webb may have picked up ten light years from us, as far back as the late 1940s if not earlier? Will explain when I see you. Thank you, Jim.

The time on his phone was 10:13 p.m., which meant that back east it was very early tomorrow morning. Mitchum didn't expect Spenser to respond until he was home in the White House. But less than 30 minutes later, Spenser replied.

Got your message, figured I'd answer once the sun came up. But when my head hit the damn pillow, I couldn't go back to sleep. So I lay here thinking, remembering. Then I got on the computer and confirmed it. Xmas day, 2022. Our buddy Webb found several exoplanets around ten light years from here that might sustain life but no asteroids. Can you talk right now?

Mitchum: *On a flight right now.*

Spenser: *I think I heard it was a diplomatic mission.*

Mitchum: *That's how it turned out. I thought Webb could see asteroid belts.*

Spenser: *It's designed for infrared astronomy and thanks to its high resolution and sensitive instruments, it's able to view objects that are too old or distant for the Hubble. It can see the first stars and the formation of the earliest galaxies and provides details on the atmospheric characterization of potentially habitable planets. Because of the vast distance, it's not in real time. We see snapshots of the past.*

Mitchum wondered if any of the exoplanets the Webb had seem might be Xanthe. He supposed there was no way of knowing right now. But perhaps if Rose spoke with Spenser and looked at the information Webb had gleaned so far, she might be able to pinpoint Xanthe. Maybe it was a long shot, but what the hell.

Spenser : *May I ask, why are you asking?*

Mitchum: *I'll explain when I see you. How about a lunch or dinner soon?*

Spenser: *Just give me a date.*

Mitchum: *I'll touch base when I'm back in DC. But am going to send you a couple of photos you should delete as soon as you see them.*

Spenser : *OK.*

Mitchum hm'd him the photo he'd taken of Rose with Nomad and of Rose with Helen and Whitley.

His phone vibrated within 30 seconds, and Mitchum smiled when Spenser's number showed up.

"Really something, right?" Mitchum spoke quietly.

"Holy shit, Jim. An *alien*?"

"Hold on." Mitchum got up and went into the restroom, where his voice wouldn't wake the others. "Ok, I can now talk. Her name is Rose. She's from a planet called Xanthe, ten light years from Earth. She crashed in Roswell in 1947 and when her injuries healed, she was moved to Area 51, where she has lived ever since. She's telepathic."

"You left her back there?"

"I'm going to arrange to move her to the White House."

"I'd like to be a part of that."

Perfect. Spenser's scientific background as an astronomer would be ideal in talking with Rose. "Done. Now delete those photos."

"This is utterly fantastic. So it turns out all the conspiracy "crazies" were right. All these years, we've been hiding an actual galactic alien."

"Her people are called Stell^rs. They've been around, Paul, for millions of years and have a lifespan of 1,200 years. She's 137 years old."

Spenser chuckled. "How incredible. I gather from the photo that Nomad liked her?"

"He did. Raised his paw in greeting."

"Excellent."

There was a knock at the door. "Someone wants to use the restroom. Let's talk later today."

"I'll come by," Spenser said, and disconnected.

Mitchum unlocked and opened the restroom door. Whitley stood there, yawning. "You okay?"

"Yeah, fine. Was talking to Paul Spenser."

"He should've come with us."

"Yeah, he should have." Mitchum stepped out of the restroom, and he and Whitley settled in the front two seats. "I'd like to move Rose soon, within a few weeks or so. You willing to fly back there with Paul and do it? That way Helen and I won't have the press nosing around. We could arrange for the private Gulfstream again..."

"I'll make sure of it," Whitley said.

Nomad came over to where they were sitting and sat down in the aisle. Mitchum stroked his head. "You hungry? Thirsty? Need that patch of grass back there?"

Lt. Vicki Harris, the copilot, came over with a bowl of water and set it down in front of Nomad. He lapped at it. "He came back to the grass on his own and did his business. He's such a great dog, Mr. President."

"Thank you for accommodating him."

Mitchum got up to return to his seat where he had the extra bowl and some dry food and treats. He filled the bowl and Nomad gobbled down all of it, then climbed into his row of seats and promptly fell asleep. Mitchum stroked him. "Why can't I fall asleep like that? What's your secret, Nomad?"

The dog emitted a satisfied sigh and Mitchum sat back, fixed his pillow so his head sank into it, and pulled the blanket over him.

He dreamed about the frightening Zorgons that Rose had shown them, dreamed that they were pursuing the jet. He bolted awake suddenly to the smell of food and sunlight and the captain's voice.

"We've got another hour to Maryland, folks. Vicki is bringing around breakfast."

Whitley came out of the restroom looking a lot more rested than Mitchum felt and sat down next to him. "Your take, Jim?"

"We have a lot to learn from her. Liam told me her suggestions about their aeronautical designs have been brilliant, and that she really was the big brain behind the Raider and other breakthrough technologies. He also has been working on an advanced lunar spacecraft with her, that one day soon will take us to Mars and beyond. " He paused as Vicki came over with mugs of coffee and glasses of OJ. "Thanks, Vicki."

She walked on and Whitley continued. "Are we going to introduce her to the American people?"

"Only when she's comfortable with the idea and we are ready."

"She can also stay at the VP residence, Jim, if the White House gets too busy."

"Let's see how it all plays out." "I need a bit of time tonight to think this through."

+++

Rose was in the library the next morning when Liam Powers rushed in, cell phone in hand. "Rose, it's...President Mitchum." He whispered the words, passed his cell to her, then stepped outside the door to give her privacy.

"Mr. President?"

"Rose. I was hoping Liam would be at work. How're you doing?"

"Since yesterday? Pretty good. Thanks. How was your trip back?"

"Quick. But with some interesting developments. If you're in agreement, Steve Whitley and Paul Spenser, the head of NASA, will pick you up three weeks from today to bring you here to DC. It's more secure if they do it. No media questions."

"That's fast! I'm still helping Liam with some of his designs and..."

"He can come as well. The two of you can continue your work here. Tell him we'll arrange it with his job there."

"Let me ask Liam, see if this interests him. Hold on." She covered the phone with her hand, opened the door and stuck her head out. "Liam want to come with me to the White House for a while? President Mitchum said we can continue our work there. They'll arrange things with your employer here."

His expressions shifted from one second to the next—shock, incredulity, delight. "When?"

"Three weeks."

"I'm in."

She ducked back inside the library. "He's in, Jim."

"Wonderful. Tell him Whitley will be in touch with the details."

"Okay. Hey, how's Nomad doing?"

"Today he has been sort of moping around. I think he misses all those new scents at your place."

"Tell him I'll be there soon. And thank you for doing this."

Mitchum disconnected, and she stood there, the mobile device clutched in her hand, and allowed the good feelings to wash over her, through her. She wouldn't have access to *this* library but didn't doubt that the big White House had a library to rival it.

She would make sure she had her favorites on her reading devices. Liam had given her a secure government phone and an iPad so they could trade ideas on the designs at any hour or day of the week. He'd made sure she had a pre-loaded debit card to use for eBooks on Amazon but not for physical items because outsiders couldn't deliver to Area 51.

Mitchum hadn't known whether Rose had her own phone, so he called Liam. If she did have one, she hadn't offered her number. But besides Liam, who would she contact? Epsilon on Xanthe? Or the far side of the moon? Ha. Not by phone. Her owning a phone was no more of a risk or threat than her taking a walk outside.

She opened the door and handed Liam his phone. "Steve Whitley will contact you with more information."

"Wow! Awesome! This is so great, Rose."

"What should I pack my stuff in?" she asked.

They hurried up a long, wide corridor toward her quarters. "I brought you a pack and left it in your room."

"Thanks, Liam. What does an alien wear to the White House?"

He glanced at her and laughed. "No clue. This is a first. You've got jeans and sweaters."

"And some shirts, soaps, stuff that someone bought for me."

"How long do you think we'll be there?"

She didn't know. But intuitively, as the humans called it, she felt this was the beginning of something else. Something much bigger. Something global.

She had no idea about the specifics. But as she and Liam went through the vault-like doors to her living quarters, she hoped she would have more freedom in DC to walk around, to play ball with Nomad, to actually shop for physical items online. Or in an actual store.

But she would have to cover her bluish skin. And her height? Maybe not too much. She would have to wear dark sunglasses to cover her eyes and buy a different wig so that her hair would fall longer around the sides of her face. She would have to blend in. Here in Area 51, that hadn't been a problem. Everyone who worked here knew who she was. Off and on over the decades, someone like Liam had befriended her, worked with her, and they'd become friends. She suspected these individuals had been assigned to her—to keep her safe, to tap into her skills and knowledge, *to keep an eye on her,* as these humans liked to say.

Did they file periodic reports? If so, what kind of information would those reports contain? *Rose has a sense of irony! Rose revealed her origins. Rose doesn't say much.*

But she'd never been as close to any of these individuals as she was to Liam. He seemed to genuinely enjoy her company, liked conversing with her, discovering what her life had been like. And vice versa.

Then they were through the steel doors, in her living quarters, and Liam went over to the black pack he'd left on the couch. He plucked it up, tossed it to her.

"Perfect size, Liam. Many thanks. I'm going to start organizing my things."

"Is it okay if I give the President your cell number?"

"Sure. If I hear anything, I'll message you."

"I'll do the same. I'll also get you a purse. You'll need one."

He started back through the vaults—and that's what they were, like bank vaults— and she hurried into her bedroom and opened the closet door. Not much in here. It was pretty much like Liam had said: jeans, slacks, blouses, sweater, shoes. The sizes, of course, were really large, even by human standards.

The shoes, for instance, were size 12. She was so tall that the jeans—even in the extra-large size—barely brushed her ankles. The shirts and sweaters sometimes fit her, but all too often had sleeves that were a bit too short. But she didn't care. She plucked each article of clothing from a hanger, folded it, set it at the foot of her bed until the closet was empty. Then she packed it all in the nice bag Liam had given her.

From the bureau drawer, she brought out underclothing. In the bathroom, she collected toiletries, a hairbrush, and even a small mirror. And from a bathroom drawer, she removed a special item that had been sewn into her suit when her craft had crashed. It had belonged to her mother, the Stell^r symbol for peace made from a precious stone unique to Xanthe, a transparent bluish stone that some believed held magical properties. She often wondered if this stone had saved her life when her craft had crashed. Could it save her now?

From what?

She didn't know. But sometimes she felt this threat was connected to humanity being told she'd existed all these years at Area 51.

There's an alien among us. And she has been here for decades. Headlines like that. Sites all over the Internet showing aliens, pointing out how different they were than humans... that prospect disturbed her.

But even worse would be to stay here, confined, watched, talked about, discussed at Pentagon meetings, congressional hearings, among foreign leaders. Which leaders?

Alexander Zhukov, head of Russia, might be problematic based just on what she'd read and heard about him. But the leaders of the other nuclear powers might also prove difficult accepting her and "aliens" amongst them. She wouldn't know until she was in DC, until the next step—whatever it was—unfolded. And until then, all she could do was prepare to the best of her ability for the world beyond Area 51. Now that she was packed, the end of the week couldn't get here quick enough.

Chapter 4

Synchronicity

Rose was in the library this early September morning when Liam came in with Whitley and a tall, white-haired man she assumed was Paul Spenser, head of NASA. Whitley hugged her hello and introduced her to Spenser, whose eyes widened when she extended her hand. "A pleasure, Dr. Spenser."

"This is such an honor, Rose." He grasped her hand tightly. "I have a trillion questions for you."

She smiled at that. "That will take a lot longer to answer than three plus hours in a plane."

"Are you and Liam ready to leave?" Whitley asked.

Was she?

Was it the right decision?

The right next chapter in her life?

Or was it safer to remain here, where everything was familiar, habitual?

Liam glanced at her, brows lifting, questioning her. *You ready?* "Rose?"

She looked at the three men, considered what they were offering her. A chance in the outer world, where her presence might make a big difference. She nodded. "Definitely ready," she exclaimed, and reached for the bag on the floor next to Liam that she started packing nearly three weeks ago in anticipation of this day. She slung the strap over her shoulder.

Liam said, "Ready to rock and roll, Mr. Whitley."

Rose gestured at a book on the table. "Do you think it would be okay if I borrow this book? I couldn't find it on my device."

Spenser glanced at the title. "*Synchronicity: An Acausal Connecting Principle.* Great choice. Carl Jung was brilliant."

"Sure, it's yours, take the book," Whitley smiled. "I'll let them know."

"Let who know?" Liam asked. "No one is really in charge of the library."

"Who ordered all these books?" Whitley asked.

"No idea," Liam replied. "I've worked here for five years and all these books have been here since I arrived."

Whitley scooped up the book and handed it to her. Rose slipped it into the handbag Liam had bought for her, he opened the door, and the four of them left the library. She stood for a moment in the doorway, looking back at the place where she'd spent so much time the last several decades. She would miss its familiarity. All the books she'd read over the years were at least a reminder of this place, just like the blue stone was a reminder of her mother and Xanthe.

When she walked out of Area 51 for the first time in more than 70 years, guards and soldiers watching her, watching them, elation swept through her. The sky was utterly blue and clear, and the bright sun felt good on her face. The air felt chilly, but her jacket kept her snug and warm.

They got into a large black car that Whitley drove. Liam settled in the passenger seat, Rose and Spenser rode in the back. No Secret Service agents this time.

She kept looking around at the desolation of this place, all the desert with the white sand reflecting the sunlight, and the tall graceful cacti. She didn't see any animal life, not even a bird.

"This desolation is daunting," she remarked.

Spenser nodded. "You'll probably miss it when you get to DC. So how does it feel to be out of Area 51 after all these years?"

Exhilarating.

Her telepathic response took Spenser by surprise. She could see it on his face. *Didn't Jim mention the telepathy?*

He did. But the actual experience is something else.

Whitley pulled alongside a sleek Gulfstream—she recognized it from photos and TV—and they all got out. A woman and a man, both in uniforms, stood at the top of the stairs. "Lt. Vicki Harris is the copilot and flight attendant, and Colonel Russ Morgan is the pilot," Spenser said.

At the top of the stairs, he introduced her as Rose, Area 51's best kept secret.

"Wow, this is so awesome," Vicki exclaimed with wide-eyed amazement, and handed them aluminum bottles of cold water. "Once we're airborne, I'll have some food ready for you all. What kind of food do you prefer, Rose?"

"I'm a vegan. A salad or bowl of fruit is fine, thank you."

"We've got plenty of both. Welcome aboard."

Russ Morgan took her extended hand and looked on the verge of passing out. "Such a...a pleasure, Rose."

"You and Liam and Rose will have a lot to talk about," Spenser said. "Liam is an aeronautical engineer and Rose has been working with him on designs. Rose designed the Raider as well as many other innovative aircraft."

The colonel's face lit up. "I hope one day to fly in it. Fabulous plane! Please, step into the cockpit, Rose, and have a look around."

"Thanks, Colonel Morgan. I'd love to take a look around." She had to duck to step into the plane and even then the top of her head nearly brushed the ceiling.

The first thing she saw was the open doorway to the cockpit on her left. The colonel motioned for her to step inside. A quick glance told her it was far superior to the designs and the photos she'd seen of older aircraft but nowhere close to the shuttle craft she and Fralix had flown over Roswell all those decades ago.

Rose knew that while she was pleased to help the Americans gradually develop their new technologies, she purposefully never went too far ahead. The human race was simply not ready for leapfrog space technology at this time.

"Can your consciousness merge with that of the plane, Colonel?"

He looked bewildered. "Is the Gulfstream conscious?"

"Everything possesses some form of consciousness. It's all about finding your way in."

"Is that how you flew over Roswell?"

"Yes. My copilot and I."

"Can you teach me how to do that?"

"Depends."

"On what?"

"On the craft itself and how open to it you are."

Morgan threw his arms open as if to embrace someone. "Open, open, open." He paused. "Can the pilots do that on the Raider?"

She thought about that. The Raider had been designed for a meld if you knew what you were doing. She intentionally did not activate that advanced feature.

"Technically one day, yes."

She and Spenser sat together, with Whitley and Liam across from them, their bags in the overhead compartments. She had the window seat and as the jet taxied, she got a good look at the surrounding area. So stark in its beauty, she thought, and snapped several photos with her mobile device.

"Do you use personal communication devices on Xanthe?" Spenser asked.

"In 1947 while at the lunar base, we didn't need them. Telepathy was fine for the size of the operation. And when I was on Xanthe, telepathy was how we generally communicated."

"What planet is closest to Xanthe?"

"An uninhabited planet that was about twenty light years from us. But it may not be uninhabited these days. I just don't know. I haven't been in touch with anyone on Xanthe for a very long time."

"Not even telepathically?"

"We use it when in direct proximity with each other and use other means of communication for longer distances across space." She showed him images of what happened as her lunar shuttle plunged toward Earth, and what she'd done to convince Epsilon and the Council that she and Fralix hadn't survived. "Since they think I'm dead, no one would attempt to contact me."

"So you came here from the moon base in 1947?"

"Yes."

"But we've been to the moon and even have a regular presence with a permanent lunar lab, and no one to date has found any base."

"The far side of the moon, Dr. Spenser. And the Stell^rs have stealth technology that blocks out any viewing of our base and spacecraft. President Mitchum was an astronaut, right?"

"Yes, before he entered politics. He was also an incredible pilot."

"Did he see something as an astronaut that prompted his visit to Area 51?"

"Yes, but he doesn't talk about it much. You should ask him about it."

They were airborne, the sunlight pouring through the windows on the eastern side of the aircraft. She sensed he had a practically bottomless cache of questions about other species in the universe, about abductions, UFOs, friendly and hostile aliens, the gamut. She touched his arm, her bluish skin a startling contrast to the chocolate brown of his sweater. "Look, I know you've got a lot of questions, Dr. Spenser. It..."

"Paul. Please call me Paul."

"Paul. It's easier for me to transmit images like I did with the others. Is that okay with you?"

He grinned. "Transmit away, Rose!"

Somewhere in the back of her mind, she still had that reel of images that she'd visualized to the others, so she accessed it and sent it to him. It covered everything from her early life on Andromeda to the move to Xanthe to the Zorgons and the field of asteroids that would destroy Xanthe by 2056. She showed him images of how the government had worked in 1947 with Epsilon as head of the Council.

At one point in all this, Spenser lifted his hands, his eyes popped open. "I...need to process all this, Rose."

"It's a lot, I know."

Vicki appeared with trays of food for each of them. For her it was a bowl of hot oatmeal with a bit of honey on it, two buttered biscuits, and a large bowl of fruit. She didn't get a whole lot of fruit in Area 51, so some of these chunks were unfamiliar to her.

Rose stabbed her fork into a deep yellow chunk of something and held it up. "Paul, what's this called?"

"Looks like mango."

Mango. She'd read about them. Rose bit into it and immediately knew it was the most delectable Earth food she'd ever tasted. "The tropics, right?"

"And south Florida and southern California and India. You ever had papaya?"

"Read about it. Saw some on TV, on the Internet."

He gestured at her bowl of fruit. "That deep orange chunk. Try that next."

She did and it practically melted in her mouth. "Xanthe has fruit, but not like either of these."

"We'll make sure you have all the mangos and papayas you'd like. If I show you some images from the Webb telescope, Rose, would you be able to pinpoint the approximate location of Xanthe?"

"I should be able to. But it depends on how clear the images are."

"I can show you a miniature version." He unplugged his iPad, booted it up, opened it. His fingers tapped away, and he turned the iPad so she could see the holographic image clearly. A stunning depiction of the universe. Coordinates were provided, with dates and times.

"The coordinates are a couple light years off."

"In which direction?"

"Xanthe is about three light years to the east in this image."

He brought up another image. She looked at it closely. "Go another light year east, Paul."

He tapped another few keys. And this image struck her soul. Xanthe should have been there. Instead, there were galaxies, stars, the infinite blackness of space. Her planet's absence told her that Stell^rs now used their cloaking technology to shield their planet from view. Most likely from the Zorgon probes. She said as much aloud, and Spenser looked shocked.

"That's incredible. No wonder you're helping Liam on the designs for new stealth aircraft."

"It's been enjoyable. Keeps me occupied. I'd love to see more Webb images on a larger screen."

"You will. You and Liam. At my office."

She polished off the oatmeal and fruit, and when Vicki came around with espresso, she asked for one. On Xanthe, coffee was unknown and in Area 51 it had been limited to the cafeteria. However, based on just the scent of the stuff here in the cabin, she suspected this espresso would be the best yet.

Her first sip of the espresso stunned her system. Her heart slammed into overdrive, the back of her throat lit up, and the taste of it whipped through her body like lightning. "Wow," she gasped.

"So that means Area 51 doesn't have very good coffee," Spenser remarked. "And that espresso, by the way, is Cuban. Straight out of a coffee field west of Havana. I went there in 2017, after the island was opened to US tourism, and we worked out a deal with one of the growers. It's still in effect."

"I would love to visit Cuba." And Europe and all South America and the Caribbean islands, and...

She didn't realize the rest of that sentence had gone telepathic until Spenser laughed. "Yes to all of it, Rose. In the proper time, once the world has met you."

She still wasn't sure about that part of all this but refused to fret about it now. *All in good time. Synchronicity will unfold.* She allowed herself, for just moments, to imagine herself in Cuba, eating mangos and papaya, dancing, visiting Hemingway's hangouts, and seeing for herself how people still struggled to live under their autocracy. Abject poverty. She'd read about it. Poverty so terrible that people lacked food, clean water, basics.

The Stell^rs could remedy that across the entire planet. Totally eliminate it. Render it to an ugly period of history. Cruel dictatorships still controlled the masses in so many places on Earth. It made no sense to her.

If the field of asteroids was still on a collision course with her planet, Epsilon already would be planning how to move 100 million Stell^rs to Earth. It meant Epsilon would most likely be living at the lunar base full time or on his way there now. She had no idea how Earth with its eight billion plus people could support another 100 million unless the Stell^rs implemented their most sophisticated technology, whatever it was now, all these decades later.

On the Xanthe she'd left, poverty and inequality had been unknown for eons. She suspected it was still that way. The Council was elected by the people, and its thirteen members elected a leader. Among Stell^rs, the number thirteen was considered lucky; here on Earth it was cursed and associated with the spooky part of Halloween. She grinned to herself.

In the *I Ching, the Chinese Book of Changes,* one of Earth's oldest divination systems, hexagram thirteen was called *Fellowship of Man.* She'd studied the *Ching* during the decades of her confinement, had listened to podcasts on it, and had read books about the different interpretations. She considered it one of the most profound works of this planet and didn't understand how China had become a nuclear power.

What was the hexagram for the Chinese or Russian governments? Number 23, *Splitting Apart?* Number 39, *Obstruction?* Number 6, *Conflict?* All three became, in her mind, Hexagram 47, *Oppression.* Was that how she should view this new era of her life? In terms of the 64 hexagrams in the *I Ching?*

Jung had written the introduction to this book on synchronicity in 1949, the same year that Truman had granted her access to the library. The *I Ching* was the first book she'd selected and read. Again. And again.

"You have three pennies, Paul?"

"Sure." He dug into the pocket of his pants and brought out two pennies and a quarter. "Oops. Let me find another penny."

"Or another two quarters."

In the end, she had three quarters, a piece of paper and a pen. "Okay Paul. Ask a question."

"Any question?"

"Your choice. But don't ask for a yes or no. Ask, instead, about a relationship, a situation, an event."

"Wait a minute. I know this." He sat up straighter, downed the last of his espresso. "*I Ching*, right? The coins are the giveaway."

"Uh-huh. So you know the coins are tossed six times."

By now, Vicki was standing next to them listening, and Whitley and Liam, seated in front of them, were turned around in their seats, closely watching. "So what's your question, Paul?" asked Whitley.

"Say it out loud," said Vicki, and looked anxiously at Whitley. "Do I have security clearance for this?"

Whitley made a dismissive gesture. "No NDAs, if that's what you're asking. But if you end up writing a book about these trips, Vicki, could you at least let me have a peek first at the manuscript?"

"Deal," she replied.

"My question." Spenser held the three quarters in the palm of his right hand and started to shake them. "What will happen here once Rose's existence is revealed to the world?"

Good question, she thought. But considering this was the *Ching*, she wasn't so sure she wanted to know the answer.

Spenser asked, shook the coins, and dropped them. Heads counted three, tails counted two. Sixes and nines were changing lines. Sixes changed from broken to solid, nines changed from solid to broken. Yin and yang, male and female.

Spenser tossed the coins another five times and each time, Rose counted heads or tails, with changing lines for sixes or nines. But there weren't any changing lines. They were all unbroken. This meant the situation wasn't in flux, wasn't fluid. It meant things were settled. It was destiny. Primal power, as Jung put it. Hexagram 1, *The Creative*.

"So based on the *I Ching*, it looks like your presence is going to usher in a paradigm shift for us," Spenser said. "That's my interp, Rose. What's yours?"

She liked that about Spenser, that he'd asked. "It won't be quite that easy."

"Is that what Hexagram 1 is saying?

Rose briefly shut her eyes, conjuring the other parts of this hexagram interpretation. "If memory serves, it says, 'If an individual draws this hexagram, it means that success will come to him from the primal depths of the universe and that everything depends upon his seeking his happiness and that of others in one way only, that is, by persevering to what is right.'" She paused. "And given the matrix within which the *Ching* functions, that means I'm screwed if I don't adhere to that."

Whitley laughed and rocked back in his seat. "You said screwed, Rose. That makes you very human."

Vicki rolled her eyes. "It also means an alien presence on Earth—her presence—is going to save our asses."

Did it? she wondered.

Chapter 5

Welcome to the White House

Mitchum was outside with Nomad, on the back lawn, when the black SUV pulled up behind the White House. Whitley and Powers got out first and opened the back doors for Paul Spenser and Rose. The dog saw Rose and tore away from Mitchum, barking, his leash slapping the ground.

"Nomad!" Rose called, and crouched and opened her arms.

The dog leaped at her, knocking her down on her backside, and she laughed and flung her arms around him. For long moments, they all watched the alien and the dog, rolling around on the grass, Nomad covering her face in wet, sloppy kisses. It was a bizarre image that would be forever burned into his memory.

Mitchum hurried over, whistling for Nomad, and the dog reluctantly moved away from Rose, who got to her feet, her hands slapping at her clothes—jeans, a sweater, a heavy jacket. She strode over to Mitchum, smiling.

"Good to see you, Jim."

"I'm sorry he bowled you over." He grasped her extended hand in both of his, which felt ludicrous. Her hands were much larger than his. "You okay?"

"Sure. Just a bit tired."

Powers, Spenser, and Whitley joined them, and Nomad greeted each of them, but not like he had Rose. "The White House chef has prepared dinner for all of us, so let's get you and Liam settled in."

They headed for the stairs that led to his and Laurie's private residence on the second floor. Laurie greeted them at the top of the stairs, her dark hair tumbling to her shoulders, a stunning contrast against her white sweater. "Rose! It's wonderful to meet you! And you must be Liam Powers, the engineering genius." They shook hands and she ushered them into the living room. "Rose, Liam, I'll show you to your rooms and you can freshen up before dinner." Rose was amazed at how calmly the First Lady greeted her. It was as if she was around very tall blue aliens on a regular basis. What a lovely woman she thought. Jim was a very lucky man.

Rose took her bag from Powers, and they walked up the hall with Laurie. Mitchum went into the kitchen, where Carmen was whipping up all sorts of goodies.

"It smells delicious."

She turned those dark eyes on him. "Mr. *Presidente,* was that...I just saw...a very tall, blue-skinned woman walk in here. *La señora* told me her name is Rose and that she is from...another planet... Xanthe. I've never heard of that planet."

"None of us have, Carmen."

"So she is...*una extraterrestre.* An alien. And has lived all these years in Area 51?"

He nodded.

"But she looks... *muy joven, señor.*"

"She's 137."

"*Ay, dios mio,*" Carmen whispered, and made a hasty sign of the cross on her forehead.

When Rose and Powers returned to the living room, Mitchum introduced them to Carmen. As soon as she spoke to Rose in her accented voice, Rose replied, "*Mucho gusto, Carmen. ¿De done vienes en Cuba?*"

"*Matanzas, al este de La Habana.*"

"*Quiero ir.*"

"Your Spanish... is, *como se dice*...impecable."

Mitchum's grasp of Spanish was fairly good. But the fact that Rose spoke it—and so flawlessly, with just the right accent—shocked him. Yet, why should it? She probably spoke a dozen languages.

Carmen glanced at him, then back at Rose. "Black beans and Cuban rice. How does that sound, *Señora Rose?*"

"*Señorita Rose. No estoy casada.* And I'd love some black beans and Cuban rice. Thank you, Carmen.*"

She took the small plate of black beans and rice that Carmen handed her, fork included, and sampled it. "Superb. What spices did you use?"

Carmen explained, and as Mitchum listened to them, he realized that Rose had a heightened sense of taste. What about her sense of smell? Her vision? He already knew that her intelligence far surpassed that of humans. The Stell^rs had been around two million years longer.

Helen and her husband, Adam, arrived for dinner, and Carmen shooed everyone to the dining room table, perfectly set, and brought out the dishes of food. Black beans and the yellow rice, of course, but also baked *platanos*—plantains—and a basket of warm rolls and some vegetable dish with fish. She set two bottles of wine on the table, a red and a white. She then whistled for Nomad, and they went for a walk.

"So how are relationships among Stell^rs different than they are for humans?" Laurie asked.

"Well to start, we have an average life span of around 1200 years. That factor alone makes it different. Most of us don't commit to a partner until we're over 150 years old. We stay with each other as long as we're happy. If the happiness fades after maybe a couple centuries together, we choose to move on. No hard feelings. Ever."

"That sounds remarkably civil," Helen remarked. "Since you all live so long, how large are your families?"

"Usually, one child per couple, but it depends. Women can have children well into their 200s, so if a couple moves on from each other and enters new relationships, they may have a child, too. My parents were bonded for 260 years, then they reached a point where they were no longer happy together and ended up with new partners. My mom's second partner had a daughter, so I have what you would refer to as a half-sister."

"Did you get to see them frequently?" asked Adam.

"Yes. Until Fralix and I left for Earth."

It went on like this the entire meal, all of them asking her questions and Rose patiently answering everything. When Carmen returned with Nomad, she cleared the table and brought out dessert—homemade flan—and cups of Cuban coffee, then left for the evening.

"Do you have coffee on Xanthe?" Adam asked.

"Unfortunately not, and I learned on our flight, you also have fruits we've never heard of—mango and papaya, for instance."

Spenser spoke up. "I told her she can have all the mangos and papayas she'd like."

"Absolutely," Laurie said. "We'll also set up an area for you and Liam, so you can continue your work together. But for tomorrow, Paul said he'd like to get you and Liam to his office so you can see the images from the Web telescope. How's that sound?"

"I'm eager to see them," Rose replied.

"Me, too," Powers echoed.

"Great. I'll send a car to pick you up around nine, how's that?"

"Sounds perfect," Rose said. "Okay with you, Liam?"

"Yup."

"Should I cover up my blue skin, Paul?"

Spenser glanced at Mitchum. "Jim?"

Mitchum had given a lot of thought about keeping Rose out of the public eye for now. "Can you access the images from a computer here at the White House?"

Spenser considered the suggestion. "I'd rather not. The setup we've got involves several technical applications."

Whitley's arm shot into the air like a school kid eager to interject his opinion. "My two cents? Rose has been confined to Area 51 for decades. She needs a bit more freedom of movement. Your facility has private areas, Paul."

"Plenty of them," Spenser replied. "And we have a secure underground entrance."

"Hold on, hold on," Laurie said. "Helen and I can use makeup for her face and long sleeves and slacks would do the rest."

Mitchum listened, then turned to Rose. "What's your preference?"

"As much freedom as possible. I'd like to see this city, get a sense of it and the people. Seeing it all from a car is fine. I don't have to walk around."

"Then before we bring you to my office tomorrow, I'll drive you and Liam around. How's that sound?" Spenser asked.

"That'd be great," Powers said. "I've never gotten to see DC like that."

Mitchum nodded. "I'll assign Ken to go with you, so you have Secret Service protection, too."

"Ken." Rose smiled. "One of the young men who came with you to Area 51. I like him."

"I'll message him and ask him to meet you and Liam here tomorrow morning at 8:45," Mitchum said.

"Sounds good, Jim," said Rose. "Thank you."

"I'll be ready," Powers added.

"Do you have enough warm clothes?" Helen asked.

"The ones I have don't fit great." Rose held up her long arm, showing them that the sleeve of her shirt barely reached her elbow. "It's supposed to be long-sleeved. Same problem with slacks."

"Laurie, let's take the lady for some online shopping."

"They deliver here?" Rose sounded surprised.

"It has to go through security first," Laurie said. "But we've had a lot of practice, so we usually get the purchase the same day or the next."

"You want anything more to eat, Rose?" Laurie asked.

"No, thank you. I'm good."

Helen pushed back from the table. "Great. Let's go shopping."

The women left the room and Mitchum remained seated with Spenser, Whitley, Powers, and Adam Hargraves. "My G-d, Jim," Spenser said. "When she's introduced to the world, everything will change dramatically."

"Yeah. Understatement of the century. That's what worries me."

Chapter 6

The Ladies

The First Lady's office was spacious, tidy, and as elegant as she was. Rose gravitated toward the large window behind her desk that overlooked the grounds of the White House. Lit by moon and stars, there was also plenty of outside lighting that enabled her to see the guards, the tall hedges and gate, and a pair of black SUVs.

Tomorrow she would ride in one of those SUVs through the streets of DC, a tourist from another planet. She would rather be on foot but just the thought of being out there thrilled her.

"Okay," Helen said. "We need to know your size, Rose."

Rose turned. "Extra Large is too large. I'm tall, but I'm thin like most Stell^rs are. Although if I keep eating Carmen's cooking that may change! Large fits except for the sleeves."

She held out her arms again and lifted one leg to show them how the bottom hem didn't even touch her ankles.

"I've got a tape measure."

Helen reached into her purse and brought out an aluminum tape measure and proceeded to assess Rose's arm length from shoulder to wrists, then her legs from hips to ankles. She called out the measurements as she did them, and Laurie jotted them down. Then Laurie pulled up two more chairs. "Okay, ladies. Let's take a look at what Amazon offers in women's clothing, with these measurements." She tapped the yellow tablet where she'd jotted the numbers.

Rose and Helen sat on either side of Laurie and looked at the choices that appeared. *This one, not that one, how about this one?* It had been so long since Rose had hung out just with females that initially she felt almost intimidated. But as they laughed and commiserated about some of the outfits, she loosened up and asked them what it was like to be female in 2029 on Earth.

"Well, to start, no woman has ever been elected president."

That will change.

Both women heard this telepathically. Laurie winked at Helen. "Yup, it sure will. Is there equality for women among Stell^rs?"

Granted, she had been quite young when she'd left Xanthe and only 59 when she'd crashed at Roswell. But from what she remembered, equality was never an issue. Her mother had been a pilot and a scientist and had bonded twice. She and her second partner had a daughter, Yesenia, Rose's half-sister, 23 years younger. The last time Rose had seen her, she was only 36, the human equivalent of a kid in high school. But she was already studying biology, chemistry, telepathy, and aeronautics. She didn't have any idea what Yesenia was doing now.

Female equality?

"Yes. Completely. There is no difference between men, woman, and other alien races. Earth is still a relatively young planet. One day, when you join other planetary civilizations in the stars, you'll see that the petty differences that exist today on Earth will seem utterly ridiculous."

"How long is a Stell^r pregnancy?" Helen asked.

"They last for two years. Mothers are in constant telepathic contact with their child and if it—he or she—reaches a crisis or changes its mind about the parents it has chosen, it ejects itself, what you humans call a miscarriage. No lingering problems, no threat to the mother. Ejection. All of us know what that means, what it entails."

"Well, that puts Stell^rs well beyond humans," Laurie said.

"We've also been around about two million years longer. Believe me, we've made a lot of mistakes in our own past. But we learn from them."

Or try to. She recalled only one instance when she had overheard her parents arguing. They didn't yell. They battled telepathically.

She'd been in her room, reading, and the sparring had become so intrusive that she'd slapped her hands over her ears and curled up in a ball in her bed and hummed to herself, blocking out what she could of their voices.

Not long afterward, her parents had taken her to the aviation center where her dad worked so she could see how the interstellar starships were constructed. During that trip, they'd told her they were parting amicably but that their love for her would remain their connection forever. And that had proven to be true.

Her dad had bonded with a female not long after her mother had bonded for the second time. When her mother was pregnant with Yesenia, both couples and Rose had met at that same aviation center for Rose's first training flight in the type kind of shuttle craft that had crashed in Roswell.

She gave them this story telepathically because it was easier that way and both women looked shaken. "We've got a lot to learn from you, Rose." This came from Laurie, who then put her arms around Rose, hugging her.

Helen's arms joined Laurie's and Rose's breath caught in her throat. It was the only time she'd experienced a deeply human moment as their hearts melded with hers.

+++

Usually, Rose didn't need much sleep, just a few hours. But when she woke the next morning, she was surprised to discover she'd slept for more than eight hours. By the time she went out into the dining area, the Mitchums and Powers were already eating.

"Carmen left you a feast, Rose," said Mitchum. "Help yourself. It's all on the kitchen counter."

She liked that, being treated like a member of the family rather than a guest. She went into the kitchen, where there was a large bowl of fresh fruit filled with slices of mangos and papaya, and a bowl of cold cereal with a small pitcher of milk next to it, and a banana with a note tucked under it.

Para tu cereal. Tienes cambures en Xanthe?

For your cereal. Do you have bananas on Xanthe?

With the pen on the counter, she jotted her own note under Carmen's. *Gracias. Si, tenemos cambures en Xanthe, pero son verde y no puedes comerlos.* Yes, they had bananas, but they were green and inedible.

She carried her breakfast into the dining room and joined the others at the table. Ken had arrived and sat with them, sipping at a mug of coffee. "Dr. Spenser asked me to drive you and Liam over to his office. You ready to see the sights, Rose?"

"Definitely. Which sights?"

"The Lincoln Memorial," Liam said." And the Jefferson Memorial and the Martin Luther King Memorial and..."

"And I'd love for you to see the National Mall," Ken said. "But there's a demonstration on the mall today so we'll stay clear of it."

"Demonstration for what?" Rose asked.

"For supporting the President's planetary environment initiatives to improve our Earth for the future generations in the years to come."

"But that's a positive thing. I'd love to see it."

Ken looked at Mitchum. "Mr. President?"

"Sure. But not at too leisurely a pace."

Stell^rs didn't demonstrate or protest. They didn't have any reason to do so. The Council knew telepathically what the majority of the Stell^rs needed and wanted. But when Ken drove them past the National Mall, and she saw the thousands of demonstrators carrying signs to support the President's policies, she felt a surge of hope. For humanity, for Stell^rs if and when they came here, and for herself.

For the first time, she knew she was in the right place at the right time.

Chapter 7

Epsilon

Late November 2029

The morning it happened, Jim Mitchum and Whitley were in the Oval Office, discussing how and when they might introduce Rose to the American people—and then to the rest of the world. She'd been living in the White House since September and together with Liam had finished the design for a next generation of space vehicles. Periodically she'd been working with Paul Spenser at his office, deciphering the images from the Webb telescope and searching the universe for the exoplanets she knew about.

"It may be too abrupt, Jim," Whitley said. "Maybe we need to introduce the whole thing in a different, more nuanced way that..."

Mitchum suddenly went deaf to Whitley's voice and another voice—a male voice— filled his head. *Greetings, my name is Epsilon, leader of the Council on Xanthe, ten light years from Earth. We are known as the Stell^rs. I am speaking simultaneously to the leaders of the nine nuclear powers on your planet: the United States, Russia, France, China, the United Kingdom, Pakistan, India, Israel, and North Korea. You are the caretakers of a dangerous nuclear stockpile that currently exceeds 13,000 in weaponry.*

The Stell^rs intend no harm to humanity or your planet. But if any moves are made to change the positioning of your nuclear weapons, we will know and will take action that we hope won't be necessary. I can assure you this is real and please take this communication with the utmost seriousness. We will be in touch again soon—on January 15—to discuss how, where and when we will meet. Until then, this is Epsilon, Council leader of the Stell^rs, wishing you productive, happy days ahead.

"Jim? Hey, you okay?"

Mitchum blinked and Whitley's face snapped into clarity. "Yeah, sure, why?"

"You looked like you were paralyzed."

"I...I'm stunned."

He bolted to his feet, raked his fingers back through his hair, whipped out his cell and started recording. He repeated the telepathic message he'd heard, and as he did so, Whitley stared at him.

"My G-d, Jim..."

"Yeah. Rose has mentioned this Epsilon."

"And he said he was addressing the leaders of all the nuclear powers?"

"And he named the countries."

"Maybe we should make some calls."

"Let's wait a bit," Mitchum said. "See if *we* get any calls."

"This must be connected to our knowing about Rose, to her living here." Whitley said.

"That would make sense. But according to her, Epsilon thinks she's dead, that she died in the Roswell crash."

"Then it's an astounding synchronicity, Jim."

Probably the most powerful one he'd experienced, ever. "So you didn't hear anything?"

"Nope. Nothing."

"I wonder if that was true for the other eight leaders."

"Probably. You nine all have the nuke codes. Each of you has the ultimate say."

And just then, the red phone on Mitchum's desk rang. A foreign call through the White House operator. "I bet this is Zhukov."

+++

Zhukov listened to those irritating rings and wished he'd called from his computer or his cell phone, so he could do a holographic VR call with Mitchum. Faces always held the truth, and he was fairly certain the voice he'd heard in his head—that identified itself as Epsilon—was an American trick. Elaborate, for sure, and probably the result of a chip in his brain that his enemies had injected. Except that his enemies never got that physically close to him.

On the eighth ring—yes, he counted—Mitchum finally answered. "President Alexander."

"That was quite a realistic hoax, President Jim. And such perfect Russian."

The use of their first names had started several years ago, by mutual agreement. Friendly yet formal.

Mitchum laughed. "I wish we had technology like that. Epsilon's English was also perfect."

Zhukov was taken back. He hadn't expected a response like that. "You're saying you heard it, too?"

"Yes. After it happened, I personally recorded what I remembered. I'll play it for you."

Zhukov listened. The words were exactly the ones he'd heard, in his own language. "If it wasn't technology, then it was one of your remote viewers."

"I doubt it, President Alexander. I don't think our viewers are capable of that kind of telepathy. Are yours?"

Were they? Zhukov didn't know. He'd been too busy the last few years to check in on the remote viewing program in Moscow. Whenever the unit contacted him with some bit of information they had picked up, he noted it and passed it on. Most of the time, it proved to be correct. "Yes, our viewers have that ability. So, as you Americans say, what's your angle, President Jim?"

"Assume, if you can, that the voice was real and belonged to the head of an alien race from a planet called Xanthe. If that's true, how will an alien presence revealing itself to humanity change things here on this planet, President Alexander?"

Zhukov detested the quiet calmness in Mitchum's voice. He'd strived for that when he was stressed, when faced with impossible choices, with the imponderable. But he'd never mastered it. Maybe Mitchum was naturally calm or had learned it as an astronaut, peering down on Earth from space.

There had been rumors some years back that Mitchum the astronaut had witnessed something while on the space station. *Something,* of course, translated as a UFO, UAP, whatever the Americans called them now. Did that have something to do with his recent and unscheduled flight to Area 51? Over the years, there had been numerous UAP reports from that state as well as from Arizona and New Mexico. And ever since the Congressional hearings in 2023, it had been the hottest conspiracy topic these days.

Zhukov laughed and dropped the president from Mitchum's name. "*Change* things, Jim? It would mean that your country was no longer the most powerful. It would mean *Independence Day.* You'd better get in touch with Will Smith."

"Glad you've seen it. One of my favorite movies."

"So does Area 51 look like what President Bill Pullman walked into?"

"No idea, Alexander. Haven't had a chance to walk around inside." He paused. "But it's my belief that the voice you heard in your head—that I heard that other world leaders heard—was that of an alien. My advice is let's see what happens next." He paused. "Have another call coming through. Let's touch base again soon. Good talking with you."

"You, too," Zhukov said, and doubted if that would ever be true.

Zhukov didn't want any part of the meeting this mind message communicated. How come none of his country's best Viewers saw this coming? He initially believed it was a clever hoax the Americans perpetrated. But if it was a hoax, who or what communicated the message?

He called his trusted advisors together, and they sat around a conference table in his office. Three of them: one a trusted friend, another a distant cousin, and the third his new son-in-law, Dimitri, the youngest among them at just 34. His input was valuable because it represented that of younger Russians, whose support was important.

"Dimitri, do American Viewers have the ability to communicate telepathically to a number of people at the same time?"

"If they do, I don't know about it, sir. But I suppose it's possible. A few of our Viewers may have the ability to do it. I'll look into it."

Zhukov's cousin, Ivan, a tall, thin 43-year-old guy who enjoyed playing basketball in his free time, seemed to take offense at what Dimitri said. He made a face, shook his head. "What, Dimitri? You going to test them by demanding they send you a telepathic message? Your head is so full of crap you wouldn't know telepathic from psychopathic." He then laughed, a disjointed guffaw that sounded like he had a terrible case of hiccups.

Cousin or not, Zhukov nearly tossed Ivan off the advisory board right then. But it would look bad. He was family and had plenty of sources through his participation in amateur sports and his interest in the arts. "Well, that wasn't particularly helpful, Ivan." He turned to his friend, Victor. They had known each other since they were kids on the streets of Moscow. "Viktor?"

He was a naturally pensive man and, like Zhukov, had turned 52 this year. As a psychologist by education, he'd been involved in the Viewing program when the government had taken it over 25 years ago. He had screened prospective Remote Viewers, tested them, determined whether they were fit for the position. His opinion carried a lot of weight.

He sat forward, fingers threaded together on the tabletop, his neatly trimmed beard woven with gray, making him look distinguished, wise. "What, exactly, are you asking, Alexander? Do

I think there are other intelligent species in the universe? Yes. Do I think the human mind is practically infinite, capable of almost anything? Yes, yes. Do I think America may have Viewers who can transmit telepathic messages? Sure, why not? I think we have Viewers who can do the same. But not on the scale you've described. When you were receiving that message, I knew something was happening because you looked entranced and physically paralyzed."

Zhukov agreed on both counts. It had been one of the strangest things he'd ever experienced. He'd heard the voice, the words, understood what was being said, and had felt it was genuine. But his being rebelled. His being rejected it as real or genuine. His left brain screamed, *No, no, impossible.*

But when Viktor spoke with such conviction, Zhukov knew it was true, all of it, and that Mitchum had experienced the same thing he had.

When his advisors had left, he called his Chinese counterpart, and then the leaders he knew well of the other nuclear nations: North Korean, Pakistan, China, India. Hours later, his head dropped to his arms on his desk, and he struggled to grasp the reality that the message was real. It presented a danger this planet had never faced before: an alien race that was probably more powerful than all their nukes combined. His entire sense of reality blew up, and the pathetic pieces rained down over him and lay around him like fragments of the world he'd left behind.

+++

On many mornings in the weeks Rose had been here, she spent time behind the White House, walking Nomad and tossing balls to him. But since the weather had started to warm up, she enjoyed just sitting quietly in the sunlight, her eyes shut, her thoughts wandering. Humans called it meditation, Rose thought of it as celebration.

In the middle of this morning's celebration, she suddenly sensed that something important had happened involving Mitchum. Her eyes popped open, she tried to clarify the feeling, but nothing came to mind. So she messaged Mitchum.

Did something important happen? Are you ok?

He didn't answer immediately, which struck her as odd. Over these past weeks, they had kept in close contact even if he was out of town on presidential business. She suspected he felt responsible for her. The reverse was also true. Her presence might eventually endanger him, Helen, their spouses, everyone.

Her phone hummed. Mitchum. *I received a telepathic message from Epsilon and so did the other 8 leaders of nuclear nations. I've attached my recording of what I recall about that message. Let me know what you think.*

Epsilon. Now. She tapped the recording.

Greetings, my name is Epsilon, leader of the Council on Xanthe, ten light years from Earth. We are known as the Stell^rs. I am speaking simultaneously to the leaders of the nine nuclear powers on your planet: the United States, Russia, France, China, the United Kingdom, Pakistan, India, Israel, and North Korea. You are the caretakers of a dangerous nuclear stockpile that currently exceeds 13,000 in weaponry.

The Stell^rs intend no harm to humanity or your planet. But if any moves are made to change the positioning of your nuclear weapons, we the Stell^rs will know and will take action that we hope won't be necessary. I can assure you that this is very real and please take this communication with the utmost seriousness. We will be in touch again soon—on January 15, 2030—to discuss how, where, and when we will meet. Until then, this is Epsilon, Council leader of the Stell^rs, wishing you productive, happy days ahead.

Rose listened closely to the recording, her heartbeat speeding up. She felt this meant the Stell^rs hadn't solved the problem with the asteroid field headed toward Xanthe and were preparing to relocate the population to Earth. The preliminary step was to introduce themselves to humanity and establish certain boundaries with the nine nuclear powers about their destructive weapons.

And then what? Were more Stell^r starships headed to the moon base? The base, as she'd known it, wasn't large enough to accommodate a hundred million or whatever the population on Xanthe was now. It might accommodate several hundred comfortably. If additions had been built, maybe a couple thousand.

Had Epsilon relocated there by now?

You free for a few minutes, Jim?

Sure. Where are you?

Out back with Nomad.

I'll come to you.

I'll be in the garden.

Less than ten minutes later, he appeared and Secret Service Agent Ken was with him. He stayed behind as Mitchum entered the garden and joined her on the bench in front of the fountain. "One of my favorite spots," Mitchum said, petting Nomad as the dog greeted him.

"A few minutes ago, there were two hummingbirds darting around,"

"They love the fountain. So what did you think of that recording?"

"From what I knew of Epsilon decades ago, it sounded like something he'd say."

"But in preparation for what?"

"I think his contact means they haven't destroyed the asteroids headed toward Xanthe, and he's considering his options."

Mitchum now looked worried. "You mean like moving 100 million Stell^rs here?"

She nodded. "I don't know for sure that it's happening, Jim, but it's what I suspect."

"Christ." He ran his fingers back through his hair. "What do you recommend?"

"There's not much you can do. But he at least gave you a date—January 15—for your next contact. When he contacts you again, suggest setting up a date when you can meet in person."

"But why six weeks from now?" Mitchum asked.

"I don't know."

"It's far off."

"When you live for 1200 years, six weeks is *soon*. Or as you humans say, in the blink of an eye."

"A really *slow* blink."

She rolled that around inside herself for a few minutes. "If I'm right about what's going on, Jim, maybe he'll be in touch sooner."

Chapter 8

Life on Xanthe

Earth Year 2025 on Xanthe

The Xanthe zoo was unique. Dax felt it every time he'd come here. And today he was here with his two daughters, Nika and Rita, eleven and seven respectively. He felt both elated and sad that in less than six months, he and his family would leave this planet, their wonderful home, and travel for the next ten years to Earth.

He was an agricultural expert, and his knowledge and skills were critical to the success of that interstellar trip to Earth. He and his family would be part of the first Stell^rs to arrive on Earth in 2036. He would be immediately involved in helping with the growing of fruits, vegetables, and other indigenous plants transported from Xanthe to wherever they would settle. Dax's partner, Astra, and their children were excited to be a part of the first Stell^rs to live on Earth. This relocation process was now known as the *Cradle of Hope* for the Stell^rs civilization's collective future.

He and his daughters strolled past beautiful native habitats created for the uniqueness of these animals and various creatures collected from across the galaxies. Their favorite was the six-legged Nebulox from Astralis in the Centaurus galaxy and the Glitterwing purple and yellow bird from Valeria in the Quasaris galaxy. The Nebulox had four eyes and made the cutest cooing sounds. The Glitterwing talked like a parrot and had a long memory of previous conversations with others.

Nika suddenly stopped and pointed at the Nebulox. "Papa, look how curious he is about the Glitterwing."

Their neighboring habitats allowed them to study each other without encroaching on each other's space. And right now, the Nebulox cooed audibly and the Glitterwing started talking, a quick, conversational chatter that the Nebulox seemed to understand. It cocked its head, its four eyes zeroing in on the bird, its purple and yellow wings fluttering as it kept saying, "You're my friend, we're friends, aren't we friends?"

Nebulox cooed more loudly and scurried closer to the fence on its six legs. Glitterwing chattered, "I understand your coos! We're friends, right? Friends?"

The tone of the Nebulox's coos changed. They became more drawn out, softer, more intimate. Glitterwing flew over to the fence and landed on the side, so he and Nebulox could see each other eye to eye. And then they did something that Dax had never seen before or even heard about: Glitterwing's beak gently caressed the side of Nebulox's neck in what looked to Dax like a loving caress, then flew back into its habitat.

"Friendship," Rita remarked. "Just like the Glitterwing said."

They started walking again. "We're going to miss our home, Papa," said Nika.

"Your mom and I will, too."

"But we can't wait to see the animals on Earth," Rita added.

Nika piped in. "Especially giraffes and monkeys. And we really want to explore the terrain, the cities, the cultures."

His daughters were driven by curiosity.

Some of the Stell^rs on Xanthe were currently relocating to Andromeda, where Stell^rs had lived for thousands of years. It was more distant than Earth, so fewer numbers of the Xanthe's population were able to be transported. Dax's kids hoped that maybe one day in the distant future they would all be together again on Xanthe. It was a special dream all Stell^r children shared. And now his daughters were singing about it:

In a realm beyond celestial sight
A being of wonder, clothed in light
A child of Xanthe from distant skies
Descended upon Earth, curious and wise
Welcome the unknown with an open embrace
And always demonstrate the Stell^r grace
For we are all stardust, connected in birth
In this cosmic journey to the blue planet Earth

The words, sung in their soft, beautiful voices, nearly brought Dax to tears. All their lives were about to change completely and forever.

Part Two

Pioneers

"The person who follows the crowd will usually go no further than the crowd. The person who walks alone is likely to find himself in places no one has ever seen before."

- Albert Einstein

Chapter 9

They should have Listened

On December 15, 2029, Epsilon received a communication from the two shuttle crafts that had been listening in on conversations over the presidential palaces in North Korea and Pakistan.

Epsilon, we've heard alarming conversations between the N. Korean leader and the Pakistani leader.

Can you send to me?

Certainly. Sending now.

The recording began with the North Korean leader, Lee Shin, telling the Pakistani leader, Murad Khan, that he believed the message they'd heard was part of a conspiracy plot perpetrated by the West to try to control their nuclear weapons and proliferation. Khan eagerly agreed.

Both decided to advance to DEFCON 1 of nuclear preparedness, their terms for taking their nuclear arsenals to high alert with specific targets selected.

What would you like us to do?

All this alarmed Epsilon but didn't surprise him. He knew immediately what had to be done.

I would like you to send down pulse wave beams to disable both leaders. This action would place both men in induced stasis. Their respective medical teams would be completely mystified and would hook them up to feeding and respirator equipment to keep them alive. *I also want you to immediately disable the nuclear arsenals of both countries.*

As you command, Epsilon.

He realized that at some point he would have to revisit the situation and knew he might have to incapacitate other world leaders and also disable their nuclear arsenals. January 15, 2030 would be the telling.

+++

Zhukov's concern over that initial telepathic message and his subsequent conversations with Mitchum and the leaders of North Korea and Pakistan had eaten away at him for weeks. Now the date for next direct contact—January 15—was just one week away, and he hadn't heard from any of the leaders of the other nuclear countries. Why not? Had they been silenced by these so-called aliens? Or by the Americans? The Europeans?

He swiveled around in his desk chair and went online, checking his email. Nothing here from any leader, ally or otherwise. Time to make some calls, he thought, and went on his secure line. North Korea first.

Lee Shin was a charismatic man of 44, who at five foot nine was about two inches taller than that of the average North Korean male. He was a compelling speaker, as many leaders were, and in his official capacity carried himself with a sort of quiet dignity. But in private, that dignity was replaced with a raucous dangerous disposition that demeaned and threatened the people he represented. In that raucous side, Zhukov recognized himself, the two of them hungry for the ultimate in world power and not concerned about committing murder to keep any opposition in line.

Two rings and the phone in North Korea was answered by a woman with a soft, sonorous voice. She spoke Korean. Zhukov didn't think a translator was on the line, however, he understood enough Korean to greet the woman in her own language, then announced himself in Russian. "President Zhukov calling."

The woman replied in flawless Russian. "Please hold, Mr. President."

Moments later, a man answered. Zhukov didn't recognize his voice. "I'm Eun-woo, Lee's brother. And I'm sorry to tell you that right now, machines are sustaining his life. Our best physicians can't figure out what the problem is."

Zhukov sat up straighter. "Machines? What kind of machines?"

"Medical machines, a respirator, a feeding tube..."

His hands started sweating. He felt nauseated. "What... happened?"

"We don't know. He returned from giving a public address three weeks ago, said he was tired, and laid down for a nap. Hours later I...I found him unconscious, barely breathing."

"He must have had some symptoms beforehand."

"Nothing that anyone noticed."

"What about the two men who guard him?"

"They didn't report anything other than he said he was tired and needed a nap."

"Please let me know when there's a change."

"I will, President Zhukov. Thank you for your concern."

Deeply shaken, Zhukov thanked him and disconnected from the call. For several minutes, he just sat there, hand on the receiver, and sped through the pathetically few possibilities. That Shin had a stroke, a heart attack, some major blow up in his body that might have been caused by stress.

Or by the aliens who had incapacitated him somehow.

He pressed the heels of his hands against his eyes and desperately wished he and his wife hadn't gotten divorced. He could have gone home this evening and found her at her computer, writing madly on her novel. He had yet to read any of it, but she'd promised he would be her first reader when it was done.

He suddenly couldn't remember why they'd gotten divorced.

He and Anna had met at the Academy when they were both in their mid-twenties, training for the prestigious, elite government jobs. They'd debated about Tolstoy's *War & Peace*. She believed Natasha's inner life had been brilliantly portrayed and explained her sexuality. He believed she was just a misguided woman who followed her sexual whims and didn't give a damn about anyone else. That difference of opinion had been central to his and Anna's visceral attraction to each other. But had it also spelled their death as a married couple several years ago? Or had it been longer than that? They were both so young.

"Remember," he muttered, and ground his fists against his eyes. "You know this."

And then it came to him. It had happened during Covid in 2020, when they'd had a terrible argument about the lockdown, which collapsed into that old disagreement about Natasha in *War & Peace*. Absurd, but there it was, in his face, mocking him. When he'd come home that evening, she had packed up her clothes and books and left him a note. *Am staying with my sister.*

She'd filed for divorce three days later. And that was that.

Zhukov called the Pakistani leader Murad Khan, and it was almost a repeat of what he just had experienced in the North Korea call. But it wasn't Khan or a brother or right-hand man who answered. It was his wife, Inaya, a lovely woman he'd met twice. She was in her late twenties and her voice sounded choked with grief and worry.

"I don't know what happened, Alexander. We were going to do our usual long walk one evening three weeks ago and I was waiting outside for him. After twenty minutes or so, I went back inside to see what was going on, and one of our servants was racing toward me, shouting, "Madame, it's your husband, come quickly." A sob escaped her. "He...he was on the couch, motionless, barely breathing. We rushed him to the hospital..."

"And now he's hooked up to machines?"

"Yes, yes. How..."

"The same exact thing happened to the Lee Shin three weeks ago."

"But what...does any of this mean, Alexander?"

"I don't know. But I promise you, Inaya, as soon as I find out, I'll call you."

After they disconnected, he wondered if their nuclear arsenals had been disabled. Was there a way to tell that short of trying to detonate one of them? However, that was a completely absurd thought.

He placed a call to Adhira Agarwal, the only female leader of the nine nuclear countries. He didn't know her well but was curious if she was aware of what had happened to Shin and Khan. She answered her own phone on the second ring. "Alexander, good to hear from you."

Her Russian was excellent. "Just wanted to check in with you before this January 15 contact date, Adhira."

"I appreciate that. But I'm as much in the dark as you are. Do you think it will be another telepathic message? That was so strange."

"You believe it was actually telepathic? From the alien leader? And that it wasn't some sort of trick?"

She laughed—a soft, feminine sound, not at all mocking. "I guess you have never had a telepathic experience. Otherwise, you would have recognized it as genuine. No trick. I'm looking forward to the contact next week. Quite a start to the new decade!"

"But suppose it's all an elaborate hoax to convince the nine nuclear countries to disable their arsenals?"

"I rarely use the word impossible, Alexander. But I'll use it now. If that was a genuine telepathic message from the alien leader, then I suspect they have a way of disabling all nuclear arsenals."

"And disabling humans as well, perhaps. Both Lee Shin and Murad Khan are on life support. That's too coincidental."

"But we're fine, you, me, the other five. What did they do differently?"

Zhukov suspected they had gone to DEFCON 1, and the aliens knew it and had taken action. But he had no way of proving it.

"Maybe they violated the part of the message about what would happen if any of us moved our nukes."

"We didn't."

"Same here."

"Why tempt fate until we know more?"

"Agreed."

"Well, we'll know in one week, Alexander. How about if we talk then? I'll call you this time."

"Good. I look forward to it. You take care, Adhira."

"You, too, Alexander. And think of it this way. If we discover there really is an advanced race of peaceful aliens out there, just imagine how our planet is going to change. Imagine the technology they must have!"

Yes, that was part of what concerned him. Could these aliens hear everything that was said in these private communications?

He suddenly hoped so. If they'd listened in on his conversation with Adhira, they surely were convinced that neither of them was a risk. Could they hear his thoughts as well? Could they tune in telepathically on what he was thinking right this second? And what about Adhira's thoughts. Were hers as dark and angry as his?

Surely not. Not long after they'd met, he had researched her name. It meant moon lightning. And her demeanor, her words, reflected that meaning. No wonder she successfully ruled the world's most populous country with—what? How many billions now? A billion and a half? Two billion?

He didn't understand Indian or Hindu culture, but he felt he had a solid grasp of Adhira's character. In an American western movie, she would be "a good guy."

And he would be its opposite.

It was a humbling and depressing thought, and he wondered, in this rare introspective moment, when he had changed or if he'd been born like this. He didn't have an answer.

+++

On January 14, Rose and Liam worked for several hours on their design for a people rover that could navigate the rough terrain of Mars. It was just the two of them in the spacious office Mitchum's staff had set up for them, and for countless hours since she'd arrived here at the White House, this office had been one of her havens of solitude.

But today she was distracted by the fact that Epsilon's next contact with the world leaders would be tomorrow. She desperately wished she could tune in, listen in, eavesdrop. She could do it through Mitchum, but Epsilon might detect her presence. Would there be harm in that? It wouldn't mean she was revealing herself to the entire planet but simply letting the Stell^rs know she was alive. And living in the White House. And willing to help however she could.

She debated about discussing this with Mitchum. He would be open to anything she said, he always was. But in the end, he took everything into account and made his own decision. Afterall, he was the President of the United States.

"You're really quiet, Rose. What's on your mind?" Liam asked.

"The contact tomorrow."

He straightened up, pressed his hand against the small of his back, and stretched. "What do you want to do?"

"I'd like to let them know I'm still alive and have lived here for nearly 80 years."

"Have you spoken to the President about it?"

"Not really."

"Maybe you should."

"I'm considering it."

"Does he have any idea what time tomorrow this contact may come?"

"If so, he hasn't shared it."

Liam paced now, always a sign that he was worried. "That probably means he doesn't know, Rose."

She decided to discuss it first with Laurie and messaged her. *You free for a few?*

Definitely. Meet you in the kitchen in 5 minutes.

"Be back soon, Liam."

He slyly grinned. "You go, girl."

She didn't have too far to walk—just up one hallway and down another. Nomad met her halfway, tail wagging, his ball in his mouth. Rose greeted him and held out her hand for the ball. He dropped it, and she scooped it up and tossed it down the hall. He loped after it, caught it as it bounced, then whipped around and returned to her. "C'mon, let's go see the lady of the house, Nomad. I bet Carmen has left some goodies for lunch."

Sure enough, when they entered the private residence, the delicious scents in the air told her black beans and rice had been concocted in that marvelous way Carmen had with spices. By now, Carmen and everyone else knew she didn't eat meat.

"Hey, Laurie," she called. "Nomad came in with me."

She popped out of her office and greeted the dog. "He sneaks out when I'm busy. So what's up, Rose? Let's talk in the kitchen."

"I smell tacos," she said.

Laurie chuckled. "Yeah. Carmen was here earlier. She remarked that you'd love the tacos. How're you and Liam doing on the designs?"

"Good, really good. "

They settled side by side in comfortable high back stools in the kitchen. "So, what's on your mind, Rose?"

"Tomorrow. I'd like to let Epsilon know that I'm alive and ready to help in any way I can with whatever he has in mind."

Her face lit up. "That's a great idea. Have you talked with Jim about it?"

"I wanted to run it by you first."

"Let's get Helen in on this, too. I'll message her."

While Laurie tapped away at her phone, Rose noticed that Nomad had his paws resting on the windowsill and peered out intently, tail wagging. She joined him at the window. It overlooked the grounds, where she saw Whitley, Mitchum, and Helen and their Secret Service agents standing in the driveway, talking. Helen glanced down at her phone and then looked up and saw Rose and Nomad. She flashed a thumbs up. Minutes later, she rapped at the kitchen door—two knocks, a pause, a third knock. "C'mon, in, Helen," called Laurie.

She hurried in, greeted Nomad, glanced from Rose to Laurie. "A girls' caucus in the kitchen?"

"Something like that," Laurie replied.

Helen sat on the remaining high back chair at the counter and kicked off her high heels. "Darn, these things make my feet ache."

Rose slipped off the size 12 running shoes that Liam had bought for her several years ago and removed the inner lining of the right one. The shoes hadn't fit until she'd cut away strips of fabric from the safety suit she'd been wearing the day her shuttle craft had crashed in Roswell and then fitted the strips to the insides of the shoes. The fabric was unique to Xanthe and its space program and molded itself to the contours of the shoes and then her feet.

"Try these," Rose said. "My magical linings."

She passed the linings to Helen. They no longer had a shape but looked like ordinary strips of fabric. "What should I do with them?"

"Wrap each one around a foot, slip your feet back into the heels, see if they're more comfortable."

"They're white. This will look really weird."

"Naw. The strips will go transparent."

Helen gave her a skeptical look, then wrapped the fabric around her right foot. As soon as it interacted with the heat of her body, it went transparent. "Incredible. Look, Laurie." Helen wagged her foot.

Laurie was already leaning forward, frowning, eyes widening. She reached out and touched Helen's foot. "I can't feel it. I don't get it."

Rose explained about the space suit. "I thought the guys who had found me had disposed of the suit. But one morning before Liam went to work at Area 51, he came across a top secret file on me that held a box of remnants that had been removed from the crash site and from later, when I was in the hospital. When he and I started working together on designs, he gave me the box. My space suit was in there, intact for the most part after all the testing they performed. So I took some strips from it and created the linings."

"Scissors can cut the fabric?" Laurie asked.

"If I'm using them, yes, because the suit was made for me. But no one else can cut it."

"Are you saying it possesses a form of consciousness?" Helen asked. "Is that what you're saying?"

"It's just the nature of this particular fabric."

Helen got up and walked around the room with a blissful expression on her face. "Incredible. I could run a marathon in these. That's how comfortable they are."

"What else can that fabric be used for?" Laurie asked.

"Virtually anything. If they'd grafted a piece of it onto my intestine when I was injured, I would have healed much more quickly." She reached into the back pocket of her khaki pants and drew out another strip that she always carried with her. Just in case she needed it for...well, for anything. She passed it to Laurie, who ran her fingers over it, sniffed at it, touched it to her face. "It's remarkably soft. Have you thought about the way tomorrow to let Epsilon know you're alive?"

"I honestly don't know how best to alert him."

Helen's brows shot into sharp peaks. "Is that what this caucus is about?"

"We wanted to run the idea past you," Laurie said. "Would Jim go for that?"

Helen sat down again. "Probably not. My understanding is that he wants Rose's presence to be revealed to the Stell^rs later for security and intelligence reasons."

"But I would like my people to know I'm alive and eager to help in whatever way I can."

"What do you think their plan is, Rose?" Helen asked as the VP. Rose understood that. But she also asked as a woman, a wife, a mother, a human being.

"I haven't had any contact with them for nearly 80 years, so I can only offer my opinion based on what I know from many decades ago."

Laurie nodded. "We understand that, Rose. But your opinion may be the best measurement we have."

So she telepathically fed them the images of what she now thought of as her historical movie. The Stell^rs and the early encounters with the Neanderthals, the field of asteroids that would annihilate Xanthe in 2056 and steps the Council had taken decades ago to destroy that field. "The initial telepathic contact he made leads me to believe they've failed to destroy or deter the massive field and have started evacuating Stell^rs to other places—to our base on the far side of the moon, to planets in the Andromeda Galaxy, and to our many large space stations. But Earth is probably still the preferred destination, and the contact tomorrow is the preparation for that. Then again, I may be totally wrong."

"Can you tune in telepathically to tomorrow's contact without being noticed?" Helen asked.

"I suspect it will be quite specific to the leaders of the nine nuclear countries, so the only way I could do it is by tapping into Jim. That's part of why I think he needs to know this."

"I've been messaging him," Laurie said. "He's on his way over."

The three women left the kitchen and went to Laurie's office.

+++

Mitchum had expected something like this about tomorrow's contact. *Alleged* contact. He hadn't received any confirmation that the contact date was still on. He knew Rose was in the dark about it, too, but that she would want to be prepared in the event Epsilon kept to the January 15 date.

Once he walked into his wife's office, he would be up against three formidable women with an opinion that he felt would be the opposite of his own. Just the thought of it pissed him off. He was the President, the ultimate authority, and had the final say. Yet, he realized that was his left brain screaming, his male ego rebelling, and nearly laughed out loud. He must have looked amused, though, because Ken, hurrying alongside him said, "Sir? A private joke? Or an upset stomach?"

Mitchum laughed and stopped. "You're married, Ken. How do you feel when your wife disagrees with you?"

Ken, tall, muscular, and young, looked flustered, like he'd never been asked such a personal question before. He raked his fingers through his brown, curly hair, glanced down at the floor. "Well, sir." He raised his head. "It depends on the issue. Is she the expert on whatever this is? Or am I?"

"Suppose you believe you're the expert and she disagrees."

"May I be honest, sir?"

"I don't want anything less."

"Well, it ticks me off. We argue. Both of us are attorneys, so we start sounding like prosecutor and defense, but really it boils down to man and woman. And I hate to admit it, but nine times out of ten, she's right."

"Why? Because she argues better than you do?"

"No, sir. I don't think it's that. Women perceive differently than we do. They're more right brain, intuitive. They see what we don't."

The words made him smile. Mitchum slung an arm around Ken's shoulders. "Thanks, Ken. You just saved my ass." *My marriage, two friendships I value...* "And when you write your memoir of a secret service agent book, please don't include anything about Rose or the Stell^rs and all this."

Ken's dark eyes crinkled at the corners when he grinned. "No way I'm writing any book, President Mitchum. These experiences are all mine."

Chapter 10

Holographic Hello

January 15, 2030

Epsilon's idea was simple technologically but tricky to pull off. He and other members of the Council had spent a couple of days constructing a holographic conference room.

The construction of an idea wasn't all that different from the construction of a physical structure. It started with a design. They created it within a short period of time. A piece here, a piece there, each individually completed section detailed and unique. The actual structure was more challenging. Now to make each of these sections fit seamlessly.

He wanted the world leaders to feel like they were sitting in a physical conference room, and that entailed the mental visual assembly of tables, chairs, a projector of some kind. It meant a pitcher of water in the center of the table, glasses at each leader's place, and of course, an electronic tablet for taking notes, communication, whatever. He thought it would be a nice touch to have a platter of food and small plates, too, so the leaders could snack and feel comfortable and welcomed. The food could easily be beamed to each of them.

By the 15th, they had created what Epsilon felt would work. The walls held art or images of something unique to each country. The magnificent Himalayas stood along the borders of India, Pakistan, and China, three of the nuclear powers, but also along the borders of Nepal and Bhutan. It went on one wall. On the opposite wall were photographs of human beings from every country and walk of life and age. The diversity pleased Epsilon.

For the US they chose an image of the Woodstock musical festival in upstate NY from 1969 and another of the Statue of Liberty. For Russia, it was an image from Siberia, Lake Baikal, the largest freshwater lake in the world. The Great Wall was shown for China. The Taj Mahal for India. Big Ben represented the UK, the Eiffel Tower represented France, the Western Wall for Israel. Even though the North Korean leader had been put into a coma, Epsilon made sure that an image of the Forbidden City, Pyongyang, remained. The same was true for Pakistan; Epsilon kept the image of the Badshahi Mosque.

So at 11:00 a.m. Eastern time on January 15, 2030, Epsilon sent his telepathic message to the leaders of the seven nuclear countries that remained. *Greetings, leaders. This is Epsilon, who warmly appreciates your openness to receiving this message. Before I take you to the holographic conference room, I invite some questions.*

Not surprisingly, Zhukov rudely interjected. *Why aren't the leaders of North Korea and Pakistan present?*

Epsilon felt tempted to ignore the question. But that struck him as too easy. The Stell^rs never hid from truth. *Unfortunately, both men went to DEFCON 1, the very thing I warned about during our first interaction. So we placed them in stasis and in the capable hands of their countries' medics, and we rendered their nuclear arsenals useless.*

This created a wave of powerful emotion that he both felt and saw. It pulsed in the air around them, a deeply colored wave of blues and reds punctured by darkness. Fear, awe, helplessness, shock, utter terror, acceptance, even rebellion were felt by the Stell^rs when the humans heard this. There were so many types of emotions that Epsilon lacked names for some of them.

Any other questions?

Complete silence.

Then on behalf of Xanthe and the Stell^rs, our Council invites you into our conference room.

And he and the other four Council members brought the truly magnificent holographic room around them, enclosing them inside of it, blanketing them with the sounds and scents and details of an actual physical place. The Indian leader, Adhira Agarwal, looked around the vast space, then opened an arm to the image of the Himalayas. "Many of us claim it to be ours, but in truth, it belongs to no one." Then she brought her hands together in an attitude of prayer and bowed briefly in each direction. "Thank you, Epsilon, for trying to make us feel at home."

The French leader walked up to the image of the Eiffel Tower, placed one hand against it, and held the other hand out to the group. One by one, each of the leaders touched an outstretched hand with their own, a sign of solidarity.

Epsilon materialized into view, wearing a suit made of a fabric unique to Xanthe's space program. Rose and Fralix had worn suits like this, he thought, when they'd crashed in Roswell all those decades ago. It seemed fitting to do so now. He touched his hand to that of the French leader and then to the hands of the other leaders as well. Only one triggered a negative sensation: the raging hot hand of Zhukov.

We would like you to know something about us. And he showed them the stream of images—the movie—that depicted where the Stell^rs had originated, where they had traveled across the universe, who they were at their core. Included were images of Xanthe as well—the splendid architecture of towers and arches in the cities, the vast stretches of open land, the farming areas. He even showed them visuals of Xanthe's wonderful zoo with its exotic animals like the Glitterwing and the Jumper, which vaguely resembled an Earth kangaroo except that it had six legs.

He added another visual of the planet Andromeda with its vast peaks and valleys, its domed cities, its breathtaking vista of space. He tried to give them some idea of where the Stell^rs had visited over thousands of years.

Questions?

Mitchum, the US leader, spoke up. *Epsilon, with all respect, please share with us the purpose for this contact now. Can we do something for you? What do you need from us?*

We'll explain more of the details on a date to be announced when we all next meet in person.

+++

Rose eavesdropped through Jim. He begrudgingly agreed to allow that after Rose and Helen made it abundantly clear it was the right thing to do. It wasn't a perfect system because Epsilon's communication was intended specifically for him and the other leaders. But it worked well enough for him to sense her and for them to communicate when his telepathic discussion with the leaders reached a brief silence.

In this silence, I sense you eavesdropping. Who are you?

I'm Roseaelyn.

She felt the shock that seized him.

Roseaelyn?! The Roseaelyn we lost in 1947?

Yes, the same. But I now go by my Earth name, just Rose.

She explained what had happened, the events that had led to the crash and the events that followed immediately afterward. She told him Area 51 had been her home for almost 80 years. And that was when he chose the location for the in-person meeting at Area 51. *No one else heard our discussion,* Epsilon assured her.

Then silence ended and the leaders began asking more questions.

Zhukov: *Will this contact be in person?*

Epsilon: *Yes. Details to follow soon.*

Zhukov: *Will we receive something soon?*

Epsilon: *Yes. There is quite a bit of planning needed over the next several months. It's absolutely critical that you maintain complete secrecy and silence until then.*

Mitchum: *If the leaders of seven of the nuclear nations get together, the press will find out about it and the world will know about you.*

Epsilon: *The people of Earth will know when we are ready for them to know.*

Chen: *The world does not need to know.*

The response of the Chinese leader irritated Rose. His country had experienced numerous UFO sightings, and there was speculation that both China and Russia were ahead of the US in terms of research and UFO retrieval. Of course she knew that wasn't the case. But Chen didn't want for the rest of the world to know about the Stell^rs. Why not? What was he afraid of?

The Israeli premier, Yonatan Becker, slipped into the conversation. *Should not know what, President Chen? That the Stell^rs exist? Or that we're going to meet with them?*

Chen: *Both.*

Becker: *Of course, the world should know about the Stell^rs. This kind of information is for all people, in every country on this planet.*

Rose agreed. She suspected Epsilon did, too.

The UK premier, Benjamin Harrington, now spoke up. *President Mitchum may be right about the press. How do we deal with that, Epsilon?*

Epsilon: *You don't. We do. Our cloaking technology is quite sophisticated and will shield all of you with security and privacy during your travel to meet with us.*

Mitchum: *President Bernard? Any questions? Observations?*

The French president impressed Rose as a thoughtful man. *As long as this cloaking technology is used. We don't need publicity about this visit and meeting.*

Epsilon: *I'll be in touch in the next month with the meeting date and location. Wishing you all productive and enlightening days ahead. Signing off, respectfully Epsilon, Stell^r Council Leader.*

With that, Rose felt him withdraw from Mitchum. Fortunately, she was alone in the office where she and Liam worked, so she waited for Epsilon to acknowledge her fully. Within minutes, his voice returned to her head.

It's such a delight to learn that you survived that crash, Roseaelyn...Rose... and have lived among humans for so long. We will alert your loved ones immediately. I promise that you will have a reunion with them very soon. At some future time, we'll talk about everything, about what you've learned. But for now...

Yes. For now, how can I help and what are your plans?

They spoke for the next hour. For the most part, she'd been correct about the Stell^r plans for evacuation, but they had gone much farther than that. Epsilon explained that the first starships were already en route for arrival in 2036. Onboard would be experts in various areas necessary for the Stell^r survival on Earth. They would determine where the most suitable location would be to settle the Stell^r population.

From what I've learned about humans, your existence and plans will cause mass chaos here, Epsilon. Americans have an odd phrase about such a thing. It will take time for people to wrap their heads around the realization that aliens don't just exist but are migrating here. The nuclear power countries may threaten to use their nukes on the Stell^rs. Others may end up like Shin and Khan. I suspect you also deactivated their nuclear arsenals?

Yes, we did. And yes, some of the others may have to be dealt with in the same way. We'll know more at the next meeting. And I have decided to hold the meeting in Area 51 to honor you, Rose.

That made her smile.

By the way, have any of these humans died because of your presence? Epsilon asked.

No. You won't need protective suits. These humans are not the Neanderthals. That very unfortunate tragedy with our first contact will never happen again.

Wonderful. This isn't just a relief, Rose, it's a liberation. We have avoided physical contact with Earth for nearly 40,000 years because we were so sure our presence would prove fatal for them, just as it did for the Neanderthals.

In the decades I've been here, not a single human has died because of my presence.

I will be in touch with you before I contact the leaders with more information. If you need to get in touch before then, just say so out loud and our shuttle crafts that are close to Earth and in stealth mode will transmit your request or message to me.

I'll do whatever I can to help facilitate that meeting.

Until soon, my friend.

+++

After the January 15 contact, Mitchum spent the next several days in talks with his wife, his VP, his chief of staff, and his friend, Paul Spenser, whom he now thought of as Mr. Webb Telescope Guy. They argued and debated in the conference room, walked the White House grounds, consumed strong coffee with distressing regularity. Laurie remarked that he tossed and turned all night. Nomad kept his distance.

The plan he finally settled on was simple. He would recommend the very private government airstrip within Area 51 be hidden by the Stell^r cloaking technology, and any plane that flew into it would also be rendered invisible to radar and the naked eye. Mitchum hoped their technology actually worked that way. When he ran the idea by Rose, she laughed. Plus she already secretly knew that Epsilon had chosen Area 51. But better it come from Jim to Epsilon.

They were eating breakfast together, just the two of them and Nomad, on his best behavior. The dog sat there between them, tail thumping the floor, as he waited for a morsel to drop in front of him.

"I suspect the Stell^r cloaking technology can render an entire city invisible, Jim."

"Not surprising. So then, an airport and several arriving aircraft shouldn't be a problem. Can you contact him at any time to confirm the location, Rose?"

"Not unless there's a craft that's a lot closer to Earth than the moon base. Why?"

"I'd like to verify that the technology can be used to completely hide the airstrip and arriving planes from view."

She cupped her hands at the sides of her mouth, smiled and tilted her head back. "Hey, if any of you Stell^rs are eavesdropping on us, can you ask Epsilon to get in touch? President Mitchum would like to know whether the cloaking technology can hide an airstrip and arriving planes from view of the media and radar."

Interesting, Mitchum thought, but not shocking. Nothing about these Stell^rs surprised him at this point. "Do they listen in continually?"

"Probably. My impression is that they're alert for more potential troublemakers like Presidents Shin and Khan."

"I'm pleased that Epsilon had their nuclear arsenals deactivated."

Rose's gaze met his. "He gave them fair warning."

"He may have to do that with every nuclear arsenal if the Stell^rs evacuate their populace here to Earth, Rose."

"We'll know a lot more at our next meeting."

Just as Mitchum got up with his empty dishes in hand, he heard someone speaking in his head, a deep male voice. *President Mitchum, this is Delta, Epsilon's assistant. The answer to your question is yes, and he confirms your idea of using the airstrip inside Area 51 and will implement it. More details to follow soon.*

Mitchum didn't realize he'd stopped until Rose spoke. "Your answer came through?"

"Yes. From his assistant, Delta."

"I'd like to be there, Jim."

"Of course. And so will Helen, Whitley, and Paul."

"And Nomad?" she asked, glancing at the dog, now sprawled on the floor.

"You think Epsilon and whoever else is with him will be okay with that?"

"Yes."

"Hear that, Nomad?" Mitchum said. "You're going to meet more aliens."

The dog lifted his head, looked at each of them, then barked.

"That's a definite yes," Rose remarked.

Mitchum continued into the kitchen with his breakfast dishes, rinsed them off, put them in the dishwasher. "What's on your agenda for the rest of the day, Rose?"

"Liam and I are going to work for a while, then sometime this afternoon Laurie and I are planning to do more shopping online." She brought her hands together in a silent clap. "Your wife has exquisite taste. Let me know if you hear anything else from Delta or Epsilon, okay?"

"Will do."

Mitchum hurried on out and headed to the oval office to meet with Whitley and Helen.

+++

Zhukov, after learning that the meeting would take place at Area 51 on May 1, was in a meeting all morning with his advisors. The four of them tried to hash out a plan, a strategy, for traveling to Nevada in just a week. When would they leave? On which aircraft? Would they be armed?

Before they broke for lunch, Victor made a surprising announcement. "I've invited one of our best Viewers to dine with us. We need additional insights that only a Viewer can provide."

"Which Viewer?" Zhukov asked.

"Sofiya Popov."

Who happened to be a close friend of his ex-wife, Anna. That bothered him. He didn't want her reading him and then reporting back to Anna. But Viktor was right about one thing: she was one of their best Viewers and the only woman on the team.

When she arrived, she breezed into the room in stylish pants and a lightweight blue sweater that enhanced the vivid blue of her eyes. Her light brown hair fell in graceful waves to her shoulders and her smile lit up the room. "Gentlemen, so good to see you all."

They all stood as she entered, but it was Viktor who pulled out the chair for her. "What's your pleasure for lunch, Sofiya?"

"Whatever is on that delicious-looking platter is fine with me."

Dimitri hurried over with a clean plate and silverware and set it in front of her. "There you go, Sofiya."

"What would you like to drink?" Zhukov asked.

"A splash of vodka, thank you. And a glass of water."

She helped herself to caviar, dumplings, and a bit of the stew. "So I understand you would like me to View Area 51 on June 1, correct?" She looked directly at Zhukov as she said this, then glanced at Viktor, an acknowledgement that he had asked her to help.

Victor nodded.

A smile tugged at the corners of her mouth, and she glanced around at each of them. "Considering what Area 51 is supposedly about, are you gentlemen meeting aliens who have a playful look?"

Was she just drawing a conclusion based on the conspiracy theories about Area 51 or had she viewed it already? Or had Viktor told her? "We aren't sure what to expect, Sofiya. That's why Viktor invited you here."

"Okay then." She ate a cracker with some of the delicious caviar, then tilted the shot glass of vodka to her mouth and downed it in a single gulp. "Let's get started." She reached for her handbag hanging on the back of the chair and withdrew a drawing pad and pencil. She set them on the table beside her, folded her hands together on top of the pad and sat back. "I'll see what there is to Area 51 on May 1."

She shut her eyes and went into her deep breathing, which Zhukov had witnessed several times before. He recalled a View she'd done for Anna, after her brother had gone missing during a trip to Egypt. She'd made elaborate drawings as she'd talked about what she saw. And the View was absolutely correct.

Her brother, Mikhail, had met a woman who had belonged to a gang that ultimately assaulted, robbed him, and left him for dead. Sofiya had identified the area where it happened, drawn images of the woman and her gang members, and had identified the hospital where she ultimately had found him. She had remained for weeks in Egypt with him, while he healed, then helped him find a place to live outside of Cairo. Where he still lived.

Yes, she was good. Extraordinary. So when she suddenly picked up the pencil and started sketching, he sat forward, watching the shapes that emerged. And when she spoke, he hung on every word.

"I know I'm at Area 51 because I briefly saw it. Then...it vanished; the whole area just disappeared. I also saw a number of jets and as they approached this...this invisible area, and that's what it is, *invisible*...these jets also vanish."

"Are they destroyed?" Viktor asked.

"No, I don't think so. They seem to be rendered invisible." She stopped sketching to sip from the glass of water. "I don't understand this technology. It's completely foreign to me. To all of us. It's...*alien*." Her hand and that pencil started moving again, moving so rapidly across the sketchpad that he had to really focus to see the shape that emerged. A tall being with shaded bluish skin and a large head and big, almond-shaped eyes. Not a prototypical Grey, but definitely not human. Then she started sketching in hair and clothing, and Zhukov realized the alien was female.

"Her name...I think it's the name of a flower. She's more than a century old but looks decades younger, maybe around 30 or 40. I think she speaks many languages, including Russian, and Area 51 was her home for a very long time."

"So she's an alien," Zhukov said.

"Yes, yes, of course. But you know what? She's one of the good guys, as they say in those American westerns you love to watch. Her people could annihilate us in a heartbeat. They incapacitated two of your colleagues and...and neutralized their nuclear arsenals."

Zhukov had suspected that much.

"So on May 1, we arrive in invisible jets at an invisible Area 51 and meet a tall female alien with shaded skin?"

"Bluish skin. She has been separated from the others for..."

She paused. Under her closed lids, her eyeballs flicked quickly back and forth, as if her brain struggled to process whatever she was seeing. Or maybe her perceptions struggled to make sense of an image. He didn't know. He suddenly wondered, though, if Sofiya had Viewed something in his and Anna's future that had triggered his ex-wife divorcing him. Someday he might ask. But not right now.

"Sofiya?" Viktor said. "You okay?"

Her eyes popped open. "Yes, yes, I'm okay."

Zhukov didn't think she looked okay. The color had bled out of her cheeks, her eyes flicked repeatedly from right to left, and now she was on her feet, pacing, running her fingers through her hair. "I don't know, I don't know. This is all incredibly strange. There are other aliens with this female, I don't know how many. They're all very tall. And telepathic. They..." She stopped, ran her hands over her face, and sank into the nearest chair and sobbed. "They're *good* beings, but...but incredibly powerful. Their race is...much older than the human race."

"Holy shit," Viktor murmured. "How much older? More than a million years?"

Sofia nodded yes.

"They've got over a million years on us..."

"This woman, the one with the bluish skin...she's full of surprises. I think she has been living at the White House quite a while."

Zhukov seethed that Mitchum hadn't divulged this, hadn't told him the full truth. "What do these aliens want?"

She swiped at her eyes, then went into her deep breathing mode again and picked up the pencil. She sketched madly this time, her hand moving so quickly that he had no idea what she sketched until she set the pencil down and turned the sketchpad so they could all see it. It looked like hundreds of spaceships falling from the skies.

"I think...they're evacuating their planet. And this Area 51 female alien is going to become one of the most powerful entities in this new world." She paused. "I'd like to accompany you, Alexander."

"Good idea," Dimitri remarked. "Sofiya would give you the edge."

Zhukov nodded. "I agree. But I don't know if anyone is permitted to accompany me."

"When will you know?" she asked.

"Probably when Epsilon sends his next telepathic message."

"Please keep me in mind." She glanced at her watch. "I need to get going, gentlemen." She packed up her sketchpad and pencil.

"What do we owe you, Sofiya?"

"Viktor already paid me."

"I'll walk you out," Zhukov said.

When they were outside the conference room, she turned to him. "Anna asked me to say hello."

"How's she doing?"

"Well, she got her own place. But she misses you, that's my take."

"She divorced *me*."

"And contrary to what you probably think, it's not because I Viewed her future with you."

"Then why?"

"I don't know. But she urged me to help when Viktor got in touch. She's why I came here."

"I'm grateful that you did, Sofiya. If I'm permitted to bring someone with me, I'll call you first."

She extended her hand, which he took, and they shook. Then he slung an arm around her shoulders and hugged her. "Thank you for Viewing this. I now know a lot more than I did before."

She stepped back, obviously surprised at the embrace. "I appreciate the opportunity and really hope I can tag along."

+++

Fifteen minutes after Sofiya left Zhukov's office, his private hotline from Defense Minister Sergei Sokolov was lighting up. Sokolov who was the number one supreme hawk in the Kremlin only called if it was a matter of State emergency.

"Hello Sergei, what can I do for you?"

"Alexander, I have something to tell you that may sound crazy."

"Sergei, nothing seems crazy to me these days. Get to it then."

"Ok, one of our long range Kosmos satellites detected an on/off signature of an unidentified aircraft of some kind hovering over North Korea several months ago. We also detected some type of energy wave that went from this UAP down to the surface. I did not alert you at the time since I didn't have concrete proof. And we don't think it's the Americans."

"Go on."

"Just yesterday, we noticed other abnormalities that we can't explain. The problem is they come and go in a split second. So far, I don't see any direct threat to us." "However, if this unknown entity comes into our airspace, I want to scramble a couple of our Su-75 Checkmates to engage."

Zhukov told Sokolov, "this conversation never took place. If an alien craft comes into our airspace, then you have the green light to fire on it. Do not call me, just do it."

Sergei raised his eye brows and said "alien?"

"This conversation is terminated. Just do as I instructed."

Sokolov hung up the receiver and was now even more concerned but he would do what the President ordered.

Chapter 11

Area 51

April 26, 2030

A few days before the contact at Area 51, Mitchum and Helen were meeting with Whitley and Paul Spenser to finalize shutting down the private runway at Area 51. Mitchum figured that shutting it down now, this close to contact, wouldn't draw any attention since the runway was rarely used. Also, because Epsilon was willing to use the Stell^r cloaking technology all across Area 51, he would have vehicles waiting there to transport the leaders to the conference facilities.

"Who's going with you, Jim?" Helen asked. "I'd like to."

"Me, too," Whitley said.

"Ditto," Spenser added.

"And what about your Secret Service detail?" Whitley asked.

"One or two of them go regardless," Mitchum said. "Beyond that, I don't know. Epsilon may have a limit on who all goes. Then again, it may not matter. Rose once remarked that Stell^rs can erase short term memories."

"Wow," Whitley exclaimed. "That can change the entire dynamic."

Mitchum nodded. "So I guess Area 51 doesn't have to go into lockdown beforehand because the Stell^rs will take care of it." As soon as Mitchum had said it, he knew he would not abdicate his responsibilities as a president to anyone. Human or alien.

Whitley glanced up from his iPad, where he'd been tapping away at the keys. "I've got a lot on my *talk about* list." He motioned at the device.

"I don't think Epsilon will worry about who comes along." Mitchum looked over at Spenser. "What do you think, Paul?"

Spenser's eyes crinkled at the corners. "Are you kidding? I've entertained this idea ever since I peered through a telescope for the first time when I was 14. A chance to meet more aliens like Rose? Absolutely. I'm sure the other leaders will have people accompanying them."

Whitley grinned. "You can be damn sure Zhukov won't be traveling alone. Or Chen."

It frustrated Mitchum that there hadn't been any further contact after selecting Area 51 and that in only a few days, this event was supposed to occur. He wanted to be able to plan for this momentous occasion, to figure out who would be where and when. For him, it felt like a complex chess game, so many pieces to move around, so many moves to make.

Then again, the arrival of the Stell^rs wasn't something over which he had any control. The only detail that fell within his purview was Area 51, where the jets would land, how the leaders would get from the airstrip to Area 51, what the employees were told or not told. But within the things that were his responsibility, he needed some answers. So he did what Rose had done that day they were talking. He tilted his head hack, cupped his hands at the sides of his mouth, and called out, "Hey, if any of you are listening in, please let Epsilon know we need additional information very soon so we can prepare Area 51 for contact."

Spenser chuckled. "Well, I guess that's one direct way to contact aliens. You..."

He didn't finish the sentence. He snapped forward suddenly, shock rearranging his expression, and Mitchum's first thought was that he was having a stroke. Or a heart attack.

But when the same thing happened to Helen and Whitley, he realized something else was going on. Within seconds, he heard Epsilon's clear voice in his head.

Greetings, President Mitchum. I understand your concerns. Each leader will be permitted three companions. We realize that leaders are flanked by personal guards, so each leader is allowed to have one in addition to the companions. That person's memory of the event and the memories of the respective pilots about the flights will be wiped clean. The three people in this room with you right now fit the criteria we have set for companions—a member of your staff, the second in command, and a scientific expert. With that in mind, I can open the conversation to the others.

Mitchum didn't respond immediately. He thought of Rose. He knew she'd had some contact with Epsilon several months back, so why hadn't either of them mentioned her? *Rose would like to be there.*

Absolutely. I would like her to be there a day before the meeting. On April 30. Can that be easily arranged?

Yes.

And I understand Rose has quite deep affection for your dog. So Nomad may also accompany you. Rose is also entitled to a companion—Liam. I'm having this same kind of conversation with the other six leaders, about who accompanies them.

Thank you for responding so quickly, Epsilon.

My apology for not doing so sooner.

With that, Epsilon opened the conversation to the others. *I welcome the three of you—Helen, Steve, Paul.*

Spenser: *Will this meeting be actually physical or holographic?*

Physical. Face to face. And I'm looking forward to meeting all of you in person. And I'll make some tweaks to your equipment that will allow you to see that Xanthe exists in the area that Rose pinpointed for you.

Whitley: *Should we bring anything special? What do you need? What's the purpose of all this?*

Uh-oh, Mitchum thought. He'd heard charged emotion in Whitley's question—some frustration along with bewilderment. He needed to coach his trusted Chief of Staff about his demeanor.

What followed were images of the massive field of asteroids headed toward Xanthe. *It will obliterate our planet in 2056 so it's necessary to evacuate our populace. Some of the Stell^rs have relocated already to Andromeda, to our ten space stations, and our base on Earth's moon. The rest will be evacuated to your planet starting in 2036.*

Rose had divulged as much but hearing it from the Council leader triggered a wave of dread inside Mitchum. *I'd like to suggest, Epsilon, that you don't divulge this to all the leaders at this time. It might trigger one or two of our colleagues to mobilize their nuclear arsenal.*

Whitley: *That's a worst-case scenario. What's more likely is total chaos on the planet.*

Epsilon: *Which is why we're moving slowly, methodically. I will lay out our ideas at the meeting on May 1.*

Helen: *Why do you want Rose and Liam at Area 51 the day before?*

Epsilon: *I'd like her to experience walking in there under her own volition and having the freedom to explore it. Then she can act as our guide.*

Mitchum loved the idea. How appropriate that Rose, basically imprisoned in Area 51 for nearly 80 years, should guide these world leaders into the country's most secretive place to meet with the Stell^rs. *Have you told her this?*

Epsilon: *Yes. She's delighted.*

Whitley: *Please tell us how we can help or facilitate things?*

Epsilon: *For now, just get Rose and Liam to Area 51 safely, and if you have any questions, Jim, give me a holler like you've done before.* Jim smiled.

Mitchum hoped this alien was as personable in person as he seemed to be telepathically. *Will do.*

+++

Exhilaration and dread rose and fell inside Rose. The closer the flight got to Area 51, the more pronounced these warring emotions became. This kind of internal conflict was new for her, probably the result of having lived among humans for so many decades.

She, Liam, and Ken the Secret Service agent were the only passengers on this flight. Mitchum had sent Ken because he trusted the man. So did Rose. And Ken, she knew, was key to her free movement around Area 51.

"A penny for your thoughts," Liam said, leaning closer to her. "I think that's how the saying goes."

She laughed. "It'll cost you more than that, Liam."

"Okay, okay, a thousand Satoshi."

"It's going to feel weird to be back there, with the freedom of movement Jim promised."

"I like living at the White House."

"What about your family, Liam? Where are they?"

"No family. Parents died some years back, have a sister somewhere, but she has been absent from my life since I went to work for the government. She hates the government. Back years ago, she made a name for herself as a conspiracy theorist, a queen of misinformation. She's older than me, so back then I was just getting out of grad school for aeronautical engineering, and she was fully immersed in conspiracies and misinformation. What about you, Rose? You have a sibling, right?"

"You'd call her a half-sister, born to my mother and her second partner. I don't have any idea what she's doing, who she is. I remember she always had a fascination with Andromeda, so maybe she moved there. I will find out more when the time comes...whenever that is."

Ken came over to them. "We've got another hour or so until we land. You two want anything to drink? Snack on?"

"I'd love some water," Rose said.

"Iced tea for me," Liam said. "Thanks."

"I guess I'm the flight attendant." Ken snickered. "How about snacks?"

"Whatever there is," Rose said. "Need some help?"

"Nah, nah, all good." He hurried off to the back of the plane, where the galley was located.

"Does Epsilon have a guard?" Liam asked.

"My sense is that he doesn't. No need. Stell^rs don't threaten each other. Of course, threats may come from others."

Liam pushed back in his seat and brought his stocking feet to the back of the chair in front of him. He tucked his hands under his head. "Must be nice, one of the benefits of your civilization having a million plus years over us. I'm not even sure if we would ever survive that long knowing how unstable things have been across our planet. Your arrival on the scene in 2029 couldn't have been timelier."

"We just don't have a taste for violence. Stell^rs will fight if threatened, will fight to defend, will fight for what we think is right. But we don't fight...just to fight. You could say we've been explorers of the cosmos not conquerors."

Ken returned with the iced tea, the cold water, and a plate of snacks—crackers, some sort of vegan dip, crackers, slices of cheese for Liam, and slices of avocados and oranges for Rose. He set them on the pull-down table and claimed the aisle seat across from them.

"You mind if I ask a question, Rose?"

"Ask away."

"If the Stell^rs evacuate here, 100 million of them or whatever it is, what's that going to be like? I mean, realistically? You've lived among us all these years. I figured you must have some opinion."

She had given this whole thing a lot of thought since she and Epsilon had communicated. She had no easy answers, but maybe Ken wasn't looking for easy answers. She didn't know him well enough. As Robert Heinlein had written in his 1961 novel *Stranger in a Strange Land*, she didn't *grok* Ken yet.

She'd started reading that book the day Kennedy was assassinated in 1963 and finished it when the three-day memorial for him had ended. Many times since then—and now—she had felt like that stranger in a strange land. Earth wasn't her true home, and it would never be. Xanthe was her true home. But Earth was her adopted planet because her shuttle craft had crashed here. And that, she thought, was simply the reality of it.

Had the crash been part of a greater design in her life? Perhaps. But if so, it was because she had consented to it before she was born, when the many possible ramifications of decisions were apparent, in your face. She vividly recalled sitting with her mother at one point before birth, the two of them discussing the possible results of one decision or another in her next life as Rose, the Stell^r pilot who would crash at a place called Roswell. She remembered her mother commenting that it would all be quite *weird,* yes, that was the unusual word she'd used. Weird. A human word.

The Google definition of that word was "something supernatural, uncanny." For her, it had been and was both, especially now with Liam looking at her in an odd way, apparently waiting for her to respond to what he'd said.

An opinion. Right. Her opinion about the evacuation. "It's going to be chaotic. Humans are constantly advised to embrace change, but you don't want change, not really. You like what's known and familiar."

"Will humans and Stell^rs be living together?" Ken asked.

"Yes, but probably not for a while. Humans must become accustomed to the fact that aliens are living on their planet. And the Stell^rs will need to get used to the way humans do things."

"Openness from both races." Liam said. "That's what you mean."

"Yes."

Ken tapped the face of his watch. "We're going to land within the hour. And for the next 48 hours, we'll need to get stuff prepared in Area 51."

"We're looking forward to our tour of the place, Liam."

He sat back, smiling. "I've been making notes. This is going to be intriguing."

+++

Zhukov, Viktor, and Sofiya left for Area 51 on April 29. They intended to first stay for a night with the Russian ambassador in San Francisco which was unlikely to trigger anything in the media. Zhukov planned to sport a fake beard and glasses just in case.

Sofiya had seen this in one of her recent Viewings of this trip and felt it was the most secure spot for them. On the morning of May 1, they would leave for Nevada and Area 51. Epsilon had instructed Zhukov and the other leaders about which specific runway should be used for landing. The Stell^r technology would render it and their jet and anything else around it invisible within a span of miles. Epsilon hadn't spelled out how many miles, but Zhukov suspected the area would be expansive.

It was just the three of them and two pilots on this flight. Viktor wasn't just an advisor, he was a bodyguard, the equivalent of a Secret Service agent. And Sofiya, of course, provided the Viewing information that had proven so critical these last few weeks to the decisions that he made.

Her information wasn't so full that he knew all the details of what would transpire at Area 51. But she had seen enough so that he felt he had a slight edge. And right now, he was deeply grateful for any edge.

The more time he spent with Sofiya, the greater his attraction to her, a disturbing and distracting development. She was several years younger than he was, in her mid-forties, and so far seemed unaware of his interest. But if she was so clairvoyant, how could she be unaware of it?

Then again, since she was close friends with Anna, he should keep his interest more closely guarded. The gossip mongers would love a story like that.

While he was on his laptop in a front row of the cabin, Sofiya suddenly sank into the seat beside him. "I saw something, Alexander. I was starting to doze off and saw this incredible rose, huge, a deep red, with the most exquisite petals. And I...I realized that's the female alien's name. Rose. She will be there. She'll be the one who shows us around."

"That's helpful, Sofiya, thank you."

"Hey, I'm as curious and eager for this as you are. But for different reasons."

"What do you think my reasons are?"

"Honestly? I can say this without fearing that I'll be swept up in the next roundup of dissidents?"

The way she said this, the specific words, reminded him of Anna during one of their frequent arguments. *Are you going to have me taken away in the next roundup? Is that ultimately how this marriage works?*

"I'll never have you swept up in anything for just being honest. You have my word on that."

She leaned in a little closer to him and whispered, "And how much is your word worth, Alexander?"

She was so close to him he caught the fragrance of soap and perfume on her skin. A clean, intoxicating scent. Those vivid blue eyes bored into his. He touched two fingers to her chin and kissed her. As soon as he did it, shock tore through him. He hoped Viktor hadn't witnessed this.

She pulled back slowly, touched her finger to the underside of his chin, where he would be wearing that fake beard. "That was a surprise."

"A pleasant one, I hope."

"Maybe." She gave a coy look. "And I never saw it coming. Interesting."

"But you're clairvoyant. So how can you *not* see what's about to happen in your own life?"

She lifted her bare feet to the back of the chair in front of her. "I think the toughest thing for any Viewer is to see much of anything for themselves." She shrugged. "Maybe that's nature's way of evening things out. Who knows?"

With that, she closed her eyes and turned her head away from him.

After a few minutes, he finally got up and made his way toward the middle of the plane, where Viktor was watching something on American TV. Zhukov gestured at the aisle seat. "You mind?"

"Never. What's going on, Alexander?"

"You selected and trained a lot of our Viewers. How does Sofiya rate among them?"

Viktor regarded him for a long, uncomfortable moment, then burst out laughing. "That's a serious question. Alexander, I've selected and trained dozens of viewers over the years. Some excel at particular types of views. Some are good at specifics. But I've never worked with a Viewer like Sofiya. She's versatile. She sometimes sees details that other Viewers miss. But she can be a know-it-all, too, who believes she's the only one with the right answers. Yet, her accuracy rate so far, at least that we can check, is nearly 85 percent. That's huge for Viewers because the future shifts as we make our individual and collective decisions. She gives us a tremendous advantage."

Zhukov suddenly realized Sofiya had never answered his question about what she thought his reasons were for being so eager for this encounter. Instead, like hormonal-driven teens, they'd gotten lost in the magic of that kiss.

"An advantage in avoiding peril in Area 51?" he asked.

"That and a tighter understanding of how the leaders and advisors see all this." Viktor sat up straighter. "Listen, she's good, Alexander. I'm certain the Americans have no one like her."

"They have a Stell^r, Rose, who lived in Area 51 for 80 years, and at some point last year, she moved to the White House. She lived with Mitchum and his wife. And their dog. I've seen that dog on TV. She was like a member of the family. Can you imagine?"

Viktor's eyes widened; his mouth twitched. "No, I can't."

"But the bottom-line question is simple. As a Stell^r, where does her allegiance lie? With her own kind or with Mitchum?"

"The bottom-line question, Alexander, isn't about allegiance. Is this Rose any match for Sofiya?"

Wrong question, Zhukov thought. Was Sofiya any match for Rose?

He doubted it.

The alien female definitely had the big advantage.

What did they call the females of their species? Not women. And what about the males? They weren't called men, were they? Well, it didn't matter. He would think of them as *women,* and they come from a species at least a million years older than humans. In addition to telepathy, what other paranormal abilities did they have? Could they move objects with their minds like the girl in that Stephen King movie years ago? Could they kill psychically by disrupting the functions of the brain, the body? Could they see the future? Could they *change* the future?

No, if they were able to change the future, then they would be able to alter Xanthe's future in 2056. But *what* were the limitations of their abilities? Did any limits even exist? He needed to know that. And, for him, that was what the meeting at Area 51 was really about.

Chapter 12

We control the Airspace

May 1, 2030

At 7:10 that morning, when their flight was about 90 minutes out from landing at Area 51, Mitchum sensed a palpable change in the air. He didn't know what it was—an abrupt blip in cabin pressure, in altitude or speed? No, this was different.

Even Nomad felt it. He raised his head from the aisle floor where he sprawled, gave Mitchum one of those looks that indicated discomfort, then got up and walked over to his water bowl at the front.

Mitchum drew back the window curtain and peered outside. The morning light burned in the east. Beneath them, the desert looked like its own continent, like the fictional *Dune*. Where was the aircraft's shadow? Where were the puffs or streaks of clouds? And then it hit him, of course, that they had entered the invisible zone of Stell^r cloaking technology.

Whitley suddenly snapped forward, his face limned with alarm, excitement, and awe. "Jim, it's happening."

"Yeah. Or we're being abducted and sucked up into a spaceship."

Spenser leaned forward from behind Mitchum. "Quantum. That's what it is. It's remarkable!"

Helen, sitting across the aisle, touched her index finger to her mouth. "Listen. Even the sounds are muted."

True. The four huge engines barely hummed on the massive Air Force One 747. Even here in the cabin, their voices struck Mitchum as odd, almost hollow. Lewis, one of the two Secret Service agents, quickly made his way up the aisle to the cockpit. Moments later, the captain's voice came over the PA. "Everything has disappeared from our radar. We should be flying blind, but we aren't. Something else controls us—our flight pattern, speed, direction, all of it."

129

Then Epsilon's voice came through the PA. "We now control your aircraft and will bring it in safely at the agreed upon landing strip. The cloaking covers about five square miles. We're invisible to virtually everything. I look forward to meeting everyone when you land."

A brief pause ensued, then the captain came on once more, his voice not quite as calm and steady as before. "That was, uh, well, let's see here." He cleared his throat. "We should be landing in about ten minutes. And, uh, yeah, that was weird. His voice just...just suddenly took over the PA."

Mitchum nearly got up to go into the cockpit and assure the pilot it had been strange and unsettling for all of them. But the seatbelt light blinked on, they were on final approach. He detected all the nuances of a descending large jet, but sounds were still muted. The landing was smooth, graceful, and then the giant plane stopped.

He glanced out the window and saw two dark SUVs speeding toward them. Right on schedule. He saw only one plane in the tie-down area, a Cessna 157 that reminded him of the plane on which he originally got his pilot's license. This private runway was on Area 51 property.

The pilot came forward and opened the front door, and Mitchum and his group of three—along with Nomad—stepped out into the sweltering Nevada heat. It wasn't humid, just relentless. By the time they reached the lead SUV, and their bags were loaded in the back, Mitchum anticipated the cool air inside Area 51.

He, Helen, and one of the Secret Service agents scooted into the back with Nomad and Spenser, and the other agent got into the front with the driver, an ex-military pilot Mitchum knew, Wayne Binelli. The rest of the presidential staff remained on the plane. Mitchum believed it important to fly in Air Force One as he traveled with Helen, and this Boeing was his airborne White House office and command center.

"Good to see you, Captain Binelli." Mitchum said.

"You, too, sir. I understand we're under a, uh, cloaking cover."

"Feels kind of odd," Mitchum remarked. "No shadows."

"Yeah, I noticed that."

"Is our plane the first to arrive?" Spenser asked.

"Yes, sir. I was informed that the six other flights are within an hour of here."

"What's the situation like inside Area 51?" Helen asked.

"Business as usual, Madam Vice-President. No one suspects anything unusual. I saw Rose and Liam in the cafeteria at the crack of dawn. She said she likes having the freedom to move around in there."

"Good," Helen said. "Did you know her before she came to DC?"

"Yes. I've been working here as a pilot and driver for the last seven years since I left the military. When one of our experimental jets developed a problem a few years back, none of our mechanics could figure out what was wrong, much less how to fix it. So I went to Rose. She diagnosed the problem in a few minutes and then asked me for some tools and proceeded to repair it."

That sounded about right, Mitchum thought. He also thought it was remarkable how many people had interacted with Rose over the years and had kept it a secret. "Did you pick her and Liam up when they arrived?"

Binelli nodded. "It was great to see them again."

With that, he drew up inside the Area 51 main gate, hopped out and opened the doors. Mitchum clipped on Nomad's leash, and they all got out. Binelli led them past the guards to where more security stood around. All of them saluted as Mitchum passed by, and Binelli walked with them until they reached Rose and Liam. Behind them was Secret Service agent Ken. As soon as the dog saw Rose, Nomad ran toward her, tearing the leash from Mitchum's hand.

"Nomad!" she called, crouching slightly, and throwing her arms open.

He leaped into her arms and covered her face with licks until she fell back, laughing. "Wow," Binelli said. "The dog is obviously fond of her."

"Everyone is," Liam added, and helped her to her feet.

"Thanks, Liam. Good to see you all." Rose hugged each of them hello, then motioned for them to follow her. "To the cafeteria. That's where we'll be meeting. And we've got breakfast for everyone." She glanced down at Nomad. "For you, too, big guy."

Mitchum fell into step beside her. "Any word from Epsilon?"

"Just that I should choose a suitable comfortable location for the meeting. The cafeteria is large enough to accommodate everyone. I prepared a favorite Stell^r dish, which will set them at ease."

Ken touched the earbud in his right ear. "Looks like President Zhukov is going to land first, in about 32 minutes. Jim said let's all get situated first and then, Rose, why don't you walk out with me to greet them?"

"Be glad to."

The cafeteria didn't look the same as it had when Mitchum had been here back in August last year. Tables and chairs were arranged differently, and one wall boasted an impressive painting of the desert at sunset. Another wall held a large white screen for projected images. Mitchum couldn't imagine what images Epsilon might want to show them in this way when he could do the same telepathically. Besides, the idea that the Stell^rs shot videos or snapped photos while they traveled around was humorous to him.

They sat at a large table at the back of the cafeteria next to the only window. It looked out into the large garden patio where they'd walked with Rose during their first visit. From the small adjoining kitchen, Rose and Liam brought out pitchers of juice, several pots of coffee, and platters of breakfast foods.

"What about the others?" Helen asked.

"Each group will have a breakfast native to their country and culture," Rose replied.

That impressed Mitchum.

Rose and Liam joined them at the table, and for the next 30 minutes they were just a group of friends who had come together for an unprecedented event. Then a guard poked his head inside the room. "Three more leaders just landed, Mr. President."

"Thank you. Rose?"

"Right behind you." She stood and followed Mitchum out of the cafeteria. Nomad remained behind with the others.

+++

Zhukov, Sofiya, Viktor, and one of their guards were met just inside Area 51 by President Mitchum and his Secret Service agent, and a very tall woman with bluish skin. This was what Sofiya had seen in her remote viewing of this place on May 1.

Today.

Right now.

While he made the introductions to Mitchum, Sofiya caught Zhukov's eye at one point, and he couldn't tell if that look was a *Ha-ha, told you so* or whether her own accuracy shocked her. Zhukov introduced her as, "One of my advisors and seers."

"A seer," Rose repeated. "Interesting. Do you see the future, Sofiya?"

"Sometimes."

"We'll have to talk."

"I'd love to," Sofiya replied.

They eventually joined the others in the cafeteria and within an hour, the remaining five leaders and their entourages had arrived. Each group was served food typical of his or her own country, and the tall alien woman moved gracefully from table to table, addressing each group in their native language. Her accents were flawless. Zhukov noted that the President's dog kept watching Rose.

Suddenly, four tall beings appeared in the room. Stunningly, *beamed* into the room. They wore identical tunics in different colors, but their bluish skin was visible. The tallest one strode forward first, followed by the other three. Shock radiated through Zhukov, a shock so profound that it briefly paralyzed him. All he could do was stare. Seeing them telepathically was one thing, but now all in person, he was rendered speechless. So were the others.

The beings glanced at the dog with interest, then they stopped in the middle of the room, and the leader bowed his head slightly.

"Thank you all for coming here. I'm Epsilon, leader of the Stell^r Council. To keep things simple, my companions are Beta, Gamma, and Pi."

They introduced themselves, their voices soft, pleasant, almost robotic. Like Rose, they addressed each group in their native language. Their heads were large in proportion to their bodies, their eyes were oval shaped and dark, their noses were little more than apertures, their mouths barely moved when they spoke, and their skin was a light blue. If Zhukov had run into one of these Stell^rs on the street, he knew he would have freaked and fled. But in here, among these other people, it all felt oddly serene, and he wondered if these aliens had created this sense of calmness somehow.

"For much of the time," Epsilon said, "I'll be speaking telepathically, in English, which you all understand. First, I'd like to explain why we're here. This visual I'm going to show you will explain quite a bit."

And the visual seized Zhukov, moving through his head at a leisurely yet steady pace.

+++

Rose liked watching this Stell^r movie once more but with even more detail. It helped fill in gaps in her knowledge about how her people had changed and further evolved in nearly 80 years. When she and Fralix had left the moon base in 1947, the cloaking technology was available, but it was now more advanced than she remembered. The Stell^r telepathic ability also seemed broader and more sophisticated. Or maybe it's because she had been away for these many years. Other abilities had developed among her people and flourished. Everyone now understood the inevitability of this field of asteroids destroying their home planet and fully accepted the need for the ultimate relocation of the entire population.

Part of Epsilon's mental movie was their plan, how to settle 100 million Stell^rs on Earth. "We realize this plan may be controversial," Epsilon said aloud. "But we don't have any other choice."

Everyone's eyes opened extra wide upon hearing this announcement.

"What are the consequences if we don't want you here?" Zhukov abruptly asked.

Beta spoke up. "We do not like to intimidate, but our home planet is threatened with extinction, so we intend to do everything we can to preserve our civilization."

The very polite British prime minister, Benjamin Harrington asked, "What's your time frame for inhabiting our planet, and when should we notify our governments and citizens?"

Epsilon answered this one. "We'll start landing our passenger starships on Earth in 2036. The first transports left Xanthe four years ago. As we've said before, we don't intend to harm you or your planet. You don't have the means to stop us. We don't want to threaten but can certainly provide a demonstration of what we can do."

Rose noticed how Epsilon glanced around the cafeteria, but not a single leader stood or raised a hand. No one wanted to pursue that narrative, Rose thought. Good.

"Any other questions?" Epsilon asked.

The dapper French president, Henri Bernard, stood. "You must realize that once this is announced to the world, mass hysteria will ensue. How do we contain that?"

"Please don't notify your citizens or government until we lay out more details," Epsilon replied. "I assure you—all of you—that any populace that is inconvenienced or relocated will be compensated handsomely for it, and comfortable accommodations will be built for them. We will choose a geographic location that will cause the minimal amount of disruption."

Israeli Prime Minister Yonatan Becker, spoke next. Rose estimated his age as late 40s or early 50s. The only thing she knew about him was that he was highly intelligent and well-spoken.

"Yes, Prime Minister Becker," said Epsilon. "Please, what is your question?"

"Sir, if the Stell^rs are going to occupy our planet, will we have access to the knowledge and technology your civilization has acquired over the million plus years you have preceded us?"

"Yes and no. Yes, on things that will enable your species to enjoy accelerated growth in the areas of health, food, environment, equality, and certain technologies. But when there's a possibility that knowledge can be used for destructive purposes, then the answer is no. We'll keep our mutual self-interests in mind at all times."

Rose was pleased when Jim Mitchum got to his feet. "Epsilon, we'd like a date for when this relocation will begin. Is that possible for you to share?"

"We don't have a specific date yet, but it will begin within the next couple of years."

This statement elicited a slew of questions among the crowd in the room—not just from leaders, but from their advisors, their team, everyone shouting at once. Mitchum waved his arms. "Hey, please some decorum here. One question at a time." He glanced at Gamma, who had stepped forward.

"Go ahead, President Chen," said Gamma, gesturing at Chen with one of his noticeably long, bluish arms.

"Okay, let's assume you're successful at everything you have proposed. I am curious if you ever had to deal with any adversaries during your travels across the galaxies? If you have, can you assure us *your* adversaries won't follow you here?"

"Why do you assume we have adversaries?" Epsilon asked.

"Because we all do. And surely if you have been around a million years longer than humans, you have enemies somewhere out there."

Rose sensed that Epsilon's hesitation in answering was because he hadn't anticipated that kind of question. So, she stood. "May I answer that one, Epsilon?"

"By all means, Rose."

"President Chen, I'd like to show you and everyone else in this room, a visual of the Stell^rs adversaries—the Zorgons—as I remember them from an encounter many decades ago."

The visual she shared had happened when she was moving from Andromeda to Xanthe with her family along with a small group of Stell^rs. She remembered that several Zorgon spaceships had seemingly appeared out of nowhere, their long wings shaped just like those of the creatures themselves. And through those large, transparent windows, she had been able to see the Zorgons inside their ship, reptilians so vile and treacherous that just the brush of their wings could kill you.

As they closed the distance between their spacecrafts, the pilot's voice had boomed through the intercom, explaining what was happening and what they should do. Instead of following orders, Rose had run to the special magnifying viewing window to get an even better look at them. And the eyes of the Zorgon she had seen had terrified her. They had looked like exploding galaxies, filled with fury and chaos and such incomparable power that she had wrenched away and raced to her dad, who was headed toward her, shouting at her to secure herself, to take cover.

The visual ended with their spaceship racing away from the Zorgons at the speed of light, confusing them so badly that two of the reptilian ships crashed into each other, exploded, and plunged downward.

As the visual faded, the silence in the cafeteria was so profound Rose could hear her own breath as it escaped her mouth.

"Hideous things," murmured Prime Minister Agarwal, her expression wrinkling with distaste. "Primal."

"From the dawn of time," exclaimed Zhukov.

"Horrifying," murmured Becker.

"I...feel sick," Sofiya said, and doubled over where she sat, gagging.

Rose hurried over to her with a bucket that had been used earlier for mopping. Dirty water still sloshed around in the bottom of it. Sofiya vomited as soon as the bucket was in front of her, and Rose pressed a wad of paper towels into her hand. She took hold of the woman's arm. "Let's get you to the restroom, Sofiya."

With Rose's help, Sofiya got to her feet, unsteady, sort of wobbling, like she was inebriated. Rose knew she wasn't.

She glanced back once and saw Zhukov watching them, Mitchum watching them, everyone looking at them.

Out in the hall, they stopped under an air conditioning vent in the ceiling and Sofiya leaned back against the wall, letting the cool air blow over her face. Rose could see the beads of sweat along the rim of her hairline. "I'll get you some cold water. Just stay right here."

Sofiya sank down the wall to the floor. "Okay." She pulled her knees to her chest and rested her head against them. Rose hurried off toward the café to retrieve a water bottle, baffled that just the visual of a Zorgon could make her sick enough to vomit.

+++

After Rose had helped Sofiya out of the cafeteria, Epsilon sensed the uneasy atmosphere in the room. He wasn't surprised when Zhukov's arm shot into the air. "So tell us, Epsilon. The arrival of the Stell^rs will forever change everything on our planet. How are we supposed to deal with the repercussions?"

"We'll be doing whatever we can to minimalize any repercussions."

"Like what?" Zhukov asked.

"We'll feed the hungry, banish poverty, reverse the environmental disasters now underway, and provide some advanced technology to everyone for free." He paused. "And that's just the beginning."

"When did you send Rose to Earth?"

"Perhaps you should hear this from Rose herself." Epsilon looked at Pi, who nodded and left the room. Moments later, Rose returned alone.

"I'll be glad to answer your question, President Zhukov. In 1947, my copilot and I left our base on the far side of the moon and cruised around the U.S. southwest, searching for evidence of America's growing nuclear proliferation. Our shuttle craft malfunctioned and crashed in Roswell. Fralix, my copilot, was killed. I was severely injured. Two marvelous surgeons helped to save my life. After my injuries were healed, I was moved here to Area 51, where I lived for 80 years. Several months ago, President Jim Mitchum moved me to the White House. Anything else, President Zhukov?"

Zhukov wanted desperately to believe she was out of her mind, on drugs, a nut case. But he knew she wasn't any of those things. She was Rose, a Stell^r who had crashed in Roswell in 1947, just like all the urban legends said. "Just one question. How's Sofiya doing?"

"Pi stayed with her. She's better. And I should get back out there with her."

Rose nodded at Epsilon and left the room with the same grace Zhukov had noted when she had entered.

+++

When Rose returned, Sofiya was sipping at the bottle of cold water and every now and then rolled it over her face and across the back of her neck and her shoulders. "You okay?" Rose lowered herself to the floor beside her.

"Better. Thank...you for helping me out here. I... that...those reptiles...made all this so sickening real..." She set the bottle of water on the floor between them. Looked at Rose, her eyes intense. "I've been...sensitive all my life...but what you did..." She shook her head. "I...I would never be able to do that."

"How do you see the future?"

"I...honestly don't know. Sometimes I'll be going about my day, and something will pop into my head, and I let it...unfold. If it's in black and white, I know it's just a possibility. If it's in color and...and I'm talking incredible technicolor, okay? And if I can see some of the details—not all, just some—then I know it has a particularly good chance of happening."

"What do you see in the future for me?"

She picked up the bottle and rolled it across her forehead, pressed it to her cheeks, sipped from it. Then she set it down and looked at Rose again. "I...I..." She squeezed her eyes shut, and for long moments her eyeballs flicked back and forth under her eyelids, as if she were locked into REM and dreaming. "You're in...full color." She spoke softly. "An indescribable blue, deeper than the color of your skin. You and Alexander Zhukov are arguing...I can't hear what you two are saying...but I can tell by his body language that he's really...aggravated..." She stopped. The blood drained from her face. Her eyes snapped open.

Rose thought she looked panicked. "And..."

Her head snapped toward Rose, then her fingers grasped Rose's thin blue wrist and she leaned closer. "Listen to me." Such a soft, soft voice but so urgent. "Alexander is NOT your friend. Deep within himself...he's *evil.*"

Rose realized that what Sofiya was saying was a betrayal of the man who employed her. She had learned that humans betrayed each other for a variety of reasons. Greed, profit, power, ignorance. But what she saw and heard here, now, with this young woman, was that whatever she'd seen about Rose's future had slammed her into complete terror. And that kind of terror was what Rose the child had felt that moment when she'd peered into the eyes of the Zorgon.

That terror—its tenor, its power, its overwhelming inscription in memory—united them, Stell^r and human. Two females of different species. Rose realized she had met an actual human friend who, until moments ago, had been on the opposing human side.

"Thanks, Sofiya. I'll keep that in mind." Then Rose stroked her hair and erased her memory of that betrayal.

+++

Mitchum and the Indian President had spoken earlier, and when he looked at her now, he could almost see her questions. "I know you've got some questions for Epsilon, President Agarwal. Go ahead."

"Thank you, President Mitchum." She pressed her hands together in an attitude of prayer and bowed her head. Then her arms swung to her side, and she turned toward Epsilon. "Do Stell^rs ever go hungry? Do any of your people live on the streets of your planet?"

Mitchum noticed how Zhukov clenched his fists and imagined he did it to prevent himself from having a meltdown. He also imagined what was going through his head— outrage because he thought her questions were a waste of time.

"Hunger is unknown on Xanthe. So is homelessness."

"Can you help to banish both in India?"

"We can help *you* do that, President Agarwal."

"Then, welcome," she said.

Mitchum noticed Zhukov rolling his eyes.

"Is there anything else we should know at this time, Epsilon?" Mitchum asked.

"I believe we have covered everything." He glanced at the other three Stell^rs.

Pi spoke up. "We have asked Rose to come back in."

She reappeared moments later with Sofiya. She went over to Epsilon and the others, and something passed between them. Then, in his head, Mitchum heard her soft voice. *Epsilon thinks I should share this information with you, Jim. Sofiya warned me that Zhukov is not our friend and that deep within, he's evil.*

Mitchum: *I thought she was his confidante.*

Epsilon: *We will continually monitor him.*

Rose: *Her terror of Zhukov and his power is genuine.*

Mitchum: *That's good to know, Rose. Thank you.*

Rose: *I will keep all of you up to date.*

Epsilon: *We will do the same.*

Then Epsilon turned to the others in the room. "I thank you all for coming. I will be in touch shortly."

Zhukov stood. "Can you give us a more specific date, Epsilon?"

"On August 1. It will be virtual and telepathic. Thank you all for your cooperation and making the trip here to meet with us. Travel safely home."

With that, Epsilon, Pi, Beta, and Gamma beamed out of the room leaving everyone silent and utterly astonished.

+++

Before Zhukov and his entourage left, Rose communicated telepathically with Sofiya. *Let's stay in touch. 575-772-9083. My personal cell.*

It's amazing, your voice comes through so clearly. My number is 514-988-5674. A Montreal area code. Alexander is paranoid about American cell companies. What's the range for your telepathy? Maybe we don't need cells. I'll be in Moscow.

It might work. Message me when you get back and I'll try it.

Can you teach me how to communicate like you do?

Teach you? You're already doing it.

Only because you initiated it.

We'll practice. You're a natural.

Thank you, Rose. We'll be in touch.

The beginning of a friendship, Rose thought. But at some point she would have to confess that she had wiped Sofiya's memory about what she'd said concerning Zhukov.

Chapter 13

Zhukov & The Sindikat

Two days after that meeting at Area 51, Zhukov had recovered from jet lag and placed a call to President Chen. He'd given the events a lot of thought and made the call on the most secure line he had, which he hoped was secure enough to block any Stell^r from hearing it.

Chen answered on the first ring. "Alexander. I was just about to call you."

"We need to talk, Wei."

"Are we sure this line is secure?"

Zhukov laughed. "With the aliens out there hovering above us and their vastly superior technology? No, nothing is certain."

"Then perhaps we should meet somewhere? After all, we share more than 4000 kilometers of a border."

"You're thinking of Heihe?" Zhukov asked.

The city lay on the China-Russia border in northeast China's Heilongjiang Province. Since the end of the pandemic, Russian tourists had been crossing the border in droves for sightseeing and shopping sprees. The travel was visa-free, a major part of the allure. He could probably get into the city without being noticed, but it would require enormous preparations. Perhaps it would be safer—and it certainly would be easier—to message on their secure line.

"Let's switch," Zhukov said.

"Good idea."

Chen: *You don't think they can eavesdrop this way?*

Zhukov: *No idea. But it's probably not as easy. I'm going to call the Sindikat together. In person meeting.*

Chen: *But where?*

Zhukov: *Somewhere we won't be noticed. Some obscure spot.*

Chen: *How obscure?*

On his computer, Zhukov brought up a map of South America. Could he convince sixteen of the 50 wealthiest people in the world to meet in Quito, Ecuador? Could he and Chen and some of the others disguise themselves well enough so they wouldn't be recognized in a country that was primarily poor, with a large indigenous population primarily focused on survival? Quito was just under 10,000 feet of altitude, so it took time to acclimate, but he knew a Russian who owned and managed a small hotel just outside of Quito in Esperanza. The word, translated, meant hope. He liked that.

Zhukov: *I think Ecuador. We fly into Quito. There's a very remote town, Esperanza, where I know a hotel proprietor, a trusted old comrade. I'm looking at July 1. One month before the next meeting with Epsilon and the others.*

Chen: *Dates good. Send me other particulars.*

Zhukov: *Once I get in touch with the hotel owner, I'll contact you.*

Chen: *The Sindikat won't like this alien plan any more than we do.*

Of course not, Zhukov thought. Part of what this would mean was that the Stell^rs— not money and our power—ruled the world. *We'll see how they want to deal with things. I'll be in touch.*

He didn't bother consulting his team first. He went online and looked for Hotel Milagro in Esperanza. He hadn't been there in years but still had his comrade's private mobile number. He couldn't recall the number of rooms, whether there was a restaurant or other facilities. He was certain it had all changed since he'd been there.

The website was impressive, with a backdrop of the splendid Andes and snapshots of the town. There were 45 rooms and four cottages on the property, enough for the Sindikat's 16 leaders and the individuals who accompanied them. The restaurant looked large and comfortable, and a quick glance at the menu for various meals indicated food for every palette. Mikhail was still listed as the owner and a main phone number and email address were provided. A call would be easiest—and riskier.

So Zhukov messaged him through his government's most secure network. His own private network.

Hi Mikhail,

Hope you're doing well and still flourishing in Esperanza!

I'd like to reserve the hotel & cottages from July 1-3 for a very private get-together. Security and privacy are of paramount importance. No other guests or anyone else there unless completely trusted. I will pay you through the usual back channel to your account.

Best wishes,

Alexander

His next task was to compose a carefully worded communication to the team leader of the Sindikat, Katherine Martin. The Sindikat included three Americans, three Russians, three Europeans, three Asians, three Middle Easterners, one Australian. Each year, the group elected a new team leader. They were some of the wealthiest individuals on the planet with a combined net worth higher than every country in the world with the exception of the US, China, Japan, and Germany.

He hadn't had much personal contact with Katherine but knew that her wealth was mostly family money that had come from the buying and selling of land in Australia. Her great-grandparents had started that. She was well-liked among the group, and if she asked them to convene in Ecuador, they undoubtedly would do so. In essence, she was their leader. He was just the figurehead with nukes.

He contacted her through his private network.

Greetings, Katherine,

I hope you're doing well and that things down under are running smoothly.

Some stunning developments necessitate convening. Dates would be July 1-3 in Ecuador, where we should be safe from detection. I've asked a trusted friend/owner of a very private hotel there if we can reserve the entire hotel for those dates. As soon as I hear from him, I'll be in touch with specifics.

I know that calling this meeting is highly unusual but it's of the utmost importance.

Best,

Alexander

P.S. This development threatens everything.

Katherine replied within minutes. He liked that about her. She was prompt, on top of things.

Alexander, good to hear from you. Threatens everything? My goodness, have the aliens landed? Heard about your visit to Area 51. Ecuador would be divine. Gorgeous country. Let me know.

How do you know about Area 51, Katherine?

Got my sources. Just like you.

Zhukov started to message Mikhail again, but a response from him popped up on his screen.

Well, my friend! What a delightful surprise! Things going very well here. I have several reservations for those dates, but if you're securing the entire place for three days, I can certainly accommodate you. I imagine you'll need transportation from the Quito airport, which I can arrange. I will provide several nondescript vans with no names listed. The same way we have done it in the past.

You can pay half in advance. I know you're good for the rest of it! As you suggested, please send the payment in Bitcoin to the account you still have.

Looking forward to seeing you soon!

He immediately texted Katherine with the dates and asked her to let him know by tomorrow if everyone could make it. He explained where Esperanza was located in relation to Quito and told her about the hotel and transportation. Then he wrote Chen about the details and told Mikhail he would confirm tomorrow when he had an exact count of individuals.

With all that business taken care of, he called Viktor and asked if they could meet somewhere. "Sure, how about that Starbucks?"

There actually was a Starbucks in downtown Moscow, but it was their code word for a place on Pokrovka Street that sounded as American as Starbucks: Coffeemania. He could don a fake beard and wear glasses to test his disguise. He hoped he would be unrecognizable.

"See you in twenty," Zhukov said.

Since it was early May and gorgeous outside, he changed into casual summer clothes—no coat, no tie, no shiny shoes. Running shoes, running clothes, the bearded guy wearing glasses. And a cap. He added that at the last minute. If anything, he looked like a tourist.

He reached Coffeemania twenty minutes later and spotted Viktor at a table by a window, fiddling with his cell. What had they all done before cell phones? What had they looked at when they walked, sat, went to parties and celebrations?

Zhukov claimed the chair across from him and Viktor glanced up.

"*Ecuador?*"

It shocked Zhukov that Viktor already knew. How? Who had snitched?

Viktor leaned forward. "Katherine contacted me, asking if I was going. Am I?"

"Absolutely."

"What about Sofiya?"

Zhukov hadn't seen her since they'd returned from Area 51. He didn't want to see her. She was a distraction, a temptation, a complication. He'd asked her what had happened when Rose had taken her out into the hallway. *I vomited in a bucket she brought me, she got me cold water...other than that, I don't have any idea. I was too sick.*

Too sick? From just seeing an image of a Zorgon?

Or could the Stell^rs erase memories?

"Not sure yet about her. Tell me, Viktor, what do you recall about Area 51?"

He shrugged. "A cafeteria, a good meal, a lotta talk, that's about it."

"Talk about what?"

Viktor frowned, set his cell down, rubbed his hands over his face. "I don't really ...remember. I have fuzzy memories of things like relocating millions of aliens to Earth." His hands slipped away from his face. "Ever since we returned, Alexander, I've been fighting with my brain, trying to remember the details, the specifics. I do vividly recall that at one point you turned to me, noticeably shaken, and said, "August first. You'll be there, right, Viktor?" He paused, looking utterly miserable. "The other memories just aren't there."

"Damn, I knew it. Those aliens can wipe our memories." The words came out in a soft hiss. "It looks like it mainly affected the associates of the seven leaders. I mean, for all of this to work, they do need the leaders to understand their plan."

Viktor's expression seemed to surrender to the weight of gravity. The corners of his mouth plunged, his eyelids looked heavy, his shoulders slumped. "I agree. And that's why I think Sofiya should accompany us. Her memories of all this aren't that clear either, Alexander. But she was sick, so that may account for it. And she...*felt* things that are indisputable."

"Like?"

A server brought over coffee that Viktor apparently had ordered, and a selection of muffins and warm rolls with butter and jam. When the woman had left, Viktor leaned forward again, whispering. "She felt Rose's terror at seeing those disgusting reptilian creatures. That's why she got so violently ill. Sofiya is an empath, Alexander. So even if Stell^rs can wipe away memories, I doubt if they can wipe away feelings, emotions, impressions."

"So she's like a repository of emotional memories?" Zhukov asked.

"That's one way to describe it, yes. So, tell me. What's going to happen July first?"

"Another meeting. I'd like you and Sofiya to accompany me to Ecuador." He kept his voice low, hoping that if the Stell^rs were eavesdropping the buzz of other voices would swallow his and Viktor's. "We need to be careful about how we communicate. I think it's best here rather than the Kremlin, but otherwise, messaging. My hope is that it's more difficult for the aliens to intercept those messages sent and received that are continuously scrubbed on my private server."

"Hope to hell you're right so we don't end up like the North Korean and Pakistani leaders. So tell me, did they actually wipe all my memories clean, Alexander?"

Zhukov sipped at his coffee and helped himself to one of the muffins, sipping and nibbling as he explained. When he got to the part about how many Stell^rs would be coming to Earth, Viktor's eyes widened. "Holy crap, Alexander. A hundred million relocated aliens?"

"I think they'll do well at controlling chaos," Zhukov said, and went on to explain the Stell^r plan, at least what he knew of it. He suddenly wished he had recorded the entire thing but suspected the recording device on his cell wouldn't have worked. The Stell^rs would have disabled it.

The muffin and the coffee were gone when he finished. Viktor looked pensive. Then he grinned and folded his hands on the table and leaned forward. "When do we leave?"

"June 29. That will put us there a day or two before others arrive. We'll have Chen meet us in Tehran, then fly on together."

"Should I inform Sofiya?"

"Yes. Safer for you to do it, I think."

"Then I'll see you in..." He glanced at his phone. "Several days. Let me know time and place."

"Done."

They left the coffee shop separately. On the walk, Zhukov imagined making love to Sofiya.

Complications, distractions, he thought. But...

+++

As soon as Katherine Martin and Zhukov finished their call, she started contacting the other members of the group. *Ecuador, an important meeting on July 1. Can you be there?*

As she communicated with each member on her private, secure line, she turned her office chair so that it faced her window. It overlooked a preserve filled with wildlife— kangaroos, koalas, all of Australia's indigenous creatures. If her speculation that aliens had landed was correct, would their presence harm Australia's wildlife in any way? Would they want to run biological tests on them? Extract their DNA to create test tube replicas? To crossbreed them with creatures from their own planet? Would they seek to populate parts of this country? And if so, what would that do to her wealth? Her power here? Would the Sindikat survive?

Maybe she was jumping way ahead on all this. She didn't know for sure that Zhukov's trip to Area 51 concerned aliens. But why else would he go there? Why would the leader of one of the most powerful and repressive regimes on the planet travel there?

Once she had an affirmative answer from each of the other fifteen members, she got up and hurried into her bedroom to pack. The distance from Brisbane, where she lived, to Quito, Ecuador, was more than 8500 miles. She could leave earlier and spend a couple days shopping and sightseeing in Quito and neighboring Esperanza. The altitude in Quito was nearly 9500 feet, and that would take some time to get accustomed to. She wanted to be sure she was in tip top shape for this meeting.

On her phone, she checked the Quito weather for this time of year—sixties during the day, forties at night. Sweaters, a jacket, the right shoes. At one time, she had owned land outside of Quito and had intended to build a hacienda on it that would attract some of the country's hundreds of species of birds. But she'd sold it during the economic downturn to some obnoxious American dude who subsequently had built a hotel on it that Marriot or one of those outfits owned now.

Bad call on her part.

It would have been nice to go to her own place in Ecuador and hang out with the birds. The iguanas. The macaws and ocelots. Maybe during this trip, she would take a few days at the end to look at land along the Amazon River, which had its own unique breed of dolphins. After all, the economy over the past decade had been very good to her.

+++

In early July, Mitchum spent most of his time consulting with Whitley, Rose, and Helen about what had taken place at Area 51. They speculated about where the Stell^rs might want to settle.

"A subtropical desert would be ideal," Rose said. "The Stell^rs have the technology to turn it green, to produce food."

"Our planet has a lot of deserts," Whitley said, and projected a world map onto a screen he'd set up at the front of the room. He was big on visuals. Mitchum appreciated that about him.

Deserts were clearly delineated on the map, with the statistics provided in a column below. The Arctic and Antarctic Deserts had the greatest land masses, with over five million square miles each. But the landscape was mostly polar ice tundra, making them clear outliers. The next two largest that Mitchum saw were the Sahara, with more than 3.5 million square miles, and the Great Australian, with more than a million square miles.

The Sahara, he thought, would be an excellent choice except for the countries that bordered it: Algeria[1], Chad[2], Egypt[3], Eritrea[4], Libya[5], Mali[6], Mauritania[7], Morocco[8], Niger[9], the Sudan[10], Tunisia[11], and Western Sahara[12]. Their relationships with the US spanned the gamut from hostile to tolerant.

"Rose, how many square miles do you think 100 million Stell^rs would need?" Mitchum asked.

She studied the map in front of her, the stats. "Several hundred thousand, that's my estimate."

"Have you been told anything about their initial plans, Rose?"

Then she cocked her head, as if listening to something, and briefly shut her eyes. Mitchum and Helen exchanged a glance. Helen's brows lifted into questioning peaks, and she mouthed, *What the hell?*

Moments later, Epsilon's voice filled Mitchum's head and judging from the expressions of the others in the room, they heard him, too.

---

1.   https://en.wikipedia.org/wiki/Algeria

2.   https://en.wikipedia.org/wiki/Chad

3.   https://en.wikipedia.org/wiki/Egypt

4.   https://en.wikipedia.org/wiki/Eritrea

5.   https://en.wikipedia.org/wiki/Libya

6.   https://en.wikipedia.org/wiki/Mali

7.   https://en.wikipedia.org/wiki/Mauritania

8.   https://en.wikipedia.org/wiki/Morocco

9.   https://en.wikipedia.org/wiki/Niger

10.   https://en.wikipedia.org/wiki/Sudan

11.   https://en.wikipedia.org/wiki/Tunisia

12.   https://en.wikipedia.org/wiki/Western_Sahara

Right now, we have something a bit more pressing. It has come to our attention that Presidents Zhukov and Chen have flown to Tehran. We don't know why. We are now monitoring all their communications. Are you familiar with an Australian, Katherine Martin?

"Not offhand," Whitley replied.

"Nope," Helen said.

"She's the wealthiest woman in Australia," Mitchum said. "Why?"

She left Australia yesterday, the same day that Zhukov and Chen left.

"Why are you surveilling her?" Mitchum asked.

Because we monitor Zhukov continually, and they have had previous communications.

Mitchum said, "Rose, can you get in touch with Sofiya?"

"I can try."

"Have you been in touch since Area 51?"

"Just a brief contact several days ago where she thanked me for helping her out when she got sick."

She then shut her eyes, breathed deeply, and Mitchum waited, hoping.

+++

Rose had trouble finding Sofiya. The one time they'd messaged since Area 51 had been an experiment to see if it would go through without being tagged by security. It had gone through, so they tried a telepathic connection, and Rose hadn't been able to reach her. The distance from Washington DC to Moscow—more than 4800 miles—was apparently too far. And Tehran was even further from DC. So now, Rose called her number.

Hey, it's Rose. I have tried to reach you.

Rose! Yes! Am in Tehran.

Interesting place, You on vacation or business there?

Maybe for a day. We're headed to Ecuador. For a conference. Me, Alexander, Viktor. Wei Chen is joining us.

I'd love to see Ecuador. I've read that Quito is beautiful.

We're going to meet in Esperanza, at the Hotel Milagro.

Rose smiled at that. Hope at the Miracle Hotel. Zhukov didn't impress her as a scholar of anything, but she admired the metaphor of the location and wondered if it described what he hoped to find, to gain from this conference. *Who else will be there?*

Sofiya made a sound like laughter, but Rose heard it as a childlike giggle. *Sixteen of the wealthiest and most influential people on this planet.*

Rose conjured a vivid image of Sofiya's face in her mind and imagined her hand touching the woman's forehead and erasing her memory of most of this conversation. *Stay in touch, Sofiya.*

I will, my friend. I will.

When she was sure the connection between them had ended, she called for Epsilon. *Did you hear all that?*

I did. You going to share it with Jim?

I'd like to. He needs to know. What do you think?

Yes.

So she did. She shared it with him, Helen, and Whitley. In spite of everything Rose had learned about humans during her time living among them, she didn't understand greed. It didn't exist among Stell^rs. But it ran rampant among this species. Greed for money, power, control.

"Christ," Whitley whispered. "A cabal."

"Katherine Martin is worth something like 100 billion," said Mitchum. "Even Mackenzie Scott is worth only about 40 billion. But Katherine, unlike Scott, didn't sign any Giving Pledge and promise to give away half her wealth over the course of her lifetime."

"So what the hell does she do with it?" Helen asked.

Mitchum shrugged. "She supports some Australian causes, but other than that, I don't know. What we need to know right now the names of the other fifteen."

"I'll get on it," Whitley said, and scooted his chair over to one of the computers in the room and went to work.

Mitchum projected the map of Ecuador on the screen again, located both Quito and Esperanza. At 12,000 feet, Esperanza's altitude was higher than Quito's. It meant people dressed warmly, that Rose's skin color could be mostly hidden by a coat, scarf, and makeup. Liam or Ken could accompany her. "We'll need to be close to the Hotel Milagro to see what's going on," Mitchum said. "I'd like you to go to Ecuador, Rose. Find out what you can learn firsthand. You'd have to leave tomorrow. You can utilize your Spanish language skills, right?"

She smiled. "*Claro que sí, Jim.*"

Chapter 14

Esperanza Erupts

Ecuador July 1, 2030

Rose and Liam strolled the ancient streets of Esperanza, taking in everything around them—the small shops, the crowded open marketplace where the local people strolled and bargained, both men and women bundled up against the cold. She attracted some attention because she towered over nearly everyone else. But thanks to the makeup instructions that Helen and Laurie had given her, the color of her skin was well-disguised.

Liam glanced at the GPS on his phone. "According to this, Hotel Miracle is on the next block. What do you want to do?"

"At least take a look inside, see what I can pick up telepathically."

"By our calculations, the only people there who have seen you are Zhukov, Chen, and Sofiya."

"If Zhukov and Chen recognize me, I can wipe their memories."

"Convenient." He glanced at her. "How do you do that, anyway?"

"I'm honestly not sure. I just will it and it happens. I learned it when I was a kid, on the way to Xanthe from Andromeda. My parents showed me. However, and please don't take this the wrong way, Liam, it only works on less advanced minds. In other words, a Stell^r can't erase the short-term memory of another Stell^r. They felt it was something I needed to know because we were moving to a new place on Xanthe, and we did have transplanted species from other planets living among us."

Liam smiled at her comment and touched her arm. "Just a suggestion. But maybe you should connect telepathically with Sofiya and just eavesdrop rather than go inside."

Rose thought about that. She considered Sofiya a friend and would like to see her. They could go shopping. Feed squirrels in the park. Do something simple and ordinary that she didn't have the opportunity to do at the White House. That had never occurred in her life living among the humans. But perhaps Liam was right in this instance. "As I hear her, and repeat what I hear, can you record it?"

"Definitely. Let's find a coffee shop."

"I don't want to uncover my face."

"Then a park."

"Perfect."

El Bienvenido park was just two blocks from the hotel. They found a bench in a thicket of trees where birds sang, and the branches rustled. She spotted a giant hummingbird, a black-tailed trainbearer, and several carunculate caracara. All were colorful, unusual-looking birds. In Quito and Esperanza, there were nearly 600 species of birds.

Liam brought up his recorder on his mobile, tested it. "How do you, uh, tune in?"

"Shut my eyes..." She closed her eyes. "And go find her."

Rose found her quickly, in the lobby of the Milagro Hotel, talking with the Australian woman, Katherine. Rose kept her presence small, like she was the proverbial fly on the wall. When she spoke, her voice was quiet, and Liam scooted closer to her. She felt it. She was also aware that he positioned his phone closer to her, so the recorder would pick up her voice.

+++

Katherine was talking with Sofiya. The young woman intrigued her, and she wondered if she and Zhukov were lovers. "I didn't realize Alexander had a seer as an advisor."

Sofiya shrugged. "I came on recently, after he first learned what he's going to reveal to the conference."

Intriguing, Katherine thought. "ETs, right? That's what this is all about. I got word about his visit to Area 51."

Sofiya looked surprised. "How?"

Katherine wasn't about to reveal any of her sources. "We've had sightings in my country for years. I know just about everyone researching the field. And I know several experiencers."

"Experiencers," Sofiya repeated the word like she'd never heard it. "Oh, people who have had contact with aliens? Abductees? I've seen a couple of documentaries. Aliens. But aren't there different species of aliens?"

"From what I've learned, the Grays are mostly responsible for encounters and abductions. Has Rose ever talked about them?"

"No. She has mentioned the Zorgons, the Stell^r enemies. Reptilian things. These Stell^rs are vastly different from anything I've ever heard about the Grays."

Katherine ordered another drink for each of them, and a waiter brought them over. "You've met these Stell^rs?" Katherine asked when the waiter left.

"Yes, at Area 51."

Incredible. "This is *huge*, Sofiya. It really will change everything."

"For the better."

Ha. "Debatable."

"Why?"

How naïve she was, Katherine thought. "Honey, don't you *get* it? Money will no longer be king. The aliens will rule *us. They* will have all the power."

Sofiya frowned. "But power isn't just about money, Katherine. It's about equality. They're offering equality."

"Are they?"

"Here's something interesting I picked up," Sofiya said. "These aliens have an extensive art culture, with pieces that go back millions of years."

"Really? You actually saw the art?"

"Some of it, yes. The pieces I saw in my vision...are stunning."

One of the other members came over. "Ladies, excuse me, but we're being called into the conference room."

Katherine squeezed Sofiya's hand. "Good talking to you, hon. We need to do this again. Soon." *Very soon.*

+++

Rose's eyes popped open just as Liam turned off the recorder. "Did you get it all?"

"Yup. This is great stuff, Rose. I'm going to email it to Jim. If you're in that conference room with her, can you *see* the others?"

"I've never done that before. But I can try."

"Wait. Is what she said about Stell^r art true?"

"It was true when I was last on Xanthe. And even on the moon base."

"Wow. Awesome. How do you think Sofiya got that info?"

She suspected Sofiya had found the information during one of their telepathic connections, that the woman was more gifted than even she realized. The incredible vibrant colors of the magnificent Stell^r art subconsciously caught her attention. Incredible!

When she told Liam as much, he nodded. "Interesting. Okay, see if you can connect with her again. Let's see what happens."

Rose shut her eyes, found Sofiya more easily this time, and connected with her as she and Katherine took seats around the large conference table. She tried to sneak a peek through Sofiya's eyes but couldn't do it. A peek wasn't enough, and she was afraid that if she pushed herself too forcefully on Sofiya, the woman would sense it.

Perhaps there was another way of doing it that she simply hadn't discovered yet because she'd never had a need as deep as she did now.

She conjured her will and demanded that her eyes find a way to see what Sofiya was seeing, but without using her friend's eyes. Gradually, against the screen of her inner eyes, shapes appeared. The shapes assumed clarity, definition, and suddenly, everything in the room exploded into her awareness.

"What?" Liam whispered. "What're you seeing?"

"The room. The conference table. Zhukov holding court."

"Who else is there?"

She glanced around the table. She'd seen the photos of some of the world's wealthiest and most powerful people and recognized them all here at this table. She recited the names, then kept listening. Zhukov was relating the details about his trip to Area 51. No hands shot into the air, no one interrupted or butted in as they had at Area 51. This group listened, understood protocol and courtesy.

"We met aliens. The Stell^rs. Their technology is millions of years beyond ours. They can eavesdrop on us *if* they know where we are. That's why we're here in Ecuador. They're telepathic. President Chen was there, as well. Do you confirm what I've said so far, President Chen?"

"Absolutely." Chen's head bobbed up and down. "Four of them beamed into the Area 51 cafeteria like actors on *Star Trek*. One of them, Rose, lived for nearly 80 years in Area 51. She...spoke Chinese and Russian... and every other language flawlessly. She communicates...telepathically. Mind to mind."

This created a stir in the crowd of billionaires. One of them, a young tech star from California, *raised* his hand—it didn't *shoot* into the air. "Yes?" Zhukov said, pointing at him.

"Sir, what you've said so far is completely bonkers. Even we..." He opened his arms wide to encompass everyone in the room. "...the richest people on planet Earth, can't win against something like this."

"Of course, we can," Zhukov said quickly. "And here's how."

He stopped talking and everyone in the room looked down at their mobile devices. Rose couldn't see their devices, couldn't see what Zhukov had sent them. She withdrew quietly, rapidly, and her eyes popped open.

Liam. Park. Esperanza. The birds.

"You okay, Rose?" He pressed a container of cold water in her hand. "You look like you're going to pass out. Or something."

She sipped, grateful that he knew about her and water. When she was hydrated, she felt more normal, her abilities worked more smoothly. On Andromeda and later, on Xanthe, she had hydrated with whatever was available. Juice. The sap from trees. A piece of fruit. But here, on this planet, it always had been water that did the trick.

"Zhukov is planning something; I couldn't see it. He sent it to their mobile devices. Whatever the plan is, he thinks it will stop the Stell^rs."

"Alert Epsilon. I'm sure he and the others will figure it out. Where to next?" he asked.

"Let's walk around. I like this village."

They wandered the narrow, cobbled streets, window shopping, chatting about what they saw. Rose felt freer than she had since the day she'd crashed in Roswell. They ducked into a couple of the small shops that sold local art, sculptures, and things like tarot cards. There was even an *I Ching* book translated into Spanish. She bought it and the coins, then selected gifts for Helen, Laurie, Carmen the cook, and Sofiya.

"Have you ever been able to do this, Rose? Just walk around and look at stuff and shop?"

"Nope." She looked over at him. "This is the first time. So, thank you, Liam, for this opportunity."

He grinned in that Liam way that indicated delight, and they both laughed like a couple of kids up to no good. They weren't paying much attention to where they were going —the next strip of shops, the next road, the next drop in and shop. But suddenly, Liam stopped. So, did she.

"This road is really deeply shadowed," he said. "Not too many pedestrians, either." He fiddled with his phone. "Getting GPS for our hotel."

Nothing specific tipped her off. But Rose suddenly felt as unsafe as she had that day 83 years ago when she'd realized her shuttle had critically malfunctioned and there wasn't anything she or Fralix could do to correct it. She spun around and saw a group of shadowy figures following them, all of them heavily bundled up against the chill. The road was too darkly covered by trees to distinguish their faces, so she couldn't tell if they were just hungry kids hoping for a handout or a nefarious clutch of men.

"Liam," she said, and he looked back.

Then the group moved toward them. "Get back, Rose," Liam hissed.

She appreciated his valor, but she could take care of this. *"Hombres,"* she called out, and held her long blue fingers in front of her and wiggled them. *Come and get me.* *"Vamonos, hombres. Vamos a pelear."*

The group stopped moving. The men glanced at each other. *"La loca!"* shouted one man.

Now they swarmed toward her and Liam like hungry predators. And when they were dangerously close, she started spinning, faster and faster. During the final, dizzying spin, she kicked out both of her long legs simultaneously so that her body was airborne, and they slammed against the men, one after another, and they fell like bowling pins.

She landed right in front of them. A half dozen large men. The two nearest to her moaned and struggled to get up. The others behind them fled down the road, shouting, *"Es bruja!" She's a witch!*

Rose walked over to a man now rocking back on his heels, his face bloody, his eyes wide with terror. "Please, do not hurt me." His heavily accented plea sounded awkward in English.

"What do you want from me?" she asked in Spanish.

"I... we...were paid to...to find the very tall woman, a foreigner, and...and hurt her."

"Paid by whom?" Liam demanded. He stood next to her, clutching a gun that he pointed at this man and two others who hadn't taken off.

"Don't know...a man at the Hotel...Milagro."

She reached into his mind and withdrew an image of the man who had paid them. It was the whiz kid who had developed a series of video games now played worldwide. But she also saw him with Sofiya, the two of them dancing intimately, their heads thrown back as they laughed and commiserated and swept past the table where Zhukov sat with his Interior Minister, Viktor. And when this young man saw the expression on Zhukov's face, so did Rose. Lust. Naked sexual hunger. And a seething rage at them both.

Liam brought his weapon to within inches of the young man's forehead. "What's the man's name?"

"It doesn't matter," Rose said quietly. "I saw his face. It's Richard Williams." She looked at the frightened young man in front of them. "Richard Williams, that's his name."

His head bobbed up and down. "Y-yes."

"Time for you to run now," Liam said in English.

The young man raised his arms and got slowly to his feet—very slowly, clumsily. He started backing away from them and so did the other two men behind him. "We...go now...no problem..."

When they had backed up far enough, so they apparently felt safe, they whirled around and tore up the street, into a side alley. Liam slipped the weapon back into his coat pocket and looked at her.

"Where...did you learn...that?"

Rose took his hand and turned back toward the road with heavier pedestrian and vehicular traffic. Liam's hand vanished in hers. "Some years after I got to Area 51, one of the engineers I worked with was an expert at Tae Kwon Do. I learned from him."

"Holy cow, Rose. I've never seen anything like what you did. At one point, no part of you touched the ground."

She got a kick out of that. "Well, what do you expect from an alien, Liam?"

He exploded with what sounded like nervous laughter that quickly collapsed into genuine belly laughter. Then they reached the busier street, and she released his hand and whatever fear she'd felt evaporated.

Liam consulted the GPS on his phone and pointed off to the left. "That way."

"Would you have shot him?" she asked.

He laughed again. "The gun wasn't loaded. I've never shot a gun. I hate guns. But Jim insisted I carry one and provided the permission I needed to bring it into Ecuador."

He paused and she sensed a question in that brief silence. It was how Liam functioned. The experience, the facts, the questions. Then he assimilated it all. Mitchum's technique was different. With him, it came first as a knowing in his gut, then the experience and whatever followed. Sofiya, she thought, was much the same way. She was as intuitive as Mitchum, but she created the experience—dancing past Zhukov with the young man, flaunting it. *Hey, Alexander, look at us. Do you see how lovely and desirable I am?*

Rose felt Sofiya had done this because at some level she knew that ultimately she would betray him. But why? She had much to gain by remaining his seer, in his good graces. More power. Visibility. Wealth. Contacts. All those things might be attractive to her, but Rose felt sure that deep down, Sofiya longed to do the *right* thing.

+++

2:30 a.m.
The White House

Jim Mitchum's private phone buzzed, and he reached for it on the nightstand, saw Liam's number. His heart leaped into his throat, and he immediately clutched the mobile device and vaulted out of bed. He dashed into the bathroom, the one place where he was truly alone—no Secret Service, no Laurie, no security cams, or recorders.

"Liam?"

"Sorry about the hour, Jim. Rose finally went into her room to get some sleep. I..." Then his voice cracked. "I...something happened...today..." The story rushed out in a tumble of words.

"Are you both okay?"

"Okay. Yeah. We're okay. I've got a name. Richard Williams. The young genius techie from California who created all those video games..."

Interesting, Mitchum thought. Williams was the young man who had made his billions off the next generation video games. "Hmmm. 25 years old, the guy everyone compared to Steve Jobs." Mitchum felt the comparison was bogus. Jobs had given the world Apple technology along with smart phones. Rich had given the gaming world a way to waste their time while believing they actually accomplished something with the game.

"Tell me the rest of the details. How many were in this gang?"

The story that followed alarmed Mitchum, then surprised and shocked him. "You two should leave tomorrow since they know you are there, Liam. How did they find out?"

"Don't know for sure. But we'd like to leave tomorrow. I'm sending you the recording I made of Rose's impressions and of my conversation with this kid. Maybe you'll be able to take action against this Richard Williams."

"Probably not. It happened in a foreign country. Do you have a recording of the guy naming him?"

"I named him, and he said yes."

"Then we'll see. Stay in touch."

"I will."

Mitchum disconnected, left the privacy of the bathroom, and went into the office just off the kitchen, and messaged Paul Spenser. *You have ten minutes?*

The answer came almost immediately. Spenser was an insomniac. *Sure. News?*

Liam & Rose were assaulted on a street in Esperanza, found out the street thugs were paid by one of the richest men in the world: Richard Williams. Have no idea they even knew Rose and Liam were there.

That's very concerning.

Agreed.

Yeah. Epsilon needs to know.

Definitely.

Mitchum had sent Spenser to Esperanza as backup and was surprised when the call abruptly died. Minutes later the room suddenly lit up with Epsilon beaming in with a bewildered Spenser wearing just a T-shirt and boxer shorts. "I'll be right back," Epsilon said. "Stay here, please."

As quickly as he arrived, he beamed back out again. Spenser stumbled forward, Mitchum caught his arm, steadying him, and got him seated on the couch. "What the hell," Spenser muttered. "I was in the bathroom...messaging with you...and suddenly, the room lights up and there's Epsilon. I didn't even...have a chance to grab any clothes."

"I'll get you some clothes." Mitchum went over to the closet, opened it, selected a pair of jeans and a shirt that would fit Spenser. He scooped a pair of sneakers off the rack. "Did he say anything?"

Spenser took the clothes, stood, and pulled on the jeans, the shirt, and sat down again, fingers working at the buttons. "When he beamed into the bathroom, he said Mr. Williams was going to end up like...like the leaders of Pakistan and North Korea. I didn't have any idea what he was talking about, so he showed me a visual. Telepathically."

Uh-oh. Mitchum's thoughts slammed into overdrive. That would tell Zhukov they were onto him and might trigger something worse and more serious. "Where'd he go? Did he tell you?"

Spenser slipped on the shoes and was tying them when the room brightened again, and Epsilon appeared with Rose and Liam, each of them dressed and clutching a bag. "Wow," Liam exclaimed. "Christ. It's good to be back in the US. Thank you, Epsilon."

"We couldn't risk anything happening to either of you," Epsilon said. "One of the men that attacked you and Rose returned to the hotel and informed Richard Williams about what they'd encountered. He told Zhukov. He hasn't said anything to the others yet. Tomorrow he plans to tell them about Rose, the Stell^rs, all of it. So we will need to incapacitate Mr. Williams."

"When?" Mitchum asked.

"Within the hour. I'll be in touch."

And then he beamed out and the four of them were alone in the small office. Mitchum said, "Kitchen. I'll fix us all something to eat."

+++

Zhukov's phone woke him. A message came in from Katherine. He rolled over and sat up with the phone clutched in his hand. His cell told him it was 3:03 a.m.

Something has happened to Rich. He's been taken to a local hospital, 3 blocks from the hotel. On my way there now.

He called Mikhail and asked that the car be brought around. He was downstairs three minutes later, wrapping his heavy wool scarf around his neck and mouth and raising the hood of his jacket. The car pulled up shortly afterward, Mikhail at the wheel.

"I heard. St. Francis Hospital. Do you know what happened?"

"No."

But he had a suspicion they would find Richard on life support, hooked up to tubes and machines that would tell them the extent of the damage to the young man's body and brain. He and Katherine were the only members of the Sindikat with whom Zhukov had shared this information in any detail.

Did they follow us here, Alexander? These aliens could do that, right? Richard had burst out.

Calm down, Rich, Katherine had told him. *Calm down.*

This conversation had occurred after today's conference, when the three of them were sitting on the porch of the hotel when he'd confided all this with them. Anxiety had carved paths across Richard's face, he recalled. *They're technologically advanced aliens, so yes, they could do this. Follow us. They could be listening to us right now. Get out your devices, immediately. We'll communicate like that going forward.*

The hospital wasn't far, and when Mikhail pulled up in front, he said, "They know me here. I'll take you in."

Since Zhukov had forgotten to put on his beard, he kept his head lowered when they went into the hospital. Mikhail whispered, "Have a seat. Let me handle this."

So that was what he did. He covered his eyes and when his hands dropped to his thighs, Katherine was sitting beside him. "I...I don't know what happened. We were having a drink in the hotel bar and...and suddenly he starts choking and I thought he'd swallowed an olive or something. I...slammed my fist against his back...he kept gagging..."

"Slow down, Katherine, slow down." Zhukov patted her arm, certain this was the same MO as what had happened to the other leaders. "Have you gone in to see him?"

"Yes, just briefly. Then the doctors asked me to leave so they could start hooking him up to...to life support."

Mikhail now hurried over and gestured for them to follow him. Again, Zhukov kept his head lowered as they hurried after him through double doors and into a ward. The antiseptic odors nauseated him. His glimpses of people in the rooms, hooked up to machines, made his stomach churn. He nearly vomited when he stood in the doorway of Richard's room, two doctors hovering around him, a nurse adjusting controls on the devices, the equipment beeping, beeping.

Mikhail addressed them in fluent Spanish. The physicians responded quickly, and Mikhail translated. "He temporarily stopped breathing. They resuscitated him. They don't know yet what's wrong with him. However, he is stable but apparently in a coma. They requested the names of his next of kin to find out if they want him flown back to the US."

"I'll be in touch with them," Zhukov snapped. "And of course they will want him taken back to the US. Please prepare him for that journey."

One of the doctors, a short man with very black hair and dark eyes, looked at him. "Are you a relative?"

"I'm the President of Russia and he is here with my team and..."

"*Un momento, un momento,*" Mikhail said, quickly interceding.

The exchange in Spanish that followed was too rapid and heated for Zhukov to follow. But when the men stopped talking, Mikhail turned to Zhukov and in Russian informed him that Richard would be prepared for transport. "And you and your conference people need to be out of here ASAP, Alexander. Or we're going to have an international incident to deal with."

"I will have my plane prepared for a patient," Zhukov said, and turned and left the room. He made it outside before he had to stop and catch his breath and check his rage. He leaned against the statue of St. Francis outside the building and struggled not to heave up his lunch.

"Alexander, you okay?"

Katherine, at his side.

"I will be."

"Did...the Stell^rs do this?"

"I think so."

"But...why?"

"I don't know. After I told you both about the events at Area 51, he'd asked if this Rose was in Ecuador. I replied that I didn't think so, but if she was, she would be about six and a half feet tall, with bluish skin. I later saw him talking with a local man, young guy, a kid, really. Maybe they found her and attacked her. I'm just guessing here, Katherine."

"Well, we need to know. The group of us."

"Right now, we need to pack up our stuff and get the hell out of here.

"I'm going to tell Viktor to inform the other members to get outta here and that we'll explain more next week on an agreed upon date and time."

"I'd like to travel with you and Richard. Maybe he'll come to, and we can find out what happened. My flight won't be returning until the 10th. You can drop me off in California when you deliver Richard. I'll tell my pilot to meet me there."

They hurried out of the hospital and Zhukov called Viktor and brought him up to date.

"We need a new plan, Alexander."

"Let's discuss on the plane tomorrow."

"It might be safer to walk back to Moscow."

The car drew up shortly afterward to bring them back to the hotel.

Chapter 15

I Ching

In spite of what had happened in Esperanza, Rose had returned with gifts for her friends. Sofiya wasn't around, of course, but Helen, Laurie, and Carmen were. So on her third morning back, she entered the dining room for breakfast with a bag of presents. She also had the *I Ching* book and coins she'd bought in Esperanza.

She enthusiastically set everything on the long dining table. "My thanks to you all for making my stay here like a home." The gifts were wrapped with name tags. "Carmen, Helen, Laurie."

"*Ay, caramba!*" Carmen exclaimed. "*Gracias!*"

"*Es de Ecuador.*"

Nomad, sprawled on the floor, glanced up. "Not to worry, Nomad. I have something, for you, too."

She brought out a smaller box, also wrapped, and set it on the floor in front of him. He sniffed it thoroughly, then carefully tore off the wrapping, revealing the stuffed toy—an iguana. Nomad looked at it, glanced up at Rose, and barked twice, as if thanking her. Then he picked up the toy and carried it across the room to the window and settled down with it. Carmen opened her gift first and tears came to her eyes.

It was a pair of ceramic earrings that depicted one of the most famous spots in Havana—the 65-foot statue of Christ of Havana. "Thank you, these are...just beautiful!" And she flung her arm around Rose's shoulders.

"Put them on," Laurie exclaimed.

She slipped them on and the three of them oohed and aahed. "Now you two open your gifts," Carmen said.

For Helen, Rose had bought an exquisite crystal sculpture of the sun with the numbers 137 carved into it. "This is so gorgeous," Helen held the sculpture in the palm of her hand so that it caught the morning light streaming through the window. "Whoever designed this knew about 137, for sure."

For Laurie, the gift was a deck of tarot cards designed by an Ecuadorian seer. "How...did you know?"

"I saw a tarot deck in your office one day."

"Wow. My secret."

"Do a reading for these Stell^r events," Helen said. "Then Rose can do one of her *I Ching*s and we'll see how they compare."

"I like that idea," Rose said.

"*Yo tambien,*" Carmen chimed in.

Laurie chuckled and pushed back from the table. "I'm going to lock the door. If Jim and one of the Secret Service guys walked in..." She shook her head. "The First Lady, the VP, Rose the Stell^r, and Carmen, doing tarot and the *I Ching*...we'd be the stuff of White House gossip."

"Ha," Helen said. "We'd be on gossip websites."

Laurie sat down again, shuffled the tarot deck, and spread the cards in an arc. "It works best with specific questions."

"*Un momento.* Am I...allowed to know this question? This material?"

"*Confío en ti,*" Rose said.

Helen grinned. "My Spanish is really rusty, but I think that means you trust her."

Rose nodded.

"That's good enough for me," Laurie said. "So we take an oath. None of this goes beyond here, the four of us."

"Yes," Rose said.

"*Claro,*" said Carmen.

Helen nodded. "I'm in."

"Okay, the question. It has to be phrased exactly." Laurie looked at each of them.

"Will the Stell^r plan be successful?"

Laurie drew the first card. "The Hermit. They're wise, their plan is wise. Helen, your draw."

Helen passed her hand low over the cards, picked one, set it down. "The eight of swords."

"Ugh," Laurie said. "Okay, they feel like they're trapped and need to do this."

"Yes," Rose said.

"Your draw, Carmen," Laurie said.

Carmen reached out, selected a card and set it down. "The eight of Pentacles."

"What's emerging is a money issue." A frown jutted down between Laurie's brows. "The Sindikat?" She glanced up, biting at her lower lip. "Jim told me about them."

"Yes," Rose said. "The power of unabashed greed on your planet. My turn?"

"Draw," Laurie said.

The card Rose drew was The Hierophant. "The powers that be."

"Yes. The Stell^rs," Laurie said. "They're calling the shots. My turn."

She turned another card over, and Rose stared at it, horrified. "Death."

Carmen made a rapid sign of the cross on her forehead. *"Dios mio.* For whom?"

"I...don't know," Laurie replied. "I'll draw another card to open it up." She did.

It looked worse than the Death card, Rose thought. It showed a man face down on the ground, ten swords sticking out of his back.

"Death through betrayal," Laurie said. "Like when someone stabs you in the back."

Rose wondered if it meant Sofiya betraying Zhukov, which would spell the end of the Sindikat? But she kept her question to herself. "One more," Rose said. "The grand finale."

Helen drew this one. The nine of cups. "The wish card."

Laurie sounded relieved. "One of the two best cards in any tarot deck."

"What's the second-best card?" Rose asked.

"Focus on that question, Rose," said Laurie. "And draw another card."

She held the question uppermost in her mind and let her hand glide over the cards until she felt the urge to pick. She set the card down. The Star. "It's the Stell^r card!" Laurie exclaimed.

Rose glanced up and on the faces of her three friends she recognized shock.

"That's...the second-best card," Laurie said. "The Stell^rs are doing the right thing and this all works out in the end."

"But a lotta crap goes down in between," Helen remarked. "Can we handle it?"

"Let's ask the *I Ching*," Rose said.

"Excellent idea."

Rose thought Laurie looked relieved as she placed the cards back in their box. "So that's our question?" Laurie smiled, then asked. "Can we handle all the bad stuff that goes down in between?" They all laughed.

"Wait," Helen said. "We know the four of us can handle it, but can everyone else involved?"

"Good clarification." Rose swept up the coins in her hand, shook and tossed six times. She recorded the lines on her phone. "The hexagram is Number 36, Darkening of the Light, no changing lines. This one literally means 'wounding of the light.'"

"Yuck," Laurie snapped, and scooped up the coins. "I'd like something a lot more positive than that!" She shook the coins, dropped them.

One look and Rose knew what the hexagram was. Six unbroken lines. "Hexagram One, The Creative. My absolute favorite. The primal power, which is light giving, active, strong and of the spirit. That's how Richard Wilhelm defined it. The energy is unrestricted by any fixed conditions in space and that includes the power of time. Duration." She paused. "Let's hold onto that one."

Before anyone could respond, a rap at the door sent them scurrying—hiding the cards and coins. Carmen hurried into the kitchen; Laurie headed for the door. "Who is it?"

"It's Ken, ma'am."

"Just a second, Ken." She glanced back at the table, Helen flashed a thumbs up, so she unlocked the door and opened it.

Ken strolled in, and Rose could tell from the expression on his face that he was surprised to find them all having breakfast together. "Sorry to interrupt...a belated birthday, ladies? The President was wondering where everyone was."

"Breakfast, *Señor* Ken?" Carmen called from the kitchen.

"Just *café* if there anything left, Carmen. *Gracias*."

Carmen hurried out with a cup of espresso, handed it to him. "Fantastic," he said. "Thank you."

"I will take Nomad for a walk now," Carmen said and whistled for the dog.

Once she was gone, Ken joined them at the table with his coffee. "Any news on Richard Williams?" Rose asked.

"Still in a coma. Stell^r stasis. His medics are bewildered."

"News about Zhukov?" Helen asked.

"Nothing." Ken finished his espresso and got up. "I'll let Jim know where everyone is."

His smile, quick and enigmatic, told Rose that he suspected something private had been going on in here between the women.

+++

By the middle of July Viktor had run so many tests on Zhukov's private server that they were sure it was safe to text with the Sindikat as long as the messages were immediately scrubbed. So on the 17th, he invited the members to sign on. And then he told them nearly everything he knew about the Stell^rs.

An Asian member insisted on knowing what had happened to Richard Williams.

One of the European members fretted about whether the leaders of North Korea and Pakistan were still alive.

A Mideastern member wanted to know how the Sindikat as a group intended to handle this.

Please, one question at a time, Zhukov texted. *The leaders of Pakistan and North Korea went to DEFCON 1 right after we were first contacted by the Stell^rs. In other words, they did precisely what the aliens warned the nuclear nations not to do. When I called them to check in, I discovered both were in comas, like Richard, and the physicians were confounded about what caused it.*

As to how we should deal with this, I have several ideas which I'll bring to the table after the August 1 meeting.

The European, Henri Leveque, messaged madly. *Excuse me, Alexander, but I need more information before August 1. I need to make preparations with my company's interests.*

I understand. We all need to make preparations. But I didn't set that August 1 date. The aliens did. Any more objections? Questions?

A message from Katherine came through next. *I think we'd all better carefully consider what happened to Richard. If we appear to be rebelling against the Stell^rs, we will end up just like him. And frankly, that doesn't appeal to me in the least. I say we take a vote on convening after the world leaders meet with the Stell^rs on August 1. All in favor, message Y. All against, message N.*

Zhukov was pleased to see 14 Ys appear, and it didn't take a genius to figure out that the dissenting vote came from Henri Leveque. *As soon as I have more information, I will pass it on to you.*

He hadn't revealed that the first Stell^r starships would be arriving in just six years. He wanted to be absolutely sure of that fact—all the facts—before asking for a vote from the Sindikat about their course of action.

+++

By July 31, Mitchum had met repeatedly with Helen, Whitley, and Rose. Their gathering today in the basement of the White House was to review tomorrow's meeting with Epsilon and his team and the remaining world leaders. No Area 51 this time. It would be virtual.

"We need answers to several questions tomorrow," Mitchum said. "When will the existence of the Stell^rs be revealed to the rest of the world? It should be done through the UN."

"We need to know their timeline," Helen remarked. "So that we can adequately prepare. As we all know this will cause a profound disruption of the collective understanding of reality for the entire human race."

"We need specifics," Whitley blurted out. "Where, when, how..."

Mitchum glanced at Rose. "Your thoughts?"

"Do you want Zhukov's billionaire rogues to know all those details? Because I believe that's what will happen when he has all the specifics."

"That sounds like a trick question," Mitchum replied.

Whitley sat forward. "Actually, it sounds like a way to lure these suckers out so that the Stell^rs have reason to take them out of commission."

Helen nodded. "Not a bad idea. Flip Zhukov's plans upside down."

"The Stell^r way is to let events happen naturally and act accordingly," Rose said. "I was just curious about how the three of you saw all this. Besides, Epsilon monitors Zhukov. He'll know if and when the Russian president meets again with his Sindikat."

"It's important that the Stell^rs monitor the members of the billionaire club," Mitchum said. "I'm sure that Richard Williams didn't act entirely alone."

They spent another three hours discussing the questions, suggestions, and requests they had for Epsilon. Mitchum didn't want to come across as too demanding. But he worried about the repercussions of introducing the Stell^rs to the rest of the world. All of them knew it would change everything, and he worried about the impact of worldwide existential shock. The bottom line, though, was that the sooner humanity learned that the aliens were here, the more time people would have to acclimate themselves to this new reality. If 2036 was their target date for when the first starships would arrive, there was a lot to get done before then.

They finally broke for a late lunch, which Carmen fixed for them. She took Nomad for a walk while they ate, allowing them the privacy to continue their discussion.

Mitchum noticed that Rose listened closely. She said, "But you should do so based on how far along the Stell^r plan is."

"True," Mitchum said. "And they should do the same."

Rose smiled. "In other words, cooperation."

Chapter 16

The Sahara Plan

Early morning on August 1, 2030, Epsilon surprised the world leaders by deviating from his original plan for a virtual meeting. Instead, he intended to beam each one onto the Stell^r spacecraft that hovered completely cloaked 62 miles above Earth. This was known as the Karman line, the boundary between Earth's atmosphere and space. He would allow each leader to bring a personal advisor. He also had Rose brought on board, and she stood beside him waiting for the first two arrivals. They spoke mind to mind.

Did you inform Jim Mitchum yet about your actual plans for the Sahara? Rose asked.

Not yet. I'd like to put forth our original idea first just in case Zhukov is planning something.

That's smart, Epsilon. Are the domes ready to be built?

We have assembled most of the components on the moon base, so it's a matter of transporting them to the Sahara, which we can start to do in the next few weeks, before the announcement to the UN.

He had confided their real plans to Rose during one of their many private conversations since the events in Esperanza. She'd agreed that the Sahara was the best location. It wouldn't require relocating any humans.

Does Jim know the date yet for the UN announcement? she asked.

I haven't said anything to him yet. It will be a suggestion. He must organize that part of it.

How many domes do you anticipate building?

For 100 million Stell^rs? Planning for 18 to 20 of them, which will be the size of cities large enough to eventually accommodate approximately five million Stell^rs each.

Then the first of the guests arrived: President Agarwal and Rakesh, her husband.

Both looked shocked and shaken. But she recovered quickly and turned her dark eyes on Epsilon. "We...are humbled, Epsilon."

"I'm delighted you and your husband are here."

"Impressive," Rakesh said, looking slowly around, his gaze settling on the large side windows that provided a stunning view of Earth. "Such...incomparable beauty."

"Can you see India, sir?" Rose asked, walking over to him.

Then Zhukov and Sofiya materialized. Rose had requested that Epsilon select Sofiya instead of Viktor, and he felt it was the right choice. She grabbed onto Zhukov's arm, steadying him when he realized where they were, and urged him to the seating along the windows. Epsilon greeted them both, then turned as Mitchum and Whitley appeared onboard. Their obvious surprise turned quickly to delight, especially for Mitchum, a former astronaut. He strode toward the bank of windows where Rose stood with Rakesh. Zhukov and Sofiya sat some distance away. The Russian president looked terribly pale, and Sofiya spoke quietly to him, apparently soothing him.

"My G-d, I feel like I'm home," Mitchum exclaimed. "Not quite as high up, but high enough."

The expression on his face, Epsilon saw, was one of sheer delight, perhaps rapture. He had read that when Edgar Mitchell had peered down at Earth from space, he'd understood the numinous connections among all things, all beings, and it had shaped the rest of his life, just as it had Mitchum's.

Israel's Yonatan Becker was next, with his chief advisor.

Within minutes, the remaining leaders were on the large spaceship. As they settled on the seating along the windows, Alpha, Pi, Gamma, Beta, and Rose joined Epsilon at the front of the group. "I felt it was best to bring you all here rather than to hold this meeting virtually. It's too important. I'm now going to lay out our timeline."

Instead of Epsilon running a telepathic movie of the timeline, Alpha projected the simplest timeline into the air in front of them—straightforward, few details, no interpretation necessary.

1. August 1, 2030 - Leaders informed about where Stell^rs will settle in the Sahara.

2. January 2, 2031 - UN announcement that aliens, the Stell^rs, are here.

3. March 2031- construction begins in earnest on accommodations for the Stell^rs.

4. June 2033 - relocation begins for Stell^rs on moon base to Sahara.

5. June 2036 - first Stell^r starships arrive to Earth.

6. Between 2037-2050 - the remainder of Stell^rs arrive in waves over the next 13 years.

Mitchum was the first leader to comment. "The UN announcement has to happen earlier, Epsilon. As soon as possible. We don't want the news to appear first on social media as misinformation and conspiracy theories, and that could happen at any point. I can help to arrange the UN announcement. I will need some time to determine the best possible date."

Epsilon signaled for Alpha to end the projection. "Considering the number of people who died during the Covid pandemic from misinformation and conspiracy theories, I understand your concern, President Mitchum."

Chen commented next. "So where in the Sahara will you settle? I think it's only fair that we all know that much."

"All in good time, President Chen."

"But once you announce all this to the UN social media will explode with speculation. It certainly has its benefits, but it can also be insidious. Just look how my country was blamed for the Covid virus."

"Covid was predicted centuries ago, President Chen," said President Bernard of France. "By Frenchman Nostradamus."

Zhukov chuckled. "He also predicted a zombie apocalypse 'not far from the great millennium.'" He made quotation marks in the air with his fingers.

"Excuse me," said President Agarwal. "All countries have seers. They aren't always right. It is challenging for anyone gifted with the sight to be one hundred percent correct particularly in terms of time. Sofiya can undoubtedly attest to that."

Epsilon turned his attention on Sofiya. She looked uncomfortable. "Sometimes when I see or sense something, I doubt myself. I think it might be imagination."

Since Rose considered Sofiya a friend, Epsilon decided to explore her remark. "What do you sense about the UN announcement?"

"That president Mitchum is correct. Otherwise, news will get onto social media through unusual and unsuspected sources."

Like Zhukov? Epsilon wondered. "Anything else, Sofiya?"

"Right now, that's it, sir."

Zhukov asked, "Will there be any resettlement of humans?"

The question made Epsilon wonder how much Zhukov might know—or suspect. "Not at this time. It won't be necessary to relocate anyone other than Stell^rs."

Benjamin Harrington of the UK spoke up next. "What type of accommodations are you building for your people?"

"Giant geodesic domes."

"Will humans and Stell^rs co-exist where you settle?" Harrington went on.

"Not unless humans choose to join us."

Yonatan Becker of Israel said, "It is like the two-state solution of Israel and Palestine. For years it didn't work. And then it did when Israelis and Palestinians learned to cooperate and build mutual trust."

"Similar, but not the same," Mitchum said. "Both Israelis and Palestinians are humans. Stell^rs are another species."

Becker nodded. "True. But the situations have parallels."

While the leaders chatted like this among themselves, Epsilon conferred briefly, telepathically, with Alpha, Gamma, Pi, Beta, and Rose about moving the date for the UN reveal.

Epsilon: *Rose, you've spent so much time with these humans. What do you think?*

Rose: *Look at the chaos Richard Williams caused and that didn't involve social media. Jim Mitchum is right. If social media gets hold of this information before the UN announcement that you've stipulated six months from now, there will be conspiracy groups who arm themselves for battle with us. There may be groups that get their hands on a nuclear bomb. In some humans, there's a powerful propensity to believe falsehoods, and when they find others like themselves, they can be quite dangerous. Even for the Stell^rs.*

Epsilon trusted Rose's assessment. Observing humans from a distance yielded certain types of information. But living among them for as long as Rose had provided her with unique insights. *I believe you're right, Rose. Over the decades, we have observed destructive human chaos caused by a variety of factors. But their social media can be the worst in this regard.*

Alpha: *Perhaps it's time to contact the other members of the Council and take a vote.*

Pi: *An immediate vote?*

Gamma: *I will contact them and ask them to vote on it right now, Epsilon. I think it's that important.*

Beta: *Agreed.*

Pi: *Agreed.*

Epsilon: *Contact them, Gamma. We'll have the Council vote before these leaders are sent back to their respective countries.*

Gamma: *I will include our votes as well, Epsilon, and Alpha's.*

Epsilon: *Yes, from me.*

Gamma: *Same here.*

Gamma headed for the com area on the craft, and Epsilon turned his attention back to the group of leaders. "Are there more questions about our timeline? More suggestions?"

Zhukov, Harrington, and Bernard waved their hands. Epsilon gestured at the Russian president. "Yes?"

"When will we be told if the Council makes the UN announcement sooner than your date?"

"It's now in process, as soon as I know, you'll know. President Harrington?"

"My question is similar to President Chen's. When will we be told where exactly in the Sahara the Stell^rs will settle?"

"Once we've made that determination, you'll be informed. President Bernard?"

"Wouldn't it be simpler to relocate your people to the country represented by one of the leaders in this room?"

"Simpler, perhaps. But we deemed that given the populations and the expanses of land, one of the areas we have in mind is best."

Gamma returned to the area a few minutes later. *It's unanimous for an earlier date, Epsilon. How long will it take to arrange?*

President Mitchum said he will work on it. Jim? Epsilon now spoke directly and telepathically to Mitchum. *What's a realistic date for the UN announcement?*

I'll need at least a month to organize this unprecedented world event.

"The UN announcement will happen on September 3, 2030, " Epsilon announced.

+++

Rose slipped out of the room and found the restroom. Minutes later, Sofiya entered, just as Rose had hoped. "One month is really soon, Rose. You ready?"

"I guess I've been ready for decades. It's good to see you. How've you been?"

"I...was disgusted with what Rich Williams did. But I'm grateful you came out okay and that he ended up where he deserved to be. I wish you'd told me you were in Esperanza."

"I thought it best not to. What does your boss think?"

"He's worried. His Sindikat is planning something, I just don't what it is yet."

Rose didn't want to wipe her memory this time. She was curious about how her recollection of this conversation would affect her in the days and weeks to come. "Are they aware that they're being monitored now?"

"They suspect as much. But they believe their billions protect them."

"How?"

"No idea. I talked for a while with Rich and Katherine Martin. She thinks the Stell^r arrival means the wealthy will no longer rule. It's threatening to her. To all of them. They won't be calling the shots anymore."

Rose said, "The world needs a better way, Sofiya."

"These super powerful and wealthy people won't concede to this without a fight."

"It's a fight they'll lose, just as Rich Williams did. What does President Zhukov want?"

"To remain powerful, to keep getting paid for favors by his Sindikat."

"What do *you* want?"

Her expression revealed surprise and led Rose to think she'd never been asked this question before. "I...I..." Her eyes brimmed with tears, and she swiped her hand across her face. "I...don't ..don't want to be in Moscow anymore. I...I want to work with you."

Then she broke down completely, sobbing into her hands. Rose had never seen such raw, naked emotion. She had witnessed human terror, happiness, joy, even sadness, but never something like this, such a profound and terrible despair.

Rose slipped her arm around Sofiya's shoulder. "I'd love to work with you." She grabbed some paper towels out of the dispensary on the wall, pressed them into Sofiya's hand. "Let me see what I can do."

"I...I'll keep you informed about...Alexander's agenda, plans, whatever might impact you. But I think...he's interested, you know?"

Interested? "In what?"

"In *me*, Rose. He has made certain suggestions, certain...overtures...I just act...oblivious."

Rose didn't know much about the dance of human sexuality, except from books she'd read, movies she'd seen. Among Stell^rs, sexuality was much more obvious. "I appreciate your help, Sofiya. I'll see what I can do and, in the meantime, if you're afraid at any time, reach out to me. Call me. *Zap* me."

"Zap you," she repeated, and grinned. "I like that. It's our code word for mind to mind."

Rose gave her shoulder an affectionate squeeze. "I should get back in there."

"Me, too."

"Separately."

"You first," Sofiya said.

Rose zapped her. *Talk soon.*

+++

Zhukov felt relieved when Sofiya returned to the cabin and sat beside him again. Her presence calmed him.

Being on this spacecraft disoriented him—the altitude most of all, but also the technology that transported him here. One moment he and Sofiya had been preparing for the virtual meeting and the next instant, a column of light touched him, and he found himself on this ship in space. With her. With other leaders. With Rose and some of the Stell^rs. And 62 miles below was Earth.

He glanced back once, and a crippling nausea gripped him. The vastness of the oceans, the verdant land, the impossible beauty of a planet where he was one of the world leaders, a man with a voice that would be rendered inconsequential if these aliens arrived. He quickly looked away, and Sofiya leaned in closer to him.

"You okay, Alexander?"

"I...feel sick," he murmured, then his stomach revolted, and he leaned over and vomited.

"Excuse me," Sofiya called out. "President Zhukov just got really sick."

Rose hurried over with damp cloth that she pressed against Zhukov's forehead. "Stretch out, sir. Hold that against your face."

Zhukov stretched out, his head on Sofiya's thighs, and shut his eyes. Humiliating. But he couldn't help it.

Someone else came over and cleaned up the mess he'd made. He heard Epsilon or one of the other aliens in his head, informing him that he and Sofiya would be beamed back to Moscow. Then, in his next breath, he felt a wonderful softness beneath him, his mattress, his bed.

Sofiya's soft voice, so calming and ubiquitous, held him, cradled him. "A fresh towel, Alexander." She pressed it into his hand, and he dropped it over his forehead and eyes.

"Better," he managed to murmur. "We are...back, right? I'm not imagining my bed?"

"It's real, Alexander. Breathe deeply." She touched something cool and fragrant to his upper lip, right under his nose. "Breathe it in, Alexander. Gamma said it will get rid of your nausea."

Gamma. That tall, blue alien that looked like a bad cartoon. At least Epsilon was stately, held himself like a good-looking man, spoke with a quiet authority. But this Gamma... Zhukov desperately wanted to peel the fabric off his lip, but his arm and hand refused to cooperate.

"A trick. It may. Be. A. Trick. Take. It. Off. Please. Sofiya."

"It's no trick." She leaned in close to him, her fingers sliding back through his hair. "Here's a fresh towel." She pressed it against this face and removed the other one.

He breathed in deeply. The fabric on his upper lip smelled of the Russian summer, of Russian waters, of the vast expanse of land that he governed, where he ruled like a king. But behind this odor was another, of rose or lavender or some curious blend of the two that soothed him, calmed him, settled his stomach. He suddenly couldn't stay awake any longer.

+++

Rose was still on the spacecraft when Sofiya contacted her. *Please tell Gamma his remedy worked. Zhukov asleep. I'm headed home.*

Stay safe and well, my friend.

She was standing next to Mitchum during this exchange with Sofiya, and he seemed to sense it. "Is he okay?"

"Who?"

"Zhukov."

"Yes. Uh, he's asleep." She looked at him. "What did you feel just then?"

"That you were communicating with Sofiya. It's easier to know things up here. In space."

"She wants to come work with me. She's very unhappy and frightened with Zhukov. I told her I'd try to arrange it, and she assured me that in the meantime, she would keep me informed about what Zhukov is up to."

"Excellent. But I think having her stay close to Zhukov in the immediate future is critical. It's important for you to gather as much intelligence on him as you can during this crucial time. Then we can arrange for her to come to the US and work with you." He turned toward the bank of windows. "In your travels, when you looked down on other worlds that you passed, did you ever feel *connected* to all of it?"

She knew this was Mitchum the astronaut speaking to her, not Mitchum the president. This astronaut had seen a UFO during his journey in space, seen it clearly and closely for a matter of minutes. She wished it had been her shuttle craft, but when it had happened her life in Area 51 was already decades old. It most likely had been a Stell^r ship from their base on the far side of the moon. She would have to ask Epsilon, one of the many questions she had for him. Or perhaps it had been an alien ship from some other planet they were not aware of.

"I always felt awed and connected to all of it. What did the UFO you saw look like?"

"Classic saucer shape but more elongated. Not very large. It had a lit dome on the top and I could see odd-looking shapes inside. Nothing clear or distinctive. It flew even with us for maybe twenty or thirty seconds, apparently curious. Or maybe monitoring us to see if we presented a threat of any kind. Then it just took off."

Rose thought it sounded like a Zorgon probe. "Did you report it?"

"Not immediately. But when I did, I was told not to mention it to the press. My reply was that people deserved to know, and that I intended to relate the incident to any reporter who would listen."

Rose smiled. "Now you get to announce it to the UN, Jim."

"I'd like you there, too, Rose."

"I'd love to be there."

"I've scheduled meetings for the day after tomorrow with our ambassador to the UN. Can you join me?"

"Of course."

Epsilon came over to them. "I'd like to thank you both for your help with all this. How are you going to approach the UN, Jim?"

"Through our ambassador. She knows everyone on the UN Council."

"Do you need us to participate?"

"No, not for this. Rose is going to be there. I think she's the best suited to approach this with me."

"Excellent."

Rose excused herself and moved around, chatting with one leader after another. President Chen seemed taken back when she addressed him in Mandarin. She towered over him so much he had to drop his head back to look at her.

"Your Mandarin is flawless, Rose."

"Thank you. It's a difficult language to master."

"Any news about how President Zhukov is doing?"

"Apparently he's sleeping."

"It *is* disorienting, being on this spaceship."

"Are you familiar with the *I Ching*, President Chen?"

His face lit up. "Of course."

She reached into the pocket of her black pants and withdrew the *I Ching* coins she'd bought in Esperanza. "If you use the coins instead of yarrow sticks, then here are several more to experiment with." She held them in the palm of her large bluish hand.

Chen quickly slipped on a pair of glasses. "May I look at them more closely?"

"Of course." She handed him the coins, and he scrutinized each one. When he looked up, delight and surprise limned his features. "These...are ancient. They date back to the time of Confucius. Where did you find them?"

She couldn't tell him she'd bought them in Esperanza. That would confirm that she'd been there. "I would like for you to have them. I've found them to be stunningly accurate in creating the hexagrams."

"I had no idea that the Stell^rs knew anything about the *I Ching*."

"It is one of my favorite divination systems that I learned here on Earth."

"Do other Stell^rs use the *I Ching*?"

"I don't think so. But I'm not your usual Stell^r."

"Have you used these coins and asked how all of this will turn out?"

"Yes. I got Hexagram One, the Creative."

His small dark eyes widened. "Excellent. It is one of the best hexagrams of the 64."

Epsilon now spoke from the front of the cabin. "We will start transporting each of you back to your home countries."

Chen looked at the ancient coins in his hand. "Thank you for these, Rose." And then this little man hugged her, an awkward embrace. "You have eased my concerns."

"I'm glad," she said.

"My first gift from an alien."

They both laughed.

+++

At exactly 1400 hours Sergei Sokolov was alerted that a UAP of unknown origin was hovering 62 miles above Siberia. As per his instruction from Zhukov, he gave the green light for two of their 5th gen Su-75 Checkmates to engage with the unidentified spacecraft. Each one of them launched 4 modified RVV-MD2 missiles at the large object or at least where they thought it was. It had only appeared for a spilt second. After they deployed the missiles, they turned and high tailed quickly back to their base.

Within 5 seconds of the missiles firing, they were vaporized by a Stell^r pulse beam.

The pilots saw them disappear on their helmet visors with complete surprise.

Epsilon checked with Gamma as to the origin of the missile firing and was told it was Russia.

He then made what appeared to be a frown and said we will deal with Zhukov at another time.

There was no need to mention any of this to the other world leaders. The priority now was to plan for the UN announcement to go off without a hitch.

Chapter 17

The Big Reveal

The next day, Arlene Mayer, the US ambassador to the United Nations, breezed into Mitchum's office, an attractive, petite woman with a flair for fashion. She wore a short-sleeved colorful cotton dress for this already hot and humid August day. She was a physician by profession and had worked at NASA when Jim was an astronaut. She was the first person besides Laurie with whom he had confided about his sighting of the UFO and she, like Laurie, had encouraged him to share what he'd seen with the press.

"Jim, so good to see you." She hugged him hello and claimed one of the two vacant chairs in front of his desk. "I heard a kind of uncharacteristic urgency in your voice on the phone. So what's going on?"

Ken slipped out of the room. Arlene noticed and frowned. "Is Ken scared of me or something?"

Mitchum smiled and shook his head. "Naw, nothing like that. I'm going to introduce you to someone. I think she'll help you understand what's going on. But please, try to not be startled."

"Okay." Arlene sat back, crossed her legs at the knees. "I'm intrigued."

Ken returned with Rose, pulled out the vacant chair for her, and she sat down. "Good to meet you, Dr. Mayer. I'm Rose." She extended her long, bony, bluish hand and Arlene stared at it for a moment, her eyes wide open, then extended her own visibly shaking hand and met Rose's gaze.

"My G-d," she whispered, then drew her hand back slightly from Rose's and held it in her palm. Her thumb moved slowly over those bones, that bluish skin. "Exquisite. And you're from where?"

"A planet in the Andromeda Galaxy named Xanthe. I'm a Stell^r. After my shuttle craft crashed at Roswell in 1947, I ended up

197

at Area 51, where I lived for nearly 80 years until President Mitchum moved me into the White House."

"Wow, I, uh, don't know what to say."

"May I show you some images, Dr. Mayer?" Rose asked. "Telepathically? Jim has seen most of these, but I'll include him, too."

"Telepa..." Arlene looked at Mitchum. "Astonishing, Jim, this is going to... well, change everything. Everywhere. And Rose, please call me Arlene."

"That's why I contacted you, Arlene," said Mitchum. "The UN has got to be the one to announce this to the world."

Arlene looked at Rose again. Sat back. Folded her hands in her lap. "Okay, let's, uh, do the mind-to-mind thing, Rose. I'm open."

For the next ten minutes, the room was silent. Rose showed Arlene most of the same images Mitchum had seen—the history of the Stell^rs, their journey from Xanthe, the Zorgon craft, the moon base—but there were also new images. Mitchum saw the enormous geodesic domes on the far side of the moon at the Stell^r base. He viewed the vast expanse of the Sahara Desert, where the Stell^rs intended to settle their civilization on Earth. Where these mammoth domes would be built. The massive sections would be transported from the moon and would be assembled in the Sahara.

The visual ended with an image from the future, of the Sahara as a flourishing green paradise with forest, flowing streams, and those geodesic domes looming from the lush landscape.

Afterward, Arlene sat there for a full minute, her stunned expression saying everything that she couldn't articulate. "The UFO you saw, Jim, when..."

"Not a Stell^r ship," Rose said. "From Jim's descriptions, I think it was an AI piloted Zorgon long range probe."

"Your adversaries," Arlene said. "Those hideous reptiles you showed me telepathically."

"Yes."

"A powerful synchronicity. Wow. Jung would love this."

"Carl Jung." Rose nodded. "I met him."

"*Jung?*" Arlene exclaimed. "*The Swiss psychiatrist?* How? When?"

Arlene now sat forward, deeply intrigued, and Mitchum took it all in with that same awe and wonder he'd experienced when he'd first met Rose in Area 51.

"Early 1961. John Kennedy had just won the presidency. Jung asked if he could meet the alien being held at what he believed was Area 51."

"But...how did he know?" Arlene asked.

"Jung wasn't just a psychiatrist. He was...a *mystic*. He sometimes dreamed the future. He saw things. I guess these days he would be considered a gifted psychic or remote viewer. So I met with him at Area 51. March 6, 1961, five months before he passed away at his home on Lake Zurich. He had written about UFOs as archetypes, I'd read his books. We talked for probably five hours. He was really the first human I talked with in any meaningful depth."

"What...did he ask you?" Arlene asked.

Rose's smile was quick, enigmatic, but Mitchum recognized it. She was enjoying herself. "He was curious about everything, every facet of my life. I felt like he was psychoanalyzing me. He asked me how I perceived our encounter." She chuckled. "I told him he was the first human I'd met who had the sensibilities of an alien. He laughed, but I figured he would go back to his castle and mull it over for weeks."

Mitchum, now sitting forward, as intently focused as Arlene. "Did you hear from again?"

"A few weeks later, a courier delivered a recording." She briefly shut her eyes, and Mitchum realized she was remembering that message. "My dear alien Rose, I had believed you were an archetype. But since meeting you in person, talking with you, that archetype has leaped to life. When you're eventually released from 51, please know you're welcome to my place on Lake Zurich. In gratitude, Carl."

Her eyes opened and she and Arlene looked at each other. Mitchum felt something pass between them, perhaps the recognition of a bond, a commonality disconnected from gender and species, but completely united in consciousness. Then Arlene turned her attention on Mitchum. "So I'm supposed to introduce this to the UN Council as the aliens are here, they're benevolent. This is disclosure."

Mitchum nodded. "But don't mention the location, the Sahara. Not yet. Epsilon their leader will do that."

"At the General Council meeting?"

"Yes." That was the plan they had decided on when they had communicated most recently. Granted, circumstances might change it, but until he learned differently, that was the story.

"All right. This will take some time. If I'm proposing a worldwide announcement about disclosure, then we need every public forum on the planet to carry that message." She looked at Rose again. "This telepathy stuff. Can you do it with, uh, eight billion people?"

"I highly doubt it," Rose replied. "Maybe Epsilon and his leadership Council can do it through a means that I'm not familiar with."

"It will be more powerful if they speak directly to the delegates of the UN's 193-member countries," Mitchum said. "I would like to have Epsilon and his Council members there—and you, Rose."

She nodded.

"Realistically? For *this*?" She ran her fingers through her straight auburn hair. "In an ideal world, I'd like to do it ASAP. I can start talking to people tomorrow, but I figure September third at the earliest is best to plan accordingly. It's a Tuesday, the first business day back at the UN after the summer hiatus."

"Perfect. That's the exact day Epsilon wanted."

Federal agencies would have to be notified to be on high alert. So would the security agencies in other countries. Mitchum fully expected chaos and violence in the aftermath of this announcement. But he would wait to notify any of them until Arlene was 100% sure of that date.

"Are you going to mention the Sahara to the countries that border it?" Arlene asked.

Mitchum had thought about this a lot. But the Sahara covered large parts of Algeria, Chad, Egypt, Libya, Mali, Mauritania, Morocco, Niger, Western Sahara, Sudan, and Tunisia and amounted to three- and a half-million square miles or 31 percent of Africa. These nations would learn about the Stell^rs through the UN announcement, but he would leave the specifics to Epsilon.

Helen suddenly poked her head in the doorway. "Arlene!" She exclaimed. "What a terrific surprise." The two women hugged hello, then Ken brought a third chair around for her and she sat to Rose's left. "Isn't Rose a delight, Arlene?"

"The understatement of the century. And a total mind blower," Arlene replied.

Mitchum brought Helen up to speed on the UN. She stabbed her fingers back through her hair. "Damn, September third, literally around the corner." She paused. "Disclosure. Finally."

"Yes, and lots of chaos," Arlene added.

"Those guys who testified to Congress back a few years ago will be delirious with excitement. So will numerous UFO groups, researchers, authors, alleged abductees..."

"Stell^rs don't abduct," Rose said. "We observe, then engage only at certain times."

"You're not familiar with the species known as the Grays?" Helen asked.

"Heard of them but that's it." And to herself, was skeptical of their existence since she was isolated for those many years at 51. "Perhaps Epsilon and the Stell^r Council know more."

"People are going to freak out," Arlene said.

"You think we should erect the barricade around the White House and Congress, Jim?" Helen asked.

"Not yet. We don't want the press to start asking questions. Once the UN announcement has been locked in, then we can do that a day or two before." He glanced at Rose. "Insights?"

"I'd like to think that humanity will surprise me and be delighted the government has finally come clean about disclosure. And while that probably will be true with certain factions, my concern is that there will be far more people who react violently. Misinformation is going to run rampant."

Helen nodded. "I agree."

Mitchum nodded. "It's a depressing conclusion about where this country is now, but I agree. And I suspect countries across the globe will be dealing with the shock and aftermath."

+++

Toward the end of August 2030, the rumor mill started buzzing, and Zhukov received several concerned emails from Katherine Martin and some of the other Sindikat members. Something, they all agreed, was happening at the UN. Something big. The pending announcement that the aliens were real and headed this way?

If that was the case, then why hadn't the Russian ambassador to the UN alerted him?

He texted Viktor to meet him at their usual coffee spot within the hour.

I'm there now, got our usual table.

On my way.

Zhukov donned his fake beard and sunglasses and 40 minutes later walked into the shop. The place was crowded, and the acoustics were poor, so if the Stell^rs were listening, it would be more difficult for them to pick out his and Viktor's voices.

As he joined Viktor at the table by the window, Viktor said, "You look worried."

"It seems to be my natural state these days."

"News about Richard Williams?"

"Nope. Nothing on that front. But there's considerable buzz that something big is brewing at the UN. Have you heard anything about it from Ambassador Averin?" Gleb Averin and Viktor were friends, and it was Viktor who had recommended him for Russian's UN ambassador. "My sense is that it's an announcement."

"About the Stell^rs?"

"Or something else equally important."

"I haven't heard from Gleb since I told him we went to Area 51 and met an alien."

"*What*?" Incensed by this news, Zhukov leaned forward. "You weren't supposed to..."

"Relax, Alexander. That was just a joke, okay?"

"Not funny. "

"We spoke about two weeks ago, just his monthly report. Nothing unusual."

"Call him."

"You're his employer, shouldn't you call him?"

"But you're his friend, so it's more likely he would confide in you than in me."

Viktor, obviously annoyed, rolled his eyes. "And what, exactly, do you want me to ask him, Alexander?"

"Is a UN announcement pending? Ask him that."

Viktor tapped away on his phone.

"Is he in the US?" Zhukov asked.

"Last I heard he was going camping in New Mexico with his family. I told him this was urgent."

A server came over and they ordered an early lunch. She left just as Viktor's phone pinged. "Is it Gleb?" Zhukov asked.

"Yes." He paused, glanced up. "You'd better take a look at this, Alexander."

He passed Zhukov his cell. *Hey Viktor, am on my way back to NY. Dr. Mayer has called an emergency General Assembly meeting for September 3. She didn't say what it concerns.*

"That's Arlene Mayer, right?" Zhukov asked. "The U.S. ambassador?"

Viktor gave him *a look*. "Damn, Alexander, if you have to ask me that, you need a vacation."

"Just making sure."

"And usually when she calls for a special meeting, she gets it because she does it so rarely."

"Ask Gleb to keep you informed."

"He will." The server brought their meals and when she left, Viktor added, "It must be the announcement about the aliens, Alexander. And maybe they'll provide additional information, too, like where in the Sahara they're going to settle."

Maybe this, maybe that. It was enough to drive Zhukov nuts.

+++

On September 3, 2030, a day that would be forever known as the big reveal, Rose was at breakfast with Liam and the Mitchum's when a column of bright white light pierced the ceiling and surrounded her. She heard Jim say, "Looks like we're on for today. I need to contact Helen."

They had known it was coming, of course, But still, it was a shock even to Rose. Then she was on the spacecraft with Epsilon and the four Council members she'd met before. It was the same area where he had brought the leaders weeks ago. Epsilon took her hand and led her over to the closest window. "The UN. There it is."

The magnificence of the structure, of the many flags that flapped in the breeze above it, told her a great deal about its inception, its ideals. "And what is the plan, Epsilon?"

"At precisely 10 a.m. Eastern Time—about three hours from now—Arlene Mayer will give a brief talk about why she has called the General Assembly together. Then you will be transported into the room and shortly afterward, so will I. And we will introduce the Stell^rs to planet Earth."

Rose drew her gaze away from the UN and looked at Epsilon. "You ready for this?"

He laughed, the first time she had heard him do so, and she loved the sound of it. Joyous. "Ready for years. How about you?"

"Beam me down, Scotty."

He slyly grinned. "I communicated with Jim Mitchum right after you were brought aboard, Rose."

"What about the other leaders?"

"They all have ambassadors on the General Assembly. All have been notified and from what we've determined, it's going to be a full house."

"Protective barriers went up around the White House and Congress in the middle of the night."

"Some of the other nuclear countries have done the same: Russia, Israel, the UK, France."

"Not China?"

"No. Then again, the regime is so oppressive there hasn't really been an uprising there since the Tiananmen Square protests in Beijing in 1989."

"Hmm. I think President Chen liked the *I Ching* coins I gave him."

"I think he trusts you, Rose, more than he trusts President Zhukov."

"Hope so."

"Sofiya is going to be at the UN announcement."

"Probably as Zhukov's personal spy."

"Good. I'm sure she'll give you a report."

"Once the announcement is made, I'd like her to come and work with me soon."

"I'll take care of it at the right time. Keep in mind, she still provides us with the best intelligence on Zhukov and who knows what his reaction will be after the announcement."

"She'll continue to be a big plus for us, Epsilon."

+++

Zhukov settled in his office, in front of the largest flat screen in the Kremlin, and both Viktor and Dimitri were with him. In the middle of the table were a bottle of vodka, three glasses, and a platter of light snacks the kitchen had prepared.

A ball of dread and anxiety had taken up residence in Zhukov's gut. The Alien Announcement. That was how he thought of it, in the same league as the Russian Revolution, Lenin, the Bolsheviks, Tolstoy, Tchaikovsky, caviar, and vodka. Actually, it was bigger than all those events combined.

The inside of the UN General Assembly appeared on the screen. Arlene Mayer, the US ambassador, walked onto the stage and stopped in front of the podium. She tapped the microphone. Off to the right, the translators adjusted their headphones, their small TV screens. Each delegate was eagerly waiting for what was going to be announced.

He spotted Gleb in one of the front rows sitting with Sofiya. They looked as if they were conversing. Good. He would message her at some point and find out what they talked about.

"Lots of anticipation there," Dimitri remarked. "You can see it."

"It's going to be a real shocker," Viktor said.

Zhukov glanced at the clock on the wall for NYC. 9:56, just four minutes away.

Arlene Mayer tapped her mic again. "I'm Dr. Arlene Mayer and I'm pleased to see the entire General Assembly here. Thank you for coming on such short notice."

The translators went to work.

"The news I'm about to deliver will change our planet forever." She paused, a dramatic pause. "An alien race has made itself known and their emissary..."

And then Rose beamed into the room, on the stage next to Arlene. The shock that tore through the large hall was visible, tangible, and continued until Dr. Mayer spoke again. "...their emissary is here with us. Rose is a Stell^r from the planet Xanthe, about ten light years from us. Rose?" The delegates sat there in shock with eyes and mouths wide open.

"In 1947..."

Zhukov knew this part of the story but was intrigued nonetheless with the precise way Rose opened her talk, repeating the introductory sentences in a dozen different languages.

Dimitri opened the bottle of vodka and poured some into each of the three glasses. "Cheers, my friends." He held up his glass. "This may be our last normal drink ever."

Zhukov picked up the remote control and switched to the state-controlled station to see how they were covering this. A reporter on a busy thoroughfare in downtown Moscow where the UN announcement was being broadcast live on a 200-foot screen, stood there aghast, staring at the image of Rose. Several hundred people in the immediate area also had stopped and watched. Some wept openly, others cheered, and others looked completely terrified and panicked.

"This is going to create some big security problems," Viktor remarked. "Did you call out..."

"Of course I did," Zhukov snapped. "Anyone who protests or riots or causes any trouble will be arrested immediately."

Zhukov gulped the vodka in his glass and switched to CNN. The Kremlin had access to all the US and international news channels, and as soon as he saw the utter chaos on Manhattan's streets, he texted Sofiya.

How are they taking the news?

All things considered, it's eerily calm in here. But outside this building, a riot. And now, spectacularly, Epsilon just beamed in with four other members of the Stell^r Council.

Viktor suddenly got up and turned on four other screens in the conference room, each one tuned to something different: Miami, Jerusalem, London, Paris. In each city, people wept, cheered, and many collapsed in the streets. He switched to Washington DC and saw a group of a thousand or more marching toward the White House. Some chanted, *Go home ETs*. It looked like a scene from a dated sci-fi movie. But this was actually happening.

His cell buzzed and lit up with calls from the members of the Sindikat. He let them all go to voicemail. He knuckled his eyes, poured himself another vodka, and despair swallowed him whole.

+++

Rose knew what was going on outside because the head of the UN security team announced it. An undercurrent of alarm ran throughout the room, and two of the security agents at the door now bolted it. One of the men touched the pod in his ear and ran toward the other security agent, and they both hurried toward the stage.

"What's happening?" She looked at Epsilon.

"A crowd is trying to get into the building. Security thinks we're in danger."

"Can you beam all of these people in here to safety?"

"It won't be necessary."

An image appeared on the massive onstage screen of the exterior of the UN. The approaching crowd was huge—thousands, some of them armed and wild, shouting and shoving, and others being swept along in the crowd. Beyond them, traffic had snarled, police sirens screeched, helicopters hovered, chaos had erupted and now ran rampant.

Moments later, a huge column of light shone down on the UN enclosing it completely. The light became translucent, so that the crowd outside of it could clearly see what it held within, the magnificent slender glass structure built from an ideology of world peace and harmony. Many in the crowd rushed toward the column of light, shouting, some waving weapons, and when they reached it, the light repelled them. Some stumbled around, others were flung back, and others spun around and sprinted away.

When Rose turned, Sofiya stood at her side, staring at the images, her face so pale that Rose thought she might keel over. Instead, she turned her gaze on Rose and stabbed her thumb over her shoulder. "Naive Gleb finally believed what I told him."

Rose glanced back. The overweight Russian ambassador to the UN had passed out, his body partially draped over the seat in front of him. The men and women around him barely noticed. Some were on their feet, shouting, and others were headed toward the bolted doors.

Suddenly, Paul Spenser, the astronomer who headed NASA, joined them. "Jim tells me it's pretty bad out there. He asked me to get you back to the White House." He paused and looked at Epsilon. "Unless you'd like to do the honors."

"No need," Epsilon said. "The crowd eventually will get bored and move on when they realize there is no way for them to enter the building." Then Epsilon made what Rose thought was an unusual statement. "I think it's time to break bread together. We have wonderful Stell^r food for everyone in here to enjoy."

Within minutes, several large tables had been beamed in with platters of unique Stell^r dishes that Pi, Beta, Gamma, and Alpha set up. There were stacks of plates and cups —the Stell^r equivalent of paper plates and cups—and Epsilon announced, "Please, line up and enjoy our Stell^r cuisine. *Alien* food. Everyone join us for a bite to eat."

Maybe they were all really hungry or it was the delectable intoxicating scent of the exotic aromas or that they really didn't want to break through the bolted doors. Or perhaps it was Epsilon's presence that drew them. Whatever the reason, everyone in the room moved toward the tables. The screen went dark, Rose heard dozens of languages spoken. The air turned festive.

People helped themselves to all the appealing dishes and took it back to their respective seats. Rose and Epsilon then continued talking to the crowd and explained that the Stell^rs would be settling in the Sahara. Far away from human civilization.

"And we will turn the sand from barren to green. We will grow enough food to feed the hungry worldwide. It will be a Stell^r gift to your planet."

Chapter 18

Construction Begins

By March 2031, now six months after the UN Announcement, Stell^r space vehicles from the far side of the moon were continuously transporting all the sections for the construction of the massive domes in the Sahara Desert. Mitchum had sent Rose and Liam as the US representatives to oversee the human team that worked alongside the Stell^rs in the actual building of the domes. Rose discovered that for the humans the most significant problem was the soaring daily temperatures—between 116-136 degrees Fahrenheit.

The bioengineered epidermis of the Stell^rs protected them from the extreme temperatures, but humans had no such protection. That second day, while Rose was inside the Sahara headquarters overseeing lunch for the teams, Liam hurried in, covered in sweat, grabbed a chair, pulled it up in front of the powerful AC unit, and sank into it. As the gelid air poured over him, his body seemed to slump to the side, and she went over to him.

"Liam? You okay?"

"This heat. I can't take this heat for longer than 30 or 40 minutes, if that. Two guys out there just passed out and were taken to medical."

"I should've given everyone the climate-controlled space suits," she said. "I'll get them."

"They're probably too cumbersome, Rose. I just don't think the human team can work in this kind of environment."

"The suits don't have to be cumbersome, Liam. The fabric can adjust to the individual wearing them. I'll show you." She handed him a bottle of cold water. "Drink some of this first."

He took the bottle, guzzled half of it, and got up. "Okay, let's see what you've got, Rose."

She went over to the supply closet and removed one of the special suits that Epsilon had given her. "Just pull this on over your clothes. Use the hood."

Rose passed it to him, and he followed her instructions. The fabric immediately molded itself to his body. "Weird," he said.

"Now step outside into the heat, see what you think."

He walked outside into the blinding light and stood there for ten minutes, walking in loose circles. "Incredible. Why didn't you offer these from the get-go, Rose?"

"My bad. It honestly didn't occur to me." She had too much going on. She sometimes felt like she was on overload, as the humans called it. "Can you get the rest of your team in here?"

"There are six of us. You have enough suits?"

"Yes. And the two who are in medical. What're their names? I have something that will revive them quickly."

"Ace and Tom."

"Okay, I'm headed to medical. Get your guys in here." She opened the closet door. "The suits are in here. Just leave my mess. I'll finish having lunch ready when I get back."

"What's your remedy for them?"

She went over to her pack, unzipped one of the many pockets, and withdrew three pills. "Epsilon gave me a handful of these." She handed him one. "Chew it. You'll feel better in seconds."

"What is it?"

"Don't exactly know. Something new."

He popped it into his mouth, chewed, and within 30 seconds, that light returned to Liam's eyes, that light she associated uniquely with him. "Wow. Rose. I feel...normal!"

"Good. I'll be back shortly. Get those guys in here."

Outside, she hopped into the solar-powered cart with the oversized wheels and a roof that was impervious to the sun. She started toward the medical facility situated about half a mile from the headquarters building, low and squat and bone white. Its roof reflected the relentlessly hot light.

She parked in front and went inside, where the cool air smelled fragrant and felt almost weightless, unlike the heat outside. One of the medics, a blond woman from Minnesota, was leaning over the counter, tapping away on her mobile. She glanced up. "Rose, what a great surprise!"

"Hey, Dr. Griffin. I hear you've got two humans who passed out from the heat?"

"They were severely dehydrated. They're recovering."

Rose approached the counter. "May I provide a Stell^r remedy? Liam just took one and recovered in less than a minute."

She straightened up, hands fixed to her hips. "What is it?"

"Not sure. Epsilon gave me a handful a few weeks back and advised me to keep them handy for the Sahara."

"May I try one first?"

"Sure."

Rose passed her one of the bright red pills in a transparent packet. She tore open the wrapping. "Swallow or chew?"

"Chew."

She did, and within fifteen seconds she started laughing. "Oh my, that is superb. I haven't felt like this since...since I don't know when. It's...c'mon, I'll take you to my two patients. I trust the judgment of you Stell^rs."

Rose wished the rest of humanity felt the same way about them. But since the UN announcement, the protests worldwide had swelled and in some cities were very violent. It had resulted in thousands of arrests. But there were many other factions of humanity who embraced the Stell^r arrival and existence—scientists, astronomers like Paul Spenser, researchers,

Ufologists, writers, experiencers, abductees, and other enlightened humans across the planet. In her darker moments—and there weren't many, but they did happen more frequently now—she focused her attention on the positive.

The Stell^r Council had accelerated initiatives around the globe to produce massive amounts of food, environmental cleanups, and delivered educational programs to clearly show how their amazing alien technology could improve the general health and welfare of every human being on Earth. Support had begun to swell from the ground up for the Stell^rs and the eventual arrival of their civilization to the African continent.

The two men—Ace and Tom—lay in beds side by side, both hooked up to IVs, but conscious. "Gentlemen, I think you know who Rose is," Dr. Griffin said. "And she has a Stell^r remedy for you two."

Ace, a big man with glasses who looked like an ex-stockbroker, grinned. "I'm ready. These IVs help, but they take too damn long."

"Great." Rose handed him a red pill.

He looked at it and laughed. "It's like—*The Matrix?* The blue pill or the red pill."

"It's the right color," Tom said, holding out his hand. "Neo could have a blue pill which would allow him to return to experiencing only the illusion or the red pill, which would enable him to understand what was actually occurring outside the illusion created by the Matrix."

"Damn, boy," said Ace. "That sounds like it came right off the Internet."

"It did, dude, it did. I was watching *The Matrix* last night and it popped into my head just now."

"Synchronicity," Rose said, and dropped the red pill into Tom's outstretched hand.

He chewed, and two minutes later, both men removed their IVs, got out of bed, and started looking for their clothes. "Hold on, hold on," Dr. Griffin said, patting the air with her hands. "Both of you. Back in bed."

"Nope," Tom said. "We're good."

"Yeah, we are," Ace echoed.

"I've got some very cool suits for both of them," Rose told Dr. Griffin. "They'll do fine."

"I'd like to see this," she said. "Okay if I come with you all?"

"Absolutely," Rose said. "I've got a cart and it's only half a mile."

"Won't be a problem," Ace said.

"Agree completely," Tom said.

They piled into the cart, the men in the back, Dr. Griffin in the passenger seat. "What's your first name?" Rose asked, distressed that she didn't know.

"Eve. You know, like Adam's boring wife."

"Ah, *that* Eve."

She looked at Rose and rolled her eyes. "Here we are in the third decade of the 21st century and the religious zealots are divided into two factions. Those who think you guys are Satanists and sex traffickers, and those who believe G-d sent you. I don't believe in heaven or hell. Do you, Rose?"

In her—what? How many years now? 84? Yes, 84 years here with humanity—no one had ever asked her this specific question. "Good and evil exist. That's what I believe. Every human religion has named good and evil. I don't. To name them like that is to empower the archetype. I do believe in the higher power of good and what you humans call love." Rose thought to herself there certainly are powerful unexplained occurrences since the beginning of known time that are mysterious and most likely will remain that way. She also liked that thought.

+++

For the first several months or so, news coming out of the countries that bordered the Sahara reported on the construction of the geodesic domes. Some fuzzy photos were provided. Zhukov marveled at how quickly two of the gigantic domes had gone up.

They clearly were using their superior alien technology to do this with such precision and remarkable speed.

He messaged Sofiya and asked her to stop by his office and View the site. She didn't respond for nearly an hour—unusual for her, she was usually quite prompt. When he finally received her reply, it included several rough drawings of what she saw—the two completed domes and several other buildings. *A medical facility, lodging for the workers, and the main building where they have a cafeteria and conference space. I've been in touch with Rose, who is there, and she has invited me to the site to observe the construction.*

By all means go. Find out everything you can. Let me know where you fly into, and I'll arrange your ticket.

No need. She will have me teleported in.

Beamed in where? To what part of the desert?

No idea. I'll let you know.

None of the news reports had provided the exact location of the Stell^r construction, but drones from Libya had pinpointed a general area smack in the middle of the Sahara. Difficult to get to, unless you were beamed in, he thought. He called Katherine's cell.

She answered on the second ring. "Alexander. News? I hope. The other members are eager to get moving on our plan."

"Sofiya is being teleported in so once she's there, we'll know more. We have the weapons ready. And a way to deliver them. We just need to pinpoint the exact location."

He brought up a map of the Sahara on his computer. "The Libyan drones launched last night identified an area near the middle of the immense desert." He read off the coordinates to her.

"Too close to the town of Sebha, Libya," she said. "Our private satellite images show these dome structures in a completely arid part of the desert."

"Coordinates?"

She read them off and he entered them in his computer. When the image came up, he enlarged it. The pair of domes were visible from outer space and so were several other structures in the vicinity. No town or village within hundreds of miles. Good. If possible, he preferred to limit the numbers of innocents killed in this attack. Just the Stell^rs and whoever was helping them.

But what about Sofiya? She couldn't go to the Sahara, not yet. Not now. But if he told her that, she probably would give Epsilon permission to beam her there just to defy him. So he wouldn't mention it. And if she perished...it was due to *her* choice, not his. Yes, he felt comfortable with that.

"How much advance notice do you need to do this?" Katherine asked.

"24 hours' notice. How much time do you need to prepare things on your end?"

"I can make a couple of calls on the most secure line on the planet. The tentative target date for now is August 22. Temperatures over 120F are forecast."

"Excellent," Zhukov said. "Maybe from space it'll look like the sun itself has exploded."

Katherine smiled at that mental image.

+++

Mitchum liked the idea of Sofiya joining the Sahara team. Rose had texted him about it. Epsilon could have brought her in months ago. But that would have stoked Zhukov's suspicions. This way might be less controversial. She could accompany Rose to the US to assist her with an engineering project.

He received regular reports from Epsilon, Liam, and Rose on the progress of the domes. He, Steve Whitley, and Paul Spenser would travel there to see the progress in person. A trip as secretive as the one to Area 51 not so many years ago. Ken accompanied them but no Nomad this time. He was getting along in years, his muzzle starting to turn gray, and he hoped that at some point Epsilon would inform him of some cure for aging dogs. It was more than 5800 miles—nearly twice the distance to Area 51—and twice as long to get there.

They arrived early on the morning of the 23rd. The sun had just risen, but the outside temperature was already 115 degrees, hardly balmy. "Damn, how's anyone work out in this heat?" Spenser muttered, tugging a cap down lower over his forehead.

"I'm sure Rose has figured it out," Whitley remarked.

Rose pulled up in a large solar-powered cart with open sides and a roof and enough space for their bags. No special climate suit for her, Mitchum thought, and wondered about the humans.

Once they were in the cart and had started moving, he could see the domes in the distance, one half-completed, two others standing tall and magnificent. He spotted workers, too, around the incomplete dome, and several of them wore those special suits.

"You want to take a look?" Rose gestured at the domes.

"Definitely," Mitchum replied.

"May I take pics?" Spenser asked.

"Sure. Liam has taken hundreds, at every stage."

"You gave all the humans those adaptive suits," Whitley remarked.

"Yes, Stell^rs don't need them."

"Your blueish skin?" asked Spenser.

She nodded. "Along with some bioengineering. It all evolved over the centuries as temperatures became more extreme."

Rose pulled up in front of the incomplete dome and they all got out. The stifling heat immediately brought beads of sweat to Mitchum's face. But it wasn't just the heat. He sensed something very wrong about all this but couldn't pinpoint it, couldn't clarify it.

He hurried over to one of the men wearing a special suit, Ken right behind him. "Excuse me."

Liam glanced up. "President Mitchum! And the team! Wow, so glad you are all here." He gestured for them to follow him. "You gotta see how these pieces are fitted together."

They trotted after him, into the incomplete dome. Despite the fact that it was wide open at the top, the air in here felt pleasant, strangely cooler. "Over here," Liam called, motioning at them again.

They joined him at the far side, where Liam ran his fingers across several pieces of the dome. "See this?"

Mitchum looked closely and saw what he was referring to. Even though it was obvious there were several large pieces here, they fit together so seamlessly it looked as if they had been mathematically matched. The precision astonished him. He rapped his knuckles against the surface.

"How impervious is it?" he asked.

"To heat, air attacks, giant worms from *Dune*..." Spenser added.

Liam laughed. "All that and more. C'mon outside, I'll show you."

They followed him to the eastern exterior of the incomplete dome, Rose trailing along behind them. Here, he picked up a blowtorch that was on the ground, switched it on and held the flame so close to the tile that there should have been some type of mark. But the tiles didn't have even a scorch mark.

"And now I'd like to show you something else I came across just before you all arrived." He gestured at a small area where the sand had been transformed into greenery—not grass, exactly, but a kind of wildness with long weeds and wildflowers. In the middle of it, digging had been conducted, and that was where Liam stopped. At the edge of a shallow hole.

He pointed at an object that looked like it was trying to make friends with the dirt and sand or with the greenery and flowers. "Jesus," Whitley murmured. "It looks like a small tactical explosive device."

"And gladly it didn't go off and no radiation fallout," Rose said.

"Thank G-d," Mitchum said. "Do the Stell^rs know about this, Rose? Does Epsilon?"

"I don't know but guessing yes."

"This is what you found right before we arrived?" Mitchum asked Liam.

"Yeah. I was digging out here to see how deep the bottom of the dome went and...and my shovel hit it."

"Was there noise last night? Any loud sounds?" Whitley asked.

"I didn't hear anything," Liam replied.

"Me, either," Rose said. "And nothing was reported." She crouched and ran her fingers along the side of the device, then placed her palm against the exterior. "It had a mate."

"That's around here?" Spenser balked.

"Yes, I think so."

"Let's take a look at the completed domes," Liam suggested. "Maybe the mate targeted one of them."

"It had to have been delivered from somewhere by either a very sophisticated controlled drone or launched from an aircraft," Mitchum said. "And there would have been some sound. There are very few bad actors that could have pulled this off. I have my suspicions on who it might be."

They walked back to the cart. Liam drove, and Rose brought out an iPad. "I'm checking the computer radar for last night."

"Isn't there usually someone monitoring it?" Spenser asked.

"Yes. Since the device didn't detonate and was most likely on a timer, I highly suspect that Epsilon or someone else on the Council knew about it, took care of it, and rendered it inoperable," Rose replied.

Up close, the completed dome looked spectacular. Mitchum figured it was miles across and a half mile high, spacious enough for a city with buildings, shops, and homes. The Tacoma Dome, the largest wooden dome arena in the world, was 530 feet in diameter and 152 feet tall and would look dwarfed next to this marvel.

They all moved through it, vigilant for any disturbance in the Earth. Mitchum finally spotted something on the Northeast side, where there were large circular-shaped windows like portholes on a boat. The sand here looked disturbed, as if the windows had been open when a wind had blown through.

He snapped a photo with his cell and called the others over. Liam had a hand shovel now, and when Mitchum gestured at the disturbed sand, Liam crouched and gently ran the edge of the shovel back and forth across the sand, carefully moving it from one side to the other. It didn't take long to expose another explosive device, about the size of the first one. It lay so shallow in the sand that Mitchum wondered how the hell both had gotten in here. He snapped a couple more photos, then went outside, Ken hurrying alongside him, to take a look at the exterior.

"Stealth mini tactical nukes?" Ken remarked. "Do we have anything like that?"

"Yes. But I'm surprised that some other country does, too. They were created in great secrecy."

They stopped at a spot about even with the location of the explosive device inside. Mitchum rolled up his right sleeve and dug his hand down through the sand, searching for anything unusual. Liam used the shovel to clear the sand away. Rose dug her long, bony fingers and hand down through the sand on the other side of where Mitchum crouched.

"Well, well." She suddenly pulled her hand out of the sand and held out a piece of dark metal the same color as the missile. She placed it in the palm of her left hand so they could all see it. Inscribed on it were a couple of words in Russian. "The words mean *go deep*."

"What's its purpose?" Spenser asked.

Rose's fingers closed over it, she briefly shut her eyes. Mitchum realized she was reading the metal just as she had done when she'd placed her hand against the surface of the first missile and announced it had a mate. "It's sophisticated," she finally said. "I think it expanded or something when it struck the sand and then burrowed down deep enough so it could end up inside the dome."

"How deep does the dome base go?" Whitley asked.

"I don't know," Rose said. "The base of it was already here when Liam and I arrived."

"Any estimates, Liam?" Mitchum asked.

"At least several hundred feet, that would be my guess."

"Rose, can you contact Epsilon and find out the specifics?"

"I've been sending him messages since you all arrived. The..."

And suddenly a column of light pierced the top of the dome and struck the ground and vanished. Epsilon now stood there. "It's the work of Zhukov and his billionaire cronies. We disemboweled the missiles and eliminated any possible radiation leak. Remotely, of course. And then we created a simulated explosion that was detected by Russian satellites, so they think it went off."

"And now?" Mitchum asked.

"Is Zhukov in a coma like the other two leaders?" Whitley asked.

"Not yet. But when he is, it will be him along with his fellow bad players. All of them."

"But...that consists of...some of the wealthiest people on the planet," Mitchum said. "There will be scrutiny and a lot of suspicion if they all suddenly vanish."

"That's something to consider, Epsilon," Rose said.

Epsilon gave her his full attention, his large oval eyes seeming to dominate his thin face. "You're our human expert, Rose. What do you suggest?"

She slid her hand into the pockets of her dusty jeans and looked down at the ground. Mitchum couldn't tell if she was considering

Epsilon's question or if she was actually studying the nuclear device. When she raised her head, she was smiling. "I think you shouldn't do anything right now. Watch them. Listen to them. Make a move when they do something threatening. I'd like to work with Sofiya. I invited her here. She knows Zhukov well, and I can access her memories about him *and*... we learn from each other."

"We can grant her amnesty," Mitchum said. "If it comes to that."

"Or we can," Epsilon added.

"She certainly had no advance information on this, Rose said."

"When is she arriving?" Whitley asked.

"Tomorrow," Rose replied, then looked at Epsilon. "Have Stell^rs ever granted amnesty to anyone from another planet?"

"If so, it was before my time, and I'm 825 years old."

"And look about 40," Spenser remarked. "Share your secret."

"Does it work for dogs?" Mitchum asked.

Epsilon frowned. "Is Nomad ill?"

"No, no, nothing like that. He's just getting on in years, sleeps a lot, doesn't have the energy he once did."

"Dudes." Whitley regarded them like they were a couple of crazy drunks on a Manhattan street corner, chatting while the city was being bombed. "We've got these two missiles..."

Epsilon gave Mitchum's shoulder a reassuring squeeze. "Not to worry about Nomad or the missile, Jim. But Steve has a good point. When Sofiya arrives here, she'll be in our shared custody."

"Love it," Rose said. "Thank you both."

"In the meantime..." Mitchum pointed at the nuke. "We need to get this one and its mate out of here."

"We'll do it," Epsilon said.

"Do your beam-me-ups ever trigger problems?" Spenser asked.

"Of course not. We rendered them nuclear duds so no worries."

Minutes later, Rose opened her arms to the magnificence of the dome. "We'll need to start building homes soon. And towns. Roads. Farms."

"We have time," Epsilon said. "When the first starships land here, we'll have at least eighteen completed domes that are self-contained. We'll be producing food. The desert will be turning green. The countries that border the Sahara will be more prosperous. The hungry will be fed. The poor will be uplifted. The power mongers here on Earth won't like any of it. At all. They will do everything to instigate rebellion."

"And you're prepared for that?" Mitchum asked. "Rebellion worse than anything we've seen so far?"

"We will be," Epsilon replied.

Chapter 19

The Sindikat Plots

Zhukov desperately wanted to interfere in the US election in 2032 to prevent Mitchum from winning a second term. But he was certain that if he did so, the Stell^rs would surely know about it. He deeply resented how they'd duped him about the missiles, tricked him until satellite images had revealed the truth—the domes still stood.

+++

On January 20, 2033, when the satellite images showed seven completed domes, he and his Sindikat watched Mitchum's second inauguration on their personal viewing devices. The growing angst in the center of his chest was shared, he knew, by the other members of his group. He and Viktor sat in Zhukov's office in the Kremlin, sharing a bottle of vodka with Badr Asfour, a Middle Eastern billionaire who'd made his wealth in oil. Asfour worried about how his fortune would dwindle down to nothing once the Stell^rs completely obliterated the world's need for oil.

He suddenly changed his video device to rock music and turned the volume up full blast to make it more difficult for the Stell^rs to eavesdrop. As Mick Jagger belted out *I Can't get no Satisfaction,* Asfour leaned in closer to Zhukov and Viktor. "I know exactly how Jagger feels. And I think there's something I can do about it."

"We're open to suggestions." Zhukov leaned forward.

"All ears, as the Americans say," remarked Viktor, and also leaned forward.

Asfour now scribbled on a paper: *Epsilon has invited representatives from the countries that border the Sahara to visit the Stell^r enclave in the Sahara. I will go and take care of Epsilon. And Rose. And any of the other Stell^rs who are present.*

How? Zhukov mouthed.

He used his index finger to spell out *poison* in the air. "That would be simplest."

"Excellent," Zhukov agreed, then held out his hand for the pad of paper and pen, which Asfour passed to him. He scribbled, *What's the date?*

Asfour shrugged. "To be announced."

Now Zhukov jotted, *What poison?*

Asfour just smiled.

"I like it," Zhukov said, and flashed a thumbs up.

Viktor remained quiet.

As it turned out, he didn't hear any more about it for weeks, then months, a period of high anxiety for him. The protests in Russia—and in Moscow particularly—were mostly in favor of the Stell^r arrival. Hundreds of arrests were made, then thousands. He had stayed out of the public eye because he feared retribution for the failed missile attack on the Stell^rs in 2031. It shocked him that it never came, but he was now extra cautious. Zhukov did have some contact with other members of the Sindikat like Katherine Martin. She expected to be in the region on personal business in December 2033 and asked if they could meet and discuss "things."

So in early December they met at the cafe where he and Viktor had in the past. Dressed for business, she looked efficient and determined as she made her way to the table where he waited, a cup of hot coffee already in front of him. That day, an old Beatles tune blasted from the vintage jukebox.

"Almost didn't recognize you with that beard and those glasses, Alex." She pulled out the chair across from him and sat down.

"You look like you're ready to take on a CEO, Katherine."

She laughed. "When I leave here, I'm headed to Dubai to do exactly that. So I hear that Sofiya changed sides? That she's working with the Americans now?"

He didn't like talking about Sofiya. She'd gone to the Sahara—and never returned. He'd heard from her once—that she was working on designs with Rose and that the Stell^rs had granted her permanent amnesty. So that was exactly what he told Katherine.

"The *Stell^rs* granted her amnesty? Really? What the hell does that even mean, Alexander?"

"No idea."

"Well, I thought you should know. I received an invitation from Epsilon to visit the Stell^r enclave on March 1, 2034."

"Did anyone else get that invitation?"

"Badr Asfour and three other members of the Sindikat. So five of us in total. We're invited to see the progress they've made in transforming the Sahara in just three years."

"It must be a trap, Katherine. It's worrisome that it's five of you."

"Why? We're all economic leaders within our respective countries."

"And you're all members of the Sindikat. We fired those missiles..."

"Yeah, I remember the fiasco, Alexander. I think it's smart that we've remained under the radar since then."

That was one way of looking at it, he thought. "So what's the plan?"

"We fly in separately with a security guard of our choice and stay in one of the completed domes where cities have been built already."

"Cities? Incredible. What kind of technology enables that so quickly?"

A server arrived with coffee for Katherine and a platter of hors-d'œuvres.

When the server left, Katherine responded. "A technology we humans could certainly use. Badr and I intend to find out how they've done this. As the Stell^rs have begun to wean the world from fossil fuels, Badr has already lost billions. And so have I since I hold major shares of stock in his company."

"Badr has a plan for the Stell^rs, did he tell you?"

The jukebox suddenly went silent, and she glanced around nervously, her expression screaming the very thing he was thinking: *did the Stell^rs do that?* But to his relief, another song came on, some loud Russian tune about betrayal. Katherine leaned forward her voice quiet. "Yes, he told me. What do you think?"

"Well, we need to do something. That much is clear. Keep me posted on all this, Katherine."

"I will. I definitely will." She picked up an hors d'oeuvre and bit into it delicately.

+++

Rose, Sofiya, and Liam had moved into one of the homes built in Dome 1. It was comfortable for the three of them, and on their days off, Liam worked with the team on interior designs for the other domes. He also observed and chronicled how she and Sofiya taught and learned each other's psychic skills.

From Sofiya, Rose was learning how to sense the future. And from her, Sofiya was learning to perfect her telepathy. They were doing it now, as they walked through the town inside Dome 1 with Liam headed to the market.

Hey, Rose, we should figure out a way to teach Liam how to do this.
I think he already knows how; he just doesn't use it.

Liam glanced over at them. "Can you ladies do a reading of this area?"

"What're we looking for?" Rose asked.

"Any threat to our security."

"You know something we don't, Liam?" Sofiya asked.

"Ha. That'll be the day."

"Did that request come from Jim or Whitley?"

"All they told me was to keep an eye out."

His verbiage sounded odd to Rose. *Keep an eye out,* as though they had an all-seeing eye that hung from the roof of the dome, watching everything. "Let's detour through the park for a few minutes," Rose suggested.

It was the largest park in Dome 1, replete with trees, flowers, and ponds where Xanthe fish swam that they replicated at the moon base. Epsilon and the Council had created these biological marvels from extracted chromosomes, and the same was true of the birds that flitted through the trees singing. They settled on a bench in front of the pond. "Your recorder on, Liam?"

"On and ready."

Rose and Sofiya shut their eyes and Liam started speaking in a soft, quiet voice. "You're looking specifically for any threat to our enclave here in the Sahara. Or to humans or Stell^rs who are here."

Rose's eyes flicked from side to side, searching for anything unusual or threatening. Her sight took her to a dining hall where the entire Stell^r Council was in attendance with a number of guests, some of whom she recognized from that trip to Ecuador. Platters of food were brought out—Stell^r dishes, delectables from other countries. Some sort of celebration, Rose thought, but when?

"What are you seeing, Sofiya?" Liam asked.

"A huge dining hall," she replied.

"Me, too," Rose said. "And a lot of different kinds of food."

"Epsilon stands to make a toast to the crowd..."

"And then he samples from one of the platters that holds something other than Stell^r food and... "

Rose leaped to her feet to break the connection to this future scene, but it continued to play out in front of her, around her in 3-D, the horrifying image of Epsilon choking, of his eyes rolling back in their sockets, of him stumbling forward, arms flailing as he struggled to breathe.... Several Council members rushed toward him; several others slammed the doors to the dining room...

She sank to her knees in the park, hands covering her eyes, her heart breaking. Liam and Sofiya helped her to her feet and back to the bench. "They...he...was...poisoned."

"I...I saw it, too," Sofiya stammered.

"Which platter of food was it?" Liam asked. "Could you see that?"

"I did," Sofiya said. "It was...food...from...Russia... It had been poisoned."

"Damn," Liam said.

Sofiya looked from one to the other. "When is it...these guests are coming here?"

"March first," Rose replied.

"That's next week."

"Is anyone from Russia coming?" she asked.

Liam thought a moment. "I'm not sure. I know Australia, Middle East, US, Europe..."

"I recognized several of them from Esperanza, Liam. They're from Zhukov's billionaire group."

"That explains the Russian food," Sofiya said. "Is Zhukov coming?"

Rose shook her head. "Not that I've heard."

"He has stayed off the grid since the missile attack," Sofiya said. "So this will be another instance where good ole Alexander has someone else do his dirty work."

"Or the billionaires are getting impatient," Rose added. "We need to alert Epsilon. And Jim."

"And the kitchen on the day of their visit," Liam said.

+++

Mitchum had expected something like this, some horrifying surprise that would be planned and implemented by Zhukov, but without his presence at the scene. When Rose alerted Jim to what she and Sofiya had seen happening just four days from now at the Sahara enclave, he and his team sprang into action.

He assigned a dozen agents to kitchen duty in Dome 1. The briefing was held that evening at Paul Spenser's home, with Epsilon present and Rose beamed in. The Stell^rs explained the layout of the compound, of Dome 1, and Whitley brought up the photos they had of some of Zhukov's Sindikat members.

"Do you know which of these people is responsible, Rose?" Mitchum asked.

"Not specifically," she replied. "And I don't know who else might have sampled the goodies. As soon as I...saw Epsilon choking, I leaped up and I...don't know what happened after that. Neither does Sofiya."

"How secure is that kitchen, Epsilon?" Mitchum asked. "Is it easy for others to come and go?"

"Yes."

"That should change," Mitchum said.

One of the assigned agents, 35-year-old ex-engineer Blake Russo, raised his hand. "Excuse me, President Mitchum. But I think it would be enormously helpful if all the guests wore tags with their names and country on them."

"Excellent idea. Epsilon?"

"We'll make sure of that," Epsilon said.

"Any other suggestions?" Mitchum asked the group of agents.

"Yes." Annette Dawson was one of the two women on the team, an ex-flight attendant who spoke Russian fluently. "Will we be armed?"

"Absolutely," Mitchum replied. "But discreetly."

"And will we be beamed in, like Kirk on *Star Trek*?"

"Better than Kirk," Epsilon said. "Nine p.m. sharp, from here, with your bags. Rose will accompany you."

"Any other questions?" Mitchum asked. "Suggestions?" He glanced round the room. Spenser raised his hand.

"Paul?"

"I'd like to accompany the group."

Epsilon nodded enthusiastically. "Perfect. We need an astronomer to provide a prelude."

"Done." Spenser said.

And Ken, Mitchum thought, would accompany them as well.

"One other thing," Epsilon said. "We will be transporting Zhukov in as well."

That seemed like an unnecessary complication to Mitchum. "Why?"

Epsilon looked amused. "I think you humans call it karma, Jim."

+++

On the evening of February 28, Rose and Liam gave the dozen agents a final tour of Dome 1 and its large catering facility. Each agent had a role in the kitchen routine—cooks, servers, greeters, but all of them were armed spies. Then Sofiya explained what she knew about each of the individuals in Zhukov's billionaire group and used the photos she'd taken during that time in Ecuador.

Rose was pleased that the agents had questions about these individuals. The more they knew, the better the outcome. Some of them questioned Sofiya about Zhukov, the kind of man he was, their relationship in the past, before the Stell^rs had granted her amnesty, and they inquired about her ability. Its origins. Its development. How she'd been trained and by whom. And what about this guy Viktor, who had trained her, who was one of Zhukov's advisors? Had he been part of the clandestine missile attack?

"Most likely he knew about it." Sofiya replied. "Viktor is part of just about every decision Alexander makes. Thing is, I think he acts out of complete fear of what Zhukov will do to him."

"Then shouldn't he be brought in as well?" Liam asked.

"That's not my decision," she replied.

"But would you recommend it?" asked Annette in her flawless Russian.

"Yes, I would."

Rose took note. Later that night, when she, Liam, and Sofiya were in their house on one of the narrow, cobbled roads in town, she posed the question to Epsilon. Telepathically. His appearance seconds later startled the three of them, Epsilon standing in their kitchen in human clothes—jeans and a blue work shirt so out of character that Rose laughed.

"Not quite up to snuff, huh?" Epsilon asked.

"Uh, no," she replied.

"Definitely not," Liam opined.

"I don't think Zhukov would recognize you from another Stell^r," Sofiya said.

Rose got to the point. "Can you bring in Viktor, too?"

"Why?"

"Because he's part of all of it," Sofiya replied.

"Because it will freak him out, unsettle him to the point where he'll get really careless," Rose said.

Epsilon, always democratic and inclusive, looked pointedly at Liam. "What do you think?"

"He won't know what hit him. Make the column of light the brightest thing he has ever seen."

+++

On March 1, Zhukov was eating breakfast in his private residence, his attention divided between his computer, phone, and his boiled eggs smeared with mayonnaise. A brilliant column of light shot through the ceiling of his residence, with Viktor floating somewhere inside it, and then it slammed down over him.

A breath later, he realized the Stell^rs were transporting him elsewhere. Questions coursed through him. *Where?* Where were they taking him? And why? What did they know or suspect?

Then he found himself standing next to a bewildered Viktor, the two of them in a dining room. One quick glance around told him it was one of the geodesic domes in the Stell^r enclave. Sofiya, Rose, and Epsilon stood in front of him. Epsilon spoke first. "Have a seat, gentlemen."

"What... what do you think you're doing?" Viktor demanded.

"Allowing you to see what we've accomplished here," Epsilon replied.

"I don't give a damn what you've accomplished. You and your fellow aliens just move in here like the Sahara is yours and start building these...these domes...and beaming people around like this is some episode of..."

Zhukov watched all this in horror, Viktor ranting at the head Stell^r, his face getting more flushed by the second, his eyes wilder, and then he went for his concealed weapon— which was gone. "You...you took my weapon, you..."

"No need for a weapon here," Epsilon said calmly.

Sofiya hurried over to Viktor, touched his shoulder. "You...you need to calm down, Viktor. The..."

He wrenched free of Sofiya's touch and spun around, gesturing madly at other members of the Sindikat in the dining room. "All of you, you're nuts, thinking you can win over an alien race! Just look around at these domes, at what they'd done to this desert, at how we all got here. Defeat them?" He started laughing hysterically. "You're delusional, all of you and..."

"Shut up!" screamed Badr Asfour, and lunged at Viktor, slammed into him and both men crashed into a table and then to the floor.

And then they weren't there anymore.

Zhukov backpedaled so fast he collided with someone behind them, Katherine Martin, and he grabbed her by the arm. "We need to get outta here." The two of them made a beeline toward the dining room doors.

Two very large Stell^rs blocked their way, standing against the doors with their arms crossed. Pi? Gamma? Alpha? Beta? He didn't know, didn't care. He tackled one of them, Katherine accidentally knocked into the other, and the four of them crashed through the double doors, into the desert air.

Zhukov hoped to hear the Stell^r bones crack and snap, hoped those bones would just dissolve in the scorching sun. Katherine screamed and scrambled to her feet, yelling, "Why'd you do that, Alexander? You pushed me into those doors! I don't want trouble!"

He managed to free himself from the Stell^r and bolted to his feet, aware that Epsilon and Rose and Sofiya and others were now outside, too, watching this spectacle. And then a column of light clamped down over him and minutes later he found himself barely conscious inside a spaceship headed...for where? Viktor and Asfour were here. With him.

"Welcome to the moon," said Epsilon. "You are now in our special rehab unit."

The moon? Zhukov's shock rendered him mute. He stumbled over to the closest window, a tiny round window made of something like glass and peered out. Starlight glimmered in the inky darkness. Nearly a quarter of a million miles below, he could see Earth.

"But...but..." Viktor stammered.

"Shut up, Viktor!" Zhukov snapped. "Your mouth got us into this situation."

"*My* mouth? It's your stupid Sindikat that put us here!"

+++

"Where'd he go?" Asfour exclaimed. "I want to lodge a protest. They can't do this to..."

Epsilon appeared again with three more members of the Sindikat—an American, a European, and an Asian. "More company for you."

"I'm lodging a formal protest," Asfour said.

"We found poison in your bag," Epsilon said. "You intended to kill us, Mr. Asfour."

"I knew nothing about that," Zhukov said. "I..."

"That's a lie, Alexander!" Asfour burst out.

"You knew!" This came from the European billionaire, Randolph Perry, who had made his wealth in pharmaceuticals. "You inquired about the ingredients of that poison, Alexander. You specifically wanted to know how quickly it could kill."

Zhukov vaguely recalled that. So much had been happening around that time, he'd forgotten it.

"And there were many conversations we overheard, too," Epsilon said. "About the poison and, earlier, about the tactical weapons. So we had to make a decision. Putting all of you in stasis, like the leaders of North Korea and Pakistan, seemed too easy. So we decided on the rehab unit here on our moon base."

"But we have rights," snapped Perry in his proper British accent.

"I'm the president of Russia," exclaimed Zhukov. "What you're doing breaks international laws!"

"And what you were planning and what you did with those tactical nukes violated humanity and Stell^r law." "And by the way, whether you gave the direct order or not, launching your fighter jets with missiles at all us after leaving our ship for your bed in August 2030 didn't go unnoticed."

With that, he disappeared, presumably returning to the Sahara. The five of them were left alone in the massive room with the single porthole.

+++

Katherine wasn't sure how she escaped.

When she ran out of the dome, she spotted a solar-powered cart, hopped in, and took off. She called the pilot of her plane on her satellite phone and asked him to pick her up ASAP. He was within two hours of her location and advised her to find somewhere to hide.

Hide. In a Stell^r enclave. So she turned into one of the completed domes and sat there in the stupid cart for the next two hours, periodically shaking with terror that she, too, would be beamed elsewhere. But nothing happened. No one came after her. No brilliant column of light slammed down over her.

It occurred to her that it was likely deliberate on the Stell^r part, that they were allowing her to depart, so they could keep a close watch on her, eavesdrop on her, and find out the identities of the other members of the Sindikat. She realized she needed to go into hiding somewhere. A country other than Australia. A country where she had trustworthy contacts. A country safe from the Stell^rs. But was there any such a place left on the planet?

She knuckled her eyes and struggled not to surrender to despair. Thanks to Zhukov, she had President Jim Mitchum's private number and considered messaging him. He deserved to know what these Stell^rs had done. But would these aliens block such a message?

Her message to her pilot had gone through. *Give it a try.* Her phone said it was noon here. So in DC it would be five hours earlier.

+++

Mitchum, Helen, and Whitley were in the private residence at the White House, reviewing plans for the landing of the first Stell^r crafts in 2036.

A part of Mitchum dreaded it, dreaded the protests that would follow, the misinformation campaigns, how social media and its influencers would react. He remembered all too well what had happened during the two plus years of the pandemic. There probably would be rampant conspiracy theories that these aliens were part of the deep state, robotic warriors programmed to take out anyone who didn't believe the Stell^rs were ETs.

His head ached just thinking about it.

"We're going to have to come up with a campaign to counteract all the BS that's going to appear on social media," Whitley said.

"I was just thinking the same thing," Helen said. "Some stuff is already surfacing."

Mitchum's cell buzzed. He glanced at it. *Katherine Martin.* "Odd," he murmured. "The Australian billionaire just contacted me."

Whitley glanced up, alarm in his eyes. "I thought she was at the Sahara enclave."

Mitchum read it aloud. "I thought you should know, President Mitchum, that these aliens aren't the good guys you and other leaders made them out to be. They have transported Zhukov, Viktor, and three other colleagues somewhere. Apparently, poison was discovered in Badr Asfour's belongings, and a fight broke out in the dome dining room. And now I'm in hiding, waiting for my pilot to land somewhere so I can get the hell away from them. Very far away. Rose saw what happened. Ask her where Epsilon took them."

"Christ," Helen whispered.

"Contact her, Jim," said Whitley.

"Doing it now." *Rose, what happened there? Where were they taken? Do you know?*

She didn't answer for a maddening five minutes. Then: *The Stell^r moon base, the rehab unit.*

He read this aloud and the three of them just looked at each other. "I get that they had to do something after the tactical missiles and the poison plan, but this... this is going to be construed as *very aggressive.* I'm going to ask for a meeting."

"Jim, they tried to kill Epsilon," said Rose.

+++

Not much longer, Dax thought, and hoped that the mornings when he awakened in a cold sweat were nearly done. Less than 60 days from Earth, that was it. So this morning he did what he had done way too often in the nearly ten years since his partner and daughters had been put into their sleeping pods. He made his way to the sleep area, where 9,500 of the 10,000 Stell^rs on this massive starship were in a suspended hyper sleep.

The sleeping area stretched from one end of the spaceship to the other. He found their pods easily enough and lowered a chair from the ceiling so he could sit among them. He was nearly a decade older, and they hadn't aged a day. Would this make a difference in their relationships? But ten years in a Stell^r lifetime wasn't that long. Was their love for one another large enough to accommodate for this loss of time? He expected it would.

His partner looked beautiful and ever so peaceful. Did she dream? Did his daughters dream? He checked the monitors that measured their brain waves, their breathing, all their life support functions. Normal, normal, normal. All of it.

Most of his projects were already successfully completed. His team had worked well together, just as they had on Xanthe. They would be ready to fully accelerate the seedlings and planting of all the food that 100 million Stell^rs would need for the next twenty years. He felt great pride in the accomplishment of his team under his leadership.

Part Three

The Arrival

"The human failing I would most like to correct is aggression. It may have had survival advantage in caveman days, to get more food, territory or partner with whom to reproduce, but now it threatens to destroy us all."

- Stephen Hawking

Chapter 20

Katherine is Desperate

For all intents and purposes, Katherine thought, Zhukov, Viktor and the three members of the Sindikat who had been taken somewhere were dead. She, an expat in Amsterdam, was in charge now.

Katherine had purchased a home on the outskirts of the city, on a dirt road where no one cared who came and went from the place in the cul-de-sac. The remaining members of the Sindikat were also in hiding, but when she called them together to meet at her place, they came. One by one, by car or train, but never by air.

They wore disguises, had phony passports, and had moved out of their respective countries to locales where they weren't known. She didn't ask where they were living. She didn't want to know. With Richard still in an induced Stell^r coma and the other three—where? On the far side of the moon? On a Stell^r spacecraft?—she felt the fate of the free world rested with her and the eleven who remained.

It was now March 2036 and the first passenger starships from Xanthe would be arriving in June—or so Sofiya had speculated back in Ecuador. And there had been rumors circulating in certain circles about the frenzied activity in the Sahara that had led her to believe that date might be correct. Tactical missiles hadn't worked and neither had the idea of poison. They needed to get more creative. Protests continued worldwide, but as the Stell^rs continued to grow food and feed the hungry on the planet and share aspects of their technology, most of the protesters now welcomed their eventual arrival with anticipation.

The Sahara enclave had been opened to human scientists and researchers, and she and the other members had discussed getting into the area that way. Since most of them were losing enormous amounts of their wealth, they had pooled some of their collective resources. Today, in fact, she and one of the Russian billionaires,

Dmitri Popov, walked through Amsterdam. They were headed to the home of Dmitri's contact, who had prepared credentials that proved they were art collectors with connections to museums all over the world. It had cost them one Bitcoin apiece, but if it got them into the Stell^r enclave, it would be worth every Satoshi.

During that trip to Ecuador, she'd learned from Sofiya that she had viewed the impressive Stell^r intergalactic art culture that dated back a million years. She'd learned they would be transporting it to Earth to preserve this treasure for future generations. As a gift to the humans, they would put it on exhibit in its holographic form since the physical art work would be arriving on one of the many starships.

Katherine didn't worry about being identified—she was now a redhead and had enough plastic surgery so that she barely recognized herself in the mirror. Of course, she and the others could be telepathically scanned, but not as easily as before. One of the members, a European, had found a Viewer, Lewis Carlton, who had taught them how to shield themselves. No guarantee it would work with the Stell^rs, but it was worth a try. And it gave them a defense they'd lacked before.

"You think this will work, Katherine?" Dmitri suddenly asked.

"As long as we can talk art, yes, I think so. Test question. Where's the bulk of van Gogh's work now?"

"The van Gogh museum here in Amsterdam. Okay, one for you. Where is his Starry Night exhibited?"

"Museum of Modern Art, New York. What's considered his first masterpiece?"

Dmitri thought about it. "The Potato Eaters. So we're van Gogh experts?"

"Sure. We've spent enough time in the museums here. How many pieces did he paint when he was in the asylum?"

"The asylum. Hmm. Okay, that was in Saint-Remy-de-Provence, near Arles, France. He spent a year there and produced 150 paintings. Who was the woman for whom he cut off his ear?"

"He didn't cut it off *for* her. He and Gaugin got into a heated argument, and van Gogh had one of his psychotic episodes and cut off his ear. He didn't remember afterward."

"Do you think these aliens have any artist comparable to van Gogh or Gaugin?"

She guessed their art would be astonishing, mind-blowing. After all, they'd been exploring other worlds for over a million years longer than humans had existed. "Anyway, we'll find out soon enough."

Dmitri glanced at the GPS on his phone. "One more street, then we take a left. It's not in the museum but in a house one block away from it. I met this guy through a mutual friend here in Amsterdam. His work is fake creds. His name's Harry. Probably a name as fake as ours."

The house was set back from the road, small, nothing special, except for the potted plants on the enclosed porch, where flowers bloomed and flourished. Dmitri rang the doorbell, and the man who answered was odd-looking, short and squat, probably in his late forties, early fifties, with thinning gray hair.

"Leo," he said in English, nodding, taking Dmitri's hand. "So good to see you. And you must be...Susan, correct?"

Hardly as gracious a name as Katherine, she thought, but it was the name on her fake passport. Susan Wilken of the UK. "Good to meet you, Harry."

"Come in, please, come in."

He swept his arm toward the inside of the house, and they went in. Katherine wasn't sure what she'd expected, but knew it wasn't this, a room as grand and lovely as in any palatial estate. Over the ornate fireplace hung one of Picasso's best paintings—The Old Guitarist.

"One of his best," she remarked. "Except this one is fake, Harry."

His face lit up. "But a beautiful fake, right?" He came over to her. "How did you know?"

"His fingers aren't quite right."

Harry turned to Dmitri. "You were right about her, Leo. You know how many people over the years have known it's fake? Only three."

"Wow, impressive, Susan. How'd you know?"

"His fingers are too plump."

"My office is back here," Harry said, and they followed him into the next room, just an ordinary space with a computer, printer, and a large window that looked out onto a spacious, fenced backyard. "I've got your credentials ready." He handed each of them a thick packet. "Look these over, let me know if you want or need changes."

Katherine went through her packet, but other than the certificate that she was a certified art dealer, she wasn't sure what else five million in equivalent American dollars had bought her. "So, Harry, explain all these papers to us."

"Sure, no problem." He gestured at the chairs in front of his desk. "Make yourselves comfortable, you two, and I'll go through them one at a time."

It took him half an hour to explain in detail. The papers, the certificates, gave them access to virtually any art center anywhere on the planet as critics, reviewers, collectors, movers and shakers within the art world. The big question, though, was whether any of these papers would allow them entrance to the Stell^r compound once their starships started arriving three months from now—if that June time frame was still accurate.

Just how many of these starships would be carrying art? Unknown.

How many ships would arrive initially? Also unknown.

How many Stell^rs would be on those first crafts? Another unknown.

Ever since Zhukov was taken away, there were times when Katherine missed him for the information he'd been able to attain. Details like the number of spaceships, of Stell^rs, the exact date of the arrival. The inside stuff.

Had the Stell^rs put him and Viktor and the other three Sindikat members to death? Or, if they'd been taken to their moon base, were they still up there, in a dome like the ones in the Sahara?

She desperately needed answers from a Viewer like Sofiya. Or Rose.

Fat chance of that.

Once she and Dmitri had left Harry's place, she thought about Lewis Carlton. He'd worked with them for several months, teaching them to block telepathic probing. They had told him the probes might come from the government, and he'd never asked which government. "Do you think Lewis Carlton can help us find some answers?"

"Hey, if he was good enough to work for America's Department of Defense way back, it can't hurt to ask."

+++

Jim Mitchum was on the way to the Sahara enclave with Ken and Whitley when a call came through from Aaron McHenry, a Viewer he'd known when he'd worked for NASA. He had Viewed Mitchum's first foray into space and identified the moment of his sighting of that UFO that had changed his life so dramatically. They hadn't spoken since Mitchum had been elected.

It was a holographic video call. Mitchum made sure that Whitley was close enough to see and hear the call before he took it. "Aaron, what a surprise! It's great to hear from you."

"How're you doing with all the chaos, Jim?"

Mitchum shrugged. "Which chaos? Present or future?"

McHenry, now in his late fifties, chuckled, and it changed the contours of his still handsome face but didn't touch his haunting blue eyes. "Future."

"So what did you see, Aaron?"

"Where should I start?"

"Seriously? There's that much headed toward us?"

"I guess that depends on your perception. But yeah, once the Stell^rs get here, chaos will be the name of the game. But that's not why I'm calling. It's about some other stuff. About six months ago, a woman—Susan Wilken of the UK—contacted me and asked me to train her to block telepathic probes. She and her partner, Leo Ferguson, also of the UK, trained with me for three or four months. They know me as Lewis Carlton."

Mitchum's internal alarms went off. "There's a way to block telepathic probes?"

"Yeah, sure. It's tricky, but it can be achieved."

"Did they achieve it?"

"Yes, as far as I can tell, but to varying degrees."

"You have photos of either of them?"

"Sure. I'll send them as soon as I find them. But here's the thing, Jim. I just got a call from her asking me to View the Stell^r base on the far side of the moon."

Mitchum glanced at Whitley, who mouthed, *Gotta be her, Katherine Martin.*

Makes sense. Katherine had been missing since the fiasco in the Sahara. The consensus was that she and the remaining members of Zhukov's Sindikat had gone into deep hiding. "Photos?"

"Coming through now."

The image of the woman, this Susan Wilken, resembled Katherine Marin, but only vaguely. A distant cousin. Very distant. Red hair, a longer nose, a fuller mouth, plumper cheeks. Plastic surgery? He didn't recognize this Leo Ferguson but Whitley did.

"Russian. Dmitri Popov. Member of Zhukov's Sindikat of maleficent billionaires. He has his hands in all sorts of pursuits—pharma, oil, mining of lithium, etcetera. At one time, he was Zhukov's golden boy. As the Stell^rs have made their energy technology available to the rest of us, he has lost billions."

"That's my chief of staff, Aaron. Steve Whitley. Any idea where they are now?"

"No."

"Where are you?"

"I've been living in south Miami. But I worked virtually with them."

"You going to do the same this time?" Whitley asked.

"Sure. No reason to go to them."

"Okay," Mitchum said. "Can you do this View for us? Name your price."

"No problem Jim. I already did it for myself. I got real curious. But so far, it's spotty. Very spotty. It appears that Zhukov and the others are in a dome of some kind, geodesic, but sturdier, I think. And the place outside is in complete darkness. So the far side of the moon fits. When I look out the tiny windows, I see only stars. And they're bright. Nothing else on the terrain is visible. "

"Are they treated humanely?"

"Well, let me put it this way. It certainly appears they're doing a lot better than the inmates in some of our private prisons."

Mitchum nodded. "Are they allowed access to anywhere else?"

Aaron laughed. "Like where? Central Park? Any park? No. This looks like a barren lunar surface, that's it, amigo."

"Can he communicate with anyone?" Mitchum asked.

"Zhukov seems to be trying to learn telepathy. But he doesn't have whatever it takes for mind to mind. That frustrates him. He thinks he can learn anything, so this has proven to be humiliating for him."

"Did you tell them all this?" Whitley asked.

"Nope. Told them I was working on it."

"What's their plan?"

"Well, this will sound weird. But I think their plan involves Stell^r art. Sometime in May? Yeah, May. That was the month I saw."

In June, the first Stell^r spaceships would land in the Sahara. But they wouldn't be carrying artwork not that he'd been told. Then again, in all fairness, he never had asked if the Stell^rs had any sort of artistic culture. It hadn't even occurred to him to ask.

"Would you be able to join us at the Sahara enclave? I'd like you to meet Rose, the Stell^r seer, and Sofiya, who was granted permanent asylum by the Stell^rs. She used to work for Zhukov as a seer."

"Is that where you're headed now?"

"Yes. For a meeting with the Stell^r Council the day after tomorrow. I can send a plane for you."

"Which airport?"

Mitchum glanced at Whitley, who was scrolling through his phone. "I have a pilot at Perry Airport who has a Gulfstream," Whitley said. "Will hm him now."

"I'll call you back, Aaron. In the meantime, pack your bag. How far are you from Perry?"

"Twenty miles or so. I can get there in under an hour."

"The pilot said he's available," Whitley said. "Name's Jack Foster. He'll be in hangar two."

"I'll leave as soon as I pack, Jim."

"Great."

"So this Rose. Saw her on the news. A telepath, right?"

"Like all of them. I'd like you to explain to her and the others what your training involved as far as blocking telepathic probes."

"Looking forward to this. When I asked who might be probing them telepathically, their response was "the government.""

Jim smiled. "See you tomorrow. And thank you, Aaron. I really appreciate this."

"You bet. Funny thing, Jim. Ever since you saw that UFO during your first foray into space, I had a strong hunch that something like this would play out somehow during your presidency. Until tomorrow. The Sahara. Damn."

+++

Zhukov had many complaints about his accommodations on the moon and it started with the lack of privacy. The room was spacious enough for him and Viktor, and they each had a bed, a desk, a mobile device without any way to contact Earth. They shared a bathroom, they each had a closet with clothes that had been brought to them, and there were also some books that had been transported as well. But he and Viktor were never apart.

Viktor periodically ranted and raved about their situation, and today he sounded like a madman. Zhukov finally snapped, "Viktor, shut up! Just shut up! Your rants were getting *old!*"

"*You* should be ranting, you idiot. They've taken away your power, you don't have a country to run, they've stolen everything from you. *Everything!*"

"Take a look out that tiny window, Viktor. Go ahead." Zhukov flung an arm around his neck and forced him over to the window. "See all that darkness? We're on the moon! The f-ing moon, okay? So even if we could escape, we'd die within seconds out there."

Viktor broke Zhukov's hold on him. "Don't we have rights?" He shouted the words as he backed away from the window, from Zhukov, and rubbed the back of his neck. "They... they..." Then his face seemed to collapse, and he broke down, sobbing into his hands, and plopped down on his bed, shaking his head, tears leaking through his fingers.

"Listen, my friend." Zhukov sat beside him on the bed, one arm around Viktor's shoulders. "If we despair they've won." He spoke softly and Viktor's sobs continued. "We mishandled everything about these aliens. We should have tried to befriend them, know them, welcome them even if it meant a complete annihilation of the order of things on our planet."

Viktor raised his head. "Is this how they rehabilitate us? That's what Epsilon called this place, right? A rehab center. They...they isolate us, make us yearn for our planet, for our lives, for..." He pressed his hands over his eyes then dropped them to his thighs. "They make us yearn for everything...we left behind."

"Everything we took for granted," Zhukov added, and passed him a box of Kleenex.

Viktor plucked out a couple of tissues, wiped his eyes, blew his nose. Then he looked at the box of Kleenex. "The Stell^rs use this stuff?"

Zhukov gestured at the beds. "And sheets and pillows. Or, at any rate, they provided this for our comfort and the other three guys."

"Who are deeply miserable, too. I ran into them in the gym yesterday."

"I'd like to be able to move freely around the base. I mean, we don't have weapons, we don't present any threat to them."

"Ask Ep..."

A quick rap at the door interrupted him. "Come in," Zhukov called.

One of the Stell^rs—Pi? Beta? Gamma? Alpha?—opened the door. "Gentlemen, I'd be pleased to show you around our base here."

"So you overhear everything we say?" Zhukov asked.

"Not all of it. But yes, we monitor your progress. Epsilon and the rest of the Council decided that you're now ready to venture out of your area here. What would you like to see first?"

Viktor was already on his feet, tugging at the hem of his shirt, trying to straighten his clothes. "Whatever you would like to show us."

"Excellent. I'm Pi, by the way. You can distinguish me from the others because of this mark on my arm." He held out his long, thin arm, the skin a slightly deeper blue than Rose's skin. He turned it so they could see his forearm, where he had a colorful tattoo of a hummingbird. "A young tattoo artist in San Francisco did this for me."

"It's beautiful," Zhukov exclaimed. "When...when were you in San Francisco?"

"Before we visited Washington, DC. It's a curiously accepting city. We were able to walk around as we are now. I think they thought we were in Halloween costumes." He opened the door and gestured for them to follow him.

They stepped out into a long corridor with bone white walls that held a row of windows on either side, windows that were larger than the portholes in their room. Zhukov stopped at one of them, awed by the view of Earth, of the stars, of the vast complexity of space. "It's magnificent," Zhukov said. "You Stell^rs chose well."

"As Epsilon said when he first appeared, we intend you no harm. We will help you humans with defeating hunger, poverty, and disease. We are turning your deserts green. We will help your planet avoid future environmental disasters and will turn your oceans healthy again. We truly want to harmoniously share your beautiful planet with you."

Zhukov and Viktor exchanged a glance, and Zhukov could tell he felt as overwhelmed and awed as he did. And contrite? Was that what he felt? He noted that his heart seemed to be twisting in his chest. But that often happened when terror seized him.

Pi took them into the heart of the dome and the city within it. They stood on the periphery and Zhukov took it all in, astonished at the beauty, the majesty, and the efficiency of it all. Stell^rs moved around on foot, in sleek quiet vehicles, and through beams of bright light. It resembled something from a Hollywood movie, a more sophisticated and technologically advanced *Interstellar.*

"Incredible," Viktor murmured.

"Is this the only structure on the base?" Zhukov asked.

"The only one this large. There are smaller structures for storage, supplies, for the greenhouse."

"Can we...walk around? With you?" Viktor asked.

"Certainly."

+++

Mitchum peered out the window as the jet came in for its final approach. The airstrip was new since he'd been here last. In fact, it all looked new—the numerous domes that now loomed on the surface of the shifting sands, the movement of other solar-powered vehicles, the pedestrians moving through the city visible beneath a transparent dome. Then the plane touched down and when it stopped, a vehicle drove up alongside them and Rose got out.

She looked different, although he couldn't define why. Maybe it was simply that she was mostly among her own people who relocated from the moon base. Or that she'd changed the wig. Did all Stell^r females wear wigs? It seemed that she walked taller, with greater pride, and her smile seemed broader. She embraced each of them as they came off the jet and opened the back of the vehicle so they could put their bags inside.

In the brief moments when they were in the full sun, Mitchum's face beaded with sweat, and he shrugged off his jacket and loosened his tie. It was a relief to get into the blissfully cool vehicle. He immediately messaged Laurie and Helen that they'd landed, and Rose had picked them up. He snapped several photos and texted them, too.

Then Rose got in and said, "Where to first, guys?"

"Do you have a nice park?" Whitley asked.

"Sure, several. I'll take you to my favorite one. But let's get you all settled in first. Dome 3. That's the closest thing we have to a hotel."

"We have one more on the way, Rose," Mitchum said. "Aaron McHenry. He should arrive tomorrow."

"Did you give him my personal number?"

"Yes. He'll message you when he's close to landing."

"That name is familiar. Who is he?"

"A Viewer who worked for Stargate—not the original one, but a revised Stargate, stricter protocols. He Viewed my first trip into space as an astronaut. He was contacted by two members of Zhukov's Sindikat who..."

"Katherine?"

"Yes."

"And who else?"

"Dmitri Pavlov."

"I remember him from Ecuador. He was the guy who asked how Stell^rs have sex."

"That's what they talked about in Ecuador?" Ken exclaimed.

"One thing they asked Zhukov, yes. His reply was that he didn't know and didn't want to know." She laughed, a quick, refreshing sound that told Mitchum how silly she thought it was.

When they reached Dome 3, Liam and Sofiya greeted them in the lobby. Rose touched Mitchum's shoulder. "Could you stick around here with me for a bit, Jim? Epsilon knows you have some questions about Zhukov."

"Then I'm staying," Ken said.

"Me, too," Whitley chimed in.

"Of course. I counted on that."

They walked over to a sitting area next to a large window, where food and cold drinks had been set out for them. Mitchum thought, briefly, about why the Stell^rs had whisked Zhukov, Viktor, and three of the Sindikat members off to the far side of the moon. Rose picked up what he was thinking and telepathically responded. *I Viewed the poisoning of Epsilon, and they were all behind the launching of the tactical nukes that would have killed thousands.*

"Four of your agents are still working here as cooks, Jim."

He nodded.

"We don't seek to harm anyone," Rose said.

"Zhukov and his crew probably have a different perspective on that."

"Which is exactly why Epsilon wanted to speak with you."

Mitchum, Whitley, and Ken sampled the delicious vegetarian cuisine, sipped at what tasted like iced tea, and within ten minutes, Epsilon hurried into the room with two members of the Council and Sofiya. Greetings all the way around, then they pulled up more chairs and joined them.

"I understand your concerns, Jim," Epsilon said. "But what Rose and Sofiya viewed was later confirmed when we found poison in Asfour's belongings. And poison in some of the Russian food. So it wasn't based just on what a pair of seers saw. Wasn't that your main concern?"

Interesting, Mitchum thought. Epsilon read him as well as Rose did. "I didn't know that about the poison in the food, that you actually found it. How're they doing?"

"If you'd like to ask them personally, Jim, I can transport them here,"

"Nope, no thanks. They're too dangerous, Epsilon. They tried to detonate two tactical missiles here and when that failed then tried to poison you Stell^rs. And apparently the Sindikat members who went into hiding are still up to their tricks." He told them about the call from Aaron McHenry. "So Katherine Martin and Dmitri Pavlov hired Aaron to teach them how to block telepathic probes."

"I'd like to speak to him."

"He'll be here tomorrow."

"Excellent. So until then, let us show you around our enclave. But get settled in first."

"Then I'd like to take them to the park," Rose said.

Whatever anxiety or uncertainty Mitchum had been experiencing about all this started fading away. *The aliens are here and it's not Independence Day.* It was more like *E.T.* on steroids.

Chapter 21

Billionaire Art

Early the next morning, Rose's device screen went on, and Aaron McHenry's name appeared in the ID window. She immediately took the call.

"Hi Aaron, it's Rose."

"Rose, good to speak to you. We just landed."

"I'll be right out to pick you up. Everyone is eager to speak with you."

"Okay, we'll sit tight. I assume Jim has arrived?"

"Yesterday."

"Great. See you soon."

Less than ten minutes later, she pulled up alongside the plane and stepped outside. McHenry trotted down the stairs and hurried over to the vehicle. Tall and slender, he wore dark sunglasses, a short-sleeved cotton shirt, khaki pants, and a cap pulled down low over his forehead, casting his face in shadow. The strap of his bag hung over his shoulder. She guessed he was in his mid-fifties.

She opened the door for him and extended her long slender hand. "Such a pleasure to meet you, Aaron."

"The pleasure is mutual, Rose." He gripped her hand tightly, then held onto it a moment. "I'm relishing this moment of shaking the hand of an alien. Love it."

She laughed. "Hop in. We're headed to Dome 3."

"The cool air in here is refreshing." He dabbed at his damp face with a handkerchief, then leaned forward and peered through the windshield at the domes, rising from the flat landscape in every direction. "It's astonishing, everything is...transformed. The Sahara is green! And these domes...I'm awed. How did you get them built so quickly?"

"Most of the pieces were already at our moon base. We have a great crew here putting everything together."

"But still..." He glanced at Rose. "I know your technology is advanced beyond imagination, but seeing this now, there aren't any words."

"I'm curious, Aaron. Jim told me you Viewed his first sighting. What did you see exactly?"

"I did some sketches." He reached into his bag on the floor, withdrew a sketchpad, and turned it so she could see the drawing.

Her heartbeat sped up. "A Zorgon interstellar probe. You captured it perfectly, Aaron."

"Zorgon? What's that?"

"The Zorgons are a species of advanced reptilian creatures who have been Stell^r adversaries for eons. It's interesting that Jim saw one of their long-range robotic spaceships."

"Reptiles. Ugh."

"So I understand you trained Katherine and Dmitri how to block telepathic probes?"

"Yes, but I didn't realize it was against the Stell^rs."

Rose stopped the vehicle. "Would it be okay if I telepathically probe you? Then you show me what you taught them. Let me in first, then try to block me. I'd like to understand how you do this."

"All right." He rubbed his hands against his khaki pants. "Let's give it a try."

Rose didn't need to close her eyes, but she did. Their silence filled with the noise of the breeze outside tossing sand at the vehicle. It sounded rather like rain and lured her easily into Aaron McHenry's consciousness.

It was like a comfort zone, a place relatively free of worry and concerns about the usual things humans tended to fret about. She Viewed the contours of his personal life, his 30-year marriage, a son and daughter...And then she slammed into a concrete wall.

Rose's eyes snapped open. She looked at Aaron. He already watched her, a slight smile altering the shape of his mouth. "Some paths are blocked completely, like that one for me. Personal life."

"That...has never happened before. I, uh, collided with a concrete wall."

"And it's impenetrable."

"And you taught Katherine and Dmitri how to do that?"

"I tried. They learned it to varying degrees by following a simple rule. Imagine the most important parts of your life as paths that you can block with concrete, steel, anything impenetrable."

Rose mulled this over. "So it's about the power of the person's emotions, right?"

"And their intentions and ability to focus."

"Epsilon needs to know this."

"I'll be glad to demonstrate it."

She started the vehicle again and shortly afterward, drew up in front of Dome 3. As they got out, the breeze hurled sand at them, too, and she drew a light scarf across her nose and mouth. Protective, translucent lids slid across her eyes, nictitating membranes like some animals on this planet had. Except that hers could even endure a nuclear blast. Never mind that her body would be torn to dust, her eyes would be in the rubble somewhere, still able to see.

Aaron surprised her by noticing. "Wow, third eyelids! We humans could sure use something like that. How strong are they? How much can they endure?"

"Zhukov and his Sindikat of billionaires somehow got two tactical missiles in here. We rendered them useless. But if they'd gone off, it would have been genocide. And in that carnage, there would be Stell^rs eyes still able to see because of our nictitating eyelids."

"Literally?"

"Yes."

"That's a...really disturbing image, Rose."

"It's also a fact."

He raised his arm and covered his nose and mouth with it. "No protective eyelids here. I need to get inside."

Rose liked this guy. She liked that he asked questions, just as her favorite humans had when they'd first met—Liam, Jim, Whitley, Spenser. Aaron McHenry was in their league.

+++

Epsilon and Aaron sat across from each other in a lobby enclave in Dome 3. "So Rose tells me you once Viewed for Stargate?"

"It was technically a revised version of the original Stargate. It got off the ground during Covid in 2021. I was there for almost a decade and quit when I realized how it was being used."

"Which was...?"

"You're the telepath, sir. Let's see if you can find that answer."

Interesting. A human who presented him with a genuine challenge. "And you'll show me what you taught these two students of yours?"

"Yes."

In his centuries of life, Epsilon rarely had to *think* his way into anyone's head. Usually, it simply happened, like breathing. But with this man, *thinking* didn't do it. So he *felt* his way in, creeping forward bit by bit like a worm or a snail, some small creature that had all the time in the world to figure things out. He encountered several small obstacles and found a way around them. Then he was in.

Or, at any rate, that was his initial impression. But when he glanced around, he saw that he was in what looked like an art gallery—an homage to van Gogh, Picasso, Gaugin, even da Vinci and Rembrandt. Some of each artists' paintings hung on one wall. The opposite wall was blank, except for a sign that read, *Stell^r Artists Where Are You?*

"The imposters I trained will be coming here as art experts or collectors or something along those lines," Aaron said.

"You mean these two wealthy minions of Zhukov's?"

"Hmm. The two minions who are now not quite as wealthy since you arrived. They can repel you to a certain point, that's my sense. But if you pull one of your creepy crawlers, like you just did with me, you won't have any problem probing them, Epsilon."

This man impressed him just as Jim Mitchum and a couple of other leaders of the nuclear powers had the first time he'd met them. But Aaron was markedly different. Like Rose and Sofiya, he *saw* things—possible futures? *The* future? Was there only one future per timeline? Even more importantly, he seemed to understand that the human mind had the capacity to be as competent as the Stell^r mind but was still in its infancy.

"Aaron, when you were instructing these two people, did you ever show your true face? Your physical image?"

He laughed. "No way. AI created me. And my voice was disguised. And they knew me by a different name."

"Then the day these two arrive, I'd like you to be our museum director, our art expert."

"I'd love to. But I've never seen any Stell^r art. I never knew you all had art. And Katherine seemed to think your art would arrive with the first starships in June."

Epsilon shook his head. Poor Zhukov, he thought. The man, even now after weeks in rehab on the moon, believed they would ship art in their early arrivals. But a large selection of their art was now on display in Domes Four and Five, holographic images that depicted every facet of Stell^r life on Xanthe.

"Before we go over to Domes Four and Five, where the artwork is, let me see if I found the right answer about why you left the revised Stargate." He paused. "I saw that an authority figure—your boss?—was using the program to obtain intelligence information that he didn't have clearance for."

"That was the gist of it." Then he grinned. "Very good, Epsilon."

"Rose and Sofiya are going to meet us at Dome 4. I think Jim is, too. We can take the moving walks over there. We had a corridor built between several of the domes so the heat and sand aren't an issue."

"I'm impressed with everything you've done here."

As they headed toward the connecting corridor, Epsilon asked Aaron how his abilities had developed. "Were you trained first?"

"No, I was tested and passed."

"What was the test?"

"They asked me to remote view the location of a plane that had gone down in the Bermuda Triangle in the early part of the twenty-first century, 2009, I think it was. So I did, and they located the remains of the plane and hired me."

"Was this ability something you'd had all your life?"

"When I was seven, I got really sick, high fever, some sort of virus. I ended up in the hospital, and during that time, I started seeing things. Details about the hospital personnel, future scenarios. It just continued once I was released."

So the sickness had altered something essential in his brain, his chemistry, his ability to process this kind of information. Epsilon had heard about such things. "And the ability deepened over the years?"

"The more I used it, the stronger it became."

They entered the corridor, a spacious, transparent tube filled with Sahara sunlight minus the heat. Hurrying toward them was Jim Mitchum, Ken, and Sofiya. "Jim!" Aaron shouted.

"Hey!"

They hurried toward each other and embraced in the middle of the corridor, their delight at seeing each other so obvious that he felt his mouth swing into a smile. Epsilon knew that his smile, to any human, would look awkward, unnatural.

When he reached the group, introductions had been made, and Sofiya and Aaron already were immersed in conversation.

"Aaron is going to pose as our art curator when it's time," Epsilon said.

"I've got a lot of research to do before I'm a curator for Stell^r art," he remarked.

"You'll do fine," Mitchum told him. "Now c'mon, you've got to see this exhibit, Aaron."

"As you Americans say, it's mind-blowing," Sofiya remarked.

+++

Mitchum loved being inside of Dome 4, surrounded by such eye-popping multidimensional art. The colors surpassed anything he'd ever seen in art or in nature, and even though he wasn't sure what some of the images depicted, he already had a favorite artist. A woman. Zelda. Like F. Scott Fitzgerald's wife. She painted the most exquisite birds and other animals he assumed were native to Xanthe or other planets they visited across the cosmos.

"These are...incredible," Aaron said, stopping next to Mitchum. "But if I'm going to act like a curator, I'm going to need a lot of info. What's the date for this event?"

"Probably May, a month before the first starships arrive."

"How're you going to get the word out?"

Mitchum grinned. "How long can you stick around, Aaron?"

His gesture encompassed the entire dome. "Long enough to learn about these artists and their work. I think a compelling holographic video can convince the art world to come and see this one-of-a-kind work for themselves."

Would just an exhibit of Stell^r art lure the rest of Zhukov's Sindikat out of hiding? Probably not. Mitchum thought. But maybe a philanthropic auction would. What billionaire wouldn't want to own a piece of alien art? The Stell^rs would find a terrific philanthropic use for the money, Mitchum thought.

"Hey, Epsilon," Mitchum called. "Got an idea to run past you."

Epsilon came over with Rose and Sofiya, who had joined them here in the art gallery. "Let's hear it," Epsilon said.

"Isn't it about time for Zhukov and Viktor and the other three men to have some company up there on the moon?"

"Like the rest of the Sindikat?" Sofiya asked.

"Exactly. Pick out a painting, and we'll announce an auction for it to the world's wealthiest collectors."

"Brilliant!" Rose exclaimed.

"Those billionaire boys will leap at the chance to secure one of a kind alien art," Sofiya added.

"I like it!" Epsilon nodded, then gestured at everyone to follow him. "I know just the piece. In Dome 5."

They went through another corridor into the next art gallery dome. Here, the art seemed to leap off the walls in living, breathing color, like a light show at a concert. Initially, the explosive color nearly blinded Mitchum. He had to look down at the floor, briefly shut his eyes, then looked up again. He noticed that Sofiya and Aaron had slipped on sunglasses. Good idea, he decided, and did the same. It helped.

"So which painting do you want to auction, Epsilon?"

Epsilon turned slowly in place, the brilliance of the colors enhancing and seeming to melt into the bluish hue of his skin. Then he walked over to a large holographic piece on the opposite wall and pointed his long, slim finger at it. "This one. It depicts one of my favorite spots on Xanthe. A meadow so green and lush, with that low-hanging cloudless sky, that it practically screams at you to romp. Go play. Have fun. Enjoy yourself. Many classes go out there to paint, meditate, brainstorm. There's even a source of water." He brought his finger to the lower right-hand corner of the image. "See the narrow ribbon of blue?" Without touching the image, he traced its course through the lush green. "When it reaches the horizon, it plummets over a cliff and becomes a rushing river."

"Who's the artist?" Aaron asked.

"Zelda's twin. Zee." He pointed at her fancy signature in the lower left corner.

"Identical twins?" Sofiya asked.

"Yes. Quite rare among Stell^rs. Zelda specializes in animal life and Zee specializes in landscapes. They will be on one of the first starships to arrive in June."

"But how do you place a monetary value on something like this?" Rose asked.

Mitchum stabbed his thumb at Aaron. "Ask our curator to be."

Aaron ran his fingers back through his thick hair, starting to gray at the temples. "To entice billionaires? The first piece of alien art on the planet? Oh man, how about a cool one billion?"

"And that money will be dispersed to the poor, the neediest of people," Epsilon said.

"Now *that* is a major selling point," Aaron said. "I'll need more information about her. You're going to have a lot of artists clamoring to learn these multidimensional techniques."

"Which I'm sure the twins will be glad to teach one day," Epsilon said.

Just like that, the issue had been resolved in what Mitchum considered the most feasible lure to Zhukov's in hiding Sindikat members. "Okay, Aaron, you're in charge of the holographic video that's going to sell this to the public."

"Sofiya and I would like to help," Rose said.

"And hey, Liam here." He waved his arms as he entered the room. "Count me in."

"How long will it take you to make this incredible video that's going to entice Zhukov's Sindikat?" Epsilon asked.

Aaron glanced at his team. "With this group? A week maybe two. But then the PR campaign begins to put out the word of this event."

"Let's say early April," Mitchum said. "That will give them time to make their plans to emerge from hiding and figure out how they're going to get here undetected."

"Even if we detect them, it won't matter," Epsilon said. "We won't make our move until they're here."

"Suppose some of the world leaders ask to come?" Mitchum asked. "Maybe they'd like to see the Stell^r art, too."

"Invite them," Epsilon replied.

+++

Katherine and Dmitri decided to test their phony credentials in Paris. They took the train. The fastest Eurostar maglev service took under two hours which would put them in the city of lights by noon. All they needed to know was if the creds were considered legit to people in the art business, so why not start with the Louvre?

During the train ride, they sat together, planning how they would handle this, what each of them would say. They agreed that all they wanted from this was to know the credentials would be recognized officially.

Simple.

Katherine's sources in the countries that bordered the Sahara indicated the arrival of several flights over the past several days that had originated in the US. Maybe Mitchum or some of his people were on one of those flights but maybe not. These days, the FAA masked the presidential flights; they were tracked privately.

If the US president and his team were on one of those flights, then the bottom-line question was why? Why now in early March? Had a Stell^r spacecraft landed ahead of schedule? Had Zhukov been released? What had happened that was so important that Mitchum would drop everything in DC and travel nearly 4,000 miles to the middle of a now green and flourishing desert?

But maybe that was it. Maybe he had gone there to witness the Stell^r marvels for himself, in person, rather than just seeing images from drones, satellites, and spy planes now that the domes were complete.

By the time the hovering train pulled into the Paris station, she looked like the bohemian type rather than the CEO type. But an artistic professional with class. Expensive pants that hugged her curves in just the right places, a silk blouse that exploded with color and complemented her red hair, a handbag that matched everything. Her credentials were on her phone.

Even Dmitri, who usually dressed like an eccentric slob, looked the part. Both had changed clothes in the restrooms.

When they entered the Louvre, Katherine immediately felt as if she had walked into a sanctuary. She knew that during WWII, the director of the French national museums, Jacques Jaujard, had believed that France would fall to the Germans and organized the evacuation of the museum's magnificent collection to the provinces. Good thing the man had had the foresight to do so, Katherine thought. Otherwise, the Nazis would have stolen the Mona Lisa and all the other priceless works the Louvre contained.

In fact, on August 25, 1939, the museum had been closed for three days— supposedly for repairs. The bulk of the Louvre's collection was loaded onto 203 trucks that transported 1862 wooden cases to Château de Chambord. Today, it was the largest Château in the Loire valley. During the war, the Mona Lisa was moved from Chambord to other castles and abbeys to keep it out of the hands of the Nazis. By the end of the war, it was housed at the Ingres Bourdelle Museum in Montauban, France.

Since 1966, it had been exhibited in the Louvre's largest room, the Salle des États, on a wall of its own. Because it was painted on a panel of poplar wood rather than canvas, it had warped over the centuries and developed a crack. For the last 30 years, it had been kept in a glass case that was controlled for temperature and humidity.

They went to the Salle des États first, and both just stood there, staring at the Mona Lisa, sequestered behind a railing, in solitude on the wall. Would Stell^r art surpass the Mona Lisa? How different would it be?

"Is that our angle, Dmitri?" She whispered the words so the people nearby wouldn't overhear her. "That we may have something that surpasses Mona Lisa?"

"We don't have proof. They might get suspicious and tip off the police."

"Good point." She tilted her head toward the guard standing on the other side of the room "Let's just ask to see the curator and introduce ourselves. Show our creds."

"Like what we talked about earlier."

"Right."

They headed toward the guard.

+++

Rose and Sofiya were alone in Dome 5, gathering information from Pi and Gamma about Zee and her work. They eventually would work it into a narrative for Aaron. When they took a brief break, they went into a cafe in the corridor between the two domes and chatted—sometimes telepathically, sometimes aloud.

"So tell me your impressions of Katherine Martin. I eavesdropped on you two while we were all in Ecuador."

"I just remembered something." Sofiya sounded excited. "Not long after you and I met, I was curious about whether Stell^rs had any kind of artistic culture. So I tried to View it. And...wow, I learned just how extensive and ancient it is. And I wondered if the Stell^rs would want to exhibit any of it when they arrived. And that day I talked for so long with Katherine, I told her about the Stell^r collection. And speculated about an exhibit. Her eyes lit up. She said she held a degree in art history and hoped my speculation was right."

That explained a lot, Rose thought, about what she had picked up on Katherine, random images, sensations, emotions. At her core, Katherine Martin was outrageously greedy, and wherever she saw opportunity, she made her move.

"Can you tune in on her now?" Rose asked.

"I can try."

Her eyes closed, her breathing changed. Rose eased herself into Sofiya's consciousness bit by bit until she saw what Sofiya saw, a Katherine Martin who looked entirely different than before. A redhead certainly changed by plastic surgery. Quite a bit of surgery. She was dressed oddly. And she was in a museum with a short, strange-looking man—Dmitri?

"They...they're showing their credentials to whoever is in charge of the museum. The Louvre! It's the Louvre!"

Where the Mona Lisa hung.

The man with whom they spoke approved their credentials, and then the three of them chatted about art and Paris and the changes that were coming to the planet once the Stell^rs arrived in masse.

Rose eased her way out of Sofiya's consciousness and rubbed her eyes. She had become a worrier in the months since Mitchum had invited her and Liam to live at the White House. A worrier, like humans. She disliked that about herself. Yet, she had to admit that worry often strengthened her abilities, her *intuition,* her *right brain,* as the humans said. And right now, her right brain screamed that whatever dark plans Katherine, Dmitri, and other members of the Sindikat produced might be worse than poison, than nuclear weapons, worse than any scenario humans might imagine. But how could that be?

And it might be horrifyingly simple, up close and personal: a knife in Epsilon's side, a bullet through a Stell^r forehead—hers? If that was the tactic, then the human perpetrator would have to know his or her own life would be ended as well. Were Katherine, Dmitri, or any of those other Sindikat members be ready to die to stop the Stell^rs? How great was their passion in that regard?

She worried that here in their safe domes, they might be caught off guard. But even as she considered this possibility, she knew the Viewing information gave them a distinct advantage. They would have to be prepared for virtually any possibility. After all, in Esperanza, the threat had come from a gang of local guys whose leader had been recruited by Richard, still in a comatose state in California.

The challenge with this tactic, though, was that if there were dozens of people gathered to see the Stell^r art, to participate in the auction, there would be only a limited number of Stell^rs to act as sentries. The protection would have to come primarily from humans like Ken and other Secret Service agents or any special forces whom Mitchum assigned here.

"Okay, Rose." Sofiya waved her hand in front of Rose's face. "Where are you?"

Rose blinked. Sofiya's face swam into clarity. Her session Viewing Katherine was done. And probably had been for some time. "I'm here. Just being a worrywart."

Sofiya giggled, a soft, almost childlike sound. "I've always thought that American expression was kind of funny. In Russian, we say *волноваться бородавка*. But it isn't a term you hear among many Russians."

"You don't hear it among Stell^rs, either. In fact, as kids, we're taught that worry is futile."

Sofiya shrugged. "But it has its place, Rose. It's a warning system."

"Or a distraction," Rose remarked.

"We can use everything and anything to our advantage."

"I think we should have a plan that's versatile and can change at a moment's notice. We have an advantage, you and me. The telepathy.

The day of the exhibit, one of us should be in Dome 4, the other in Dome 5, and stay in constant communication."

Sofiya nodded and raised her right hand. Rose's hand greeted it in midair. "Deal," Sofiya said.

Chapter 22

The Far Side of the Moon

Epsilon was now tying up loose ends before the starships from Xanthe started arriving.

And the first loose end was to transport the leaders of North Korea and Pakistan to the moon base. Both men were still in stasis when they arrived on the base and were taken immediately to the medical area, where Epsilon oversaw their awakening. He would transport Richard, the boy billionaire next.

Lee Shin, the North Korean leader, regained consciousness first. He bolted to a sitting position, saw Epsilon and Pi, and released a stream of Korean that basically translated as, "You blue devils again; I've dreamt about you? Where am I? What the hell have you done?"

They hadn't restrained him, and he leaped off the table and immediately took a defensive karate stance that made Epsilon smile. In flawless Korean, Epsilon said, "You have been in stasis for quite some time, President Shin, and we can revert you to that state if you prefer."

"Where...am I?" His body relaxed, arms falling to his sides as he looked around quickly, frantically. "Where have you taken me?"

"You're on the Stell^r base on the far side of the moon," Pi replied. "If you're hungry, I can take you to the dining room, where President Zhukov and Viktor are having breakfast."

"The *moon*?" His dark eyes widened so much they looked like they might pop out of their sockets. "*The freakin moon*?" He burst out laughing and laughed until tears rolled down his pudgy cheeks. Then he staggered to the closest window and peered out, gaping at the infinite darkness broken up by nothing more than starlight. His knees buckled, and he sank to the floor, weeping like a lost child.

Epsilon and Pi exchanged a glance and communicated telepathically.

Pi: *Should we leave him there?*

Epsilon: *For now. Is Murad Khan coming around?*

Pi went over to the table where Khan lay still motionless. Pi checked for a pulse. "He's alive, Epsilon."

"Help him up."

The North Pakistani leader's eyes snapped open, he raised himself on his elbows, and panic seized his expression. "This is insane, I'm...where the hell am I? What have you done to me?"

At the sound of his voice, Shin got to his feet and hurried over to Khan. "Calm down, Murad, I'm here, too. We're on the far side of the moon, on the alien's base."

"What...what does that even mean, Lee?" He swung his short legs over the side of the table. "How..."

Epsilon and Pi stepped back, giving the two men some space. Shin glanced at them, then helped Khan stand. "Over here. The window. You'll see." He whispered to Khan, but Epsilon could hear what he said. "They tell me Zhukov and Viktor are here, too."

"My last memory..."

"I know," Shin said. "They...they put us in...in...induced comas. For years!"

They reached the window and both men peered out. Khan didn't weep, his knees didn't buckle. But he pressed his face to the window, tapped his knuckles against the surface. "Not glass. I'm not familiar with this...this surface."

"It's impenetrable," Epsilon said.

Both men suddenly realized they wore only underwear. "Our clothes," Khan said "May we have our clothes?"

Pi went over to them and handed each man a neatly folded stack of clothing. "Once you're dressed, we can take you to the dining room for a meal. Zhukov and Viktor are there now."

"I would like to shower first," Shin said.

"Me, too," Khan said.

"Certainly." Epsilon opened a pair of doors that led to separate bathrooms. "We will wait here to escort you to the dining area."

"Is there soap?" Khan asked.

"And towels?" Shin chimed in.

"Everything you need," Epsilon replied.

Both men hurried through one of the open doors. *They are going to be looking for a way out,* Pi said.

Good luck with that.

Sure enough, the showers ran for less than five minutes, and when the men emerged, their hair was wet, and they were dressed in pants, shirts, and shoes. "We would like something to eat now," Shin said.

"This way," Epsilon said, and he and Pi led them up and down hallways, showed them where their quarters were with their clothes and some belongings already inside.

Neither man looked particularly happy about the accommodations. "So we are prisoners here?" Shin asked.

"You are our guests here," Epsilon said. "However, you won't be returning to your planet any time soon."

Khan spun around, fury tightening the corners of his mouth. "You have kidnapped us!"

"We have removed you as a threat to humanity and to the Stell^rs. We could have kept you in induced comas indefinitely, but believe it is much more equitable for you to live freely here on the moon base."

"Live *freely?*" Khan's laughter sounded forced, like hiccups. He stopped in the middle of the hall, threw out his arms. "How is *this* freedom?"

Such fury in such a diminutive tyrant, Epsilon thought. "President Khan, you have two choices. A life here on our lunar base or a life in stasis. It's your choice."

"That's not a choice," snapped Shin.

"It's like the choices you give your people, President Shin."

Shin looked at Khan, hoping he would defend him, but Khan shrugged and now walked on through the hallway.

+++

When Khan and Shin entered the dining area with Epsilon and one of his minions— Pi? Gamma? Alpha?—anxiety churned through Zhukov. He realized that none of them were ever going to escape this place. "Viktor, glance back," he said quietly.

Viktor did. "Shit. We've got company. Hope they have their own rooms."

Yeah, Zhukov thought. He hoped so, too. Bad enough being stuck with Viktor. But the prospect of living with these two men would be enough to lose his mind.

Khan and Shin were all smiles as they approached the table where he and Viktor sat. They both got up, and the four men shook hands and bumped fists. A server appeared, another Stell^r, of course, with two mugs of coffee and two plates heaped with what looked like a pasta dish loaded with vegetables and minus any kind of meat.

"These aliens eat pasta?" Shin asked. "And where do they grow their vegetables?"

"There's a greenhouse somewhere in this complex," Viktor said.

"What...what did they do to Lee and me?" Khan asked.

"You were in stasis for many years," Zhukov replied.

"Years?" Shin sounded incredulous. He rubbed his hands over his face. "Who...has been running my country?"

"No clue," Zhukov replied. "Since 2029. It's now 2036." Zhukov paused and looked from one man to the other. "That's seven years."

"Alexander and I have been here for..." Viktor paused, glanced at Zhukov. "Do we know? I've lost track of time."

"Me, too."

"When did they transport you up here?" Khan again. "What month? Do you know?"

Zhukov shook his head. When he and Viktor and the three members of the Sindikat initially realized where they were, what had happened, he'd kept track of the days. Now, the only thing Zhukov knew about the passage of time was that it was 2036. Time up here was skewed. Without the rising and setting of the sun, with only that infinite darkness outside broken up just by the light of the moon or stars, his life was measured by eating, sleeping, using the gym. Sometimes he had wandered around the dome, hoping to find a way out. But outside, only the lunar surface existed. It was as if he, Viktor, and the others existed in a timeless place defined only by hunger, sleep, exercise, and their frequent wandering around the dome.

He hated it.

But he'd decided awhile back that hatred was futile.

"A long time," Viktor said. "We've been here a long time."

"What's happening on Earth with these aliens?" Shin asked.

"No idea," Zhukov said.

"Well, we may have some inkling," Viktor commented. "Things around here have changed recently."

"How?" Khan asked.

"Busier, more Stell^rs traveling back and forth to and from Earth," Zhukov said. "Then they started allowing us to move around the dome, gave us a bit more freedom, as if to distract us." He spoke quietly but knew it wouldn't matter. If the Stell^rs wanted to hear what they discussed, they could eavesdrop whenever they wanted. "Maybe distract us in the hopes that we wouldn't notice how activity here has ticked upward. They're preparing for something."

"For the landing of their spaceships?" Shin asked.

"Perhaps." Zhukov nodded. "But we don't have any contact with Earth, so we don't know for sure."

"Once, fairly recently, I started coming out of the coma," Shin said. "I heard my people talking, the medics. I think they used to talk to me frequently, hoping something of what they said might reach me. And this time it did. They said the aliens have built domes in the Sahara, that their ships will land there in the future."

But when? Soon? Zhukov had no idea. Judging from the look on Viktor's face, he didn't know, either. Screw it, Zhukov thought, and got up and walked across the dining area to where Epsilon sat with some members of his Council.

"May I help you with something, President Zhukov?" Epsilon asked.

"Yes, thank you. We understand that you consider all of us dangerous. We accept that. But we think it's only fair and just if we have access to news on our planet. We aren't requesting a way to communicate with Earth. We simply would like to know what's going on."

Epsilon looked at him in such an unnerving way that Zhukov nearly glanced away. But maybe that was exactly what Epsilon wanted. "Fair enough, President Zhukov."

And suddenly, images appeared on the wall at the front of the dining room. Zhukov couldn't tell where they were coming from or what projected them. And it didn't matter. The images were the only thing that mattered—giant geodesic domes looming on a landscape that once had been the Sahara desert. He had seen satellite images before they had stupidly fired those tactical weapons into the area. But back then, it wasn't what it was now—the greenest spot on the planet. Grasses, flowers, orchards, streams and rivers, and pools of fresh water.

No words, he had no words. Nothing he said would matter. The images spoke for themselves.

"Those could be fakes!" Shin shouted from behind them.

Zhukov spun around and glared at him for shouting like a barbarian. Here on this base courtesy and its protocols prevailed.

But Epsilon seemed unfazed by the outburst. "Do you think these are fakes?" He gave a slight nod, and the images of a green Sahara were replaced by images from inside a massive starship. "This is the sleeping area on a starship now headed to the Stell^r compound in the Sahara." The image melted into a section of the giant spaceship that, from one end the other, resembled a field of chalk white pods long enough for tens of 1000's of sleeping Stell^rs.

A single figure moved among these pods, pausing here, there, touching his long bluish hand to what looked like the transparent lids of the pods. "That Stell^r is Dax, an agricultural expert who is traveling on the Celestial Dawn with his partner and two daughters. He is one of 500 out of the 1000's of Stell^rs who aren't in a sleeping pod. That's how important his skills are to the facilitation of life for our race once 100 million of us are on Earth."

The image switched again. This Stell^r, Dax, paused amid this field of sleeping pods, lowered a chair from the ceiling, and sat between two of them. He placed each hand on the lid of the pod and then leaned forward and touched his mouth to a third pod. As he rose up, his image became clearer, closer so that Zhukov could see his face. His eyes had shut, and his nearly nonexistent mouth seemed to move slightly.

Sound suddenly filled the room—a low husky voice that Zhukov assumed was Dax's. "It won't be long now. I am marking off the solar days when the three of you will leave this ship and join me as we land in our new home. Already, the Council had turned one of Earth's largest deserts into a beauty found only on Xanthe. Some of your favorite creatures will be there, Nika and Rita. Like the gorgeous Glitterwing."

Epsilon continued. "When that starship left Xanthe, his daughters, Nika and Rita, were eleven and seven in Earth years.

Youngsters. When it lands, a decade will have passed. The daughters and Dax's partner and all the others in the pods, won't have aged a single day. But Dax and the other 499 Stell^rs who weren't in hyper sleep, will have aged a decade. He worries that the age differences will impact their relationships in some way. But that would be odd since we live 1,200 years. Yet on this journey, Dax has learned what loneliness and longing are, very human emotions."

Khan's arm shot into the air, waving madly. But he didn't shout, wasn't rude like Shin. Epsilon said, "Yes, President Khan?"

"And this is how you are transporting your entire population?"

"Except for the ones on our base here."

"But...we also have families and loved ones and you have separated us. Unlike Dax, we won't see our families again."

"Yet, through the UN," Zhukov interrupted, "you said you didn't intend harm to any human, that you were coming in peace and...and here we are, the presidents of four countries, held as prisoners here on your moon base."

"We gave a single warning, President Zhukov. Remember? We said that we would retaliate if any nuclear weapons were repositioned. Presidents Shin and Khan went to DEFCON 1. You and your Sindikat managed to fire two tactical weapons into our Sahara compound. You then planned to poison us. That's why *you* and Viktor are here."

"I didn't plan any of this." Viktor spoke quietly, politely. "I just went along with it because Alexander confided in me. If I hadn't gone along with it, he would have targeted me for assassination."

"That's a damn lie!" Zhukov snapped. "You were on my Advisory Council, you went to Ecuador, to...you knew everything and never...*never*...voiced any objection. Zero, Viktor. *None.*"

Viktor just stared at him. And in that brief silence, Zhukov felt their long friendship crumbing like old bread.

"True. I didn't want to be eliminated like others who offended you." His eyes moved to Epsilon and the other Council members. "I am guilty of not wanting to be assassinated. I'm guilty of having considered fleeing to another country and not doing it because I was terrified that Alexander would send a kill team to find me." He paused, swallowed hard. "He and I have known each other since we were kids. Nine, ten years old. He was always a bully, and I knew even then that if I crossed him, if I spoke my truth, he would retaliate."

"Lies, all of it!" Zhukov shouted now. He nearly launched himself at Viktor, to strangle him, beat him up, something. But he knew that if he did, one of the Stell^rs would incapacitate him. "He's a liar!"

"Please sit down," Epsilon said.

"Why? That traitor is lying about me. He's..."

Suddenly, one of them was behind him, one of the Stell^rs, and he felt that long bony, bluish hand on his shoulder. It didn't squeeze or dig those fingers into his shoulder. It simply exerted the slightest of pressure. "Sit. Down."

Zhukov sat down.

Epsilon nodded at Viktor. "So speak your truth."

Viktor stared directly at Zhukov and then raised his arm dramatically and pointed at him. "He's a heinous, evil man whose Sindikat of the world's richest billionaires is intended to keep him in power and to keep money as king of the world. My failing is lack of courage to break away from his evil because I didn't want to die."

He sounded choked up there at the end, and Zhukov realized he was telling the truth, *his* truth, and that Epsilon and his Stell^r Council believed him. He was sure of it when he noticed the Council exchanging glances and suspected they were communicating telepathically.

Then, suddenly, a column of light descended over Viktor, and he was beamed out of the area.

+++

Rose was in Dome 5, checking the security precautions that had been set up in advance of tomorrow's auction. Security cams were in place and working and showing up clearly on her phone. She contacted Gamma in the control area to make sure she showed up on their equipment.

Hey, Gamma, just checking these cams. Do I show up?

Clearly.

On all the cams?

Everywhere.

Great.

Walk into Dome 4 through the tunnel for a check and then step outside.

Ok.

She hurried through the connecting tunnel and heard the sand pelting the exterior. Whenever she was in here, that noise seemed pervasive and reminded her of rain. Gamma messaged again.

You show up clearly in the tunnel, from all sides.

Do you think we've overdone the cams?

Nope.

As she entered Dome 4, it occurred to her that when she was dealing with other Stell^rs, VR messaging was somehow easier and more natural than telepathy. The same wasn't true with Epsilon, and she wondered why. She paused in the middle of the dome and waved at the main cam, well-hidden over the door, then stepped outside.

The wind blew hard today, and just as she drew her scarf over the nose and mouth, she noticed something unusual in the piles of sand and hurried over to it. An arm protruded from it, a man's arm, a man's fingers, human.

With one hand, she grasped hold of the man's arm and pulled while she dug at the sand with her other hand. His head appeared, and as soon as his body was free of the sand, Rose turned him over. Viktor? "What the hell."

She pulled him to a sitting position and shook him until he started coughing. She pulled a container of water from her shoulder pack, crouched in front of him, and worked the container into his hand. "Sip, Viktor. Wash the sand out of your mouth."

He released a stream of Russian words, coughed again, and brought the container shakily to his mouth.

"Sip and wash it around in your mouth and spit it out to get rid of the sand."

He did as she instructed, then ran his other arm across his eyes to wipe away the sand. "I...I..."

"C'mon, you need to get inside."

He got clumsily to his feet and stumbled through the doorway with Rose gripping one of his arms. Inside the dome, she eased him into the closest chair. "Where...am I?" he stuttered, glancing around.

"Dome 4, on the Stell^r Sahara compound."

"He...Epsilon...freed me!"

Gamma rushed into the dome. "Did you know that Epsilon had Viktor brought here?" Rose asked.

"I only knew something was happening on the base but wasn't informed what it was."

It surprised her that she felt a bit of anger about not being informed, especially now, with the auction only a day away. "We should have been alerted, Gamma."

"Agreed. I tried to contact Epsilon as soon as I walked in here, but he must still be on the lunar base."

She helped Viktor to his feet. "I'd like to get you settled in here, Viktor. It's a short walk. Can you walk okay?"

"I...I think so. Yes."

As they walked through yet another tunnel, Rose on one side of him, Gamma towering over him on the other, she asked what had happened. His story came out in stammered bits and pieces and told her a great deal about what was happening on the moon, that Zhukov apparently was there for good, along with his three Sindikat members. It also told her that whoever was governing both North Korea and Pakistan would be sounding alarms about the missing bodies of their comatose leaders.

"Is it...okay if I stay here, Rose?"

"Absolutely."

In Dome 3, she and Gamma took Viktor to one of the vacant rooms, showed him where the shower was. "I'll find you some clean clothes and stuff, Viktor."

"And I'll be glad to show you around," Gamma said. "And take you to the dining area for some coffee and anything else you would like."

Viktor stood there in the middle of the room, then turned to Rose and threw his arms around her. "Thank you," he whispered and began to cry. "Thank you."

She patted him on the back as she might a small child. "It's okay, Viktor. You're safe here from Zhukov." Her eyes met Gamma's.

I'll tend to him, Rose, Gamma's telepathic reassurance took the edge off her worry.

We still need answers from Epsilon about why he transported Viktor here.

Agreed. I'm sure he has a plan.

"Gamma will make sure you get acquainted with the compound, Viktor. And get something to eat. I'll be right back with some clothes."

As she left, she realized that his presence here might be enormously helpful in identifying any of Zhukov's operatives who might attend tomorrow's auction. Maybe that was what Epsilon had in mind?

Chapter 23

Auction in the Sahara

On May 15, 2036, Mitchum arrived with Whitley, Ken, and Nomad at three a.m. on the day of the big art auction. Rose and Epsilon stood next to one of the sleek solar-powered dune vehicles, waiting for them. Epsilon came forward, and as Nomad limped down the steps, Rose whistled loudly. "My favorite pooch!" she called. His graying snout raised up, eyes widening in that beautiful graying face. Perked up, he struggled to race down the remaining steps toward her.

Rose, of course, threw open her arms and the dog leaped—or tried to—into that welcoming embrace. Epsilon shook hands with Mitchum, Whitley, and Ken, then gestured at Nomad. "I'm glad you brought him, Jim. It gives me the opportunity to work on him."

"What does that involve, Epsilon?"

"In our greenhouse here, we've been growing something that will make him look and feel younger and should extend his life by at least five years. We used it in the early days of our life extensions. First time on an Earth canine."

It sounded miraculous to Mitchum. "Wow, this could change the entire health industry, Epsilon."

"Pharma will have a bidding war for something like that," Whitley remarked.

He smiled and said, "We won't be releasing any data on it. This is just for Nomad."

Mitchum nodded. Smart decision. Big pharma wouldn't just have a bidding war for something like this, they probably would stoop to criminal activity.

"Now tell me about Viktor. Why did you release him? I've already gotten calls from officials in North Korea and Pakistan wanting to know where their leaders are."

"Once this auction is over, I'll allow Presidents Shin and Khan to speak to their people. They're doing better than they were in their induced comas." Then, in a quiet, even voice, he recounted the events that had led him to freeing Viktor—the specifics, the generalities. "For all the months they've been on our lunar base, we've observed them, listened to them. My sense has been that Viktor went along with all this because he's utterly terrified of Zhukov. And I think he will be helpful in identifying any of Zhukov's Sindikat who venture here."

"Brilliant. Have you spoken to him about it?"

"Yes, a little while ago. He's so grateful to be away from Zhukov and off the moon that he's eager to help. The security here in the compound is tight. The first flights will arrive around eight, just five hours from now."

"How many people were invited?" Ken asked.

"We limited it to 150. All of the remaining Sindikat members are expected."

"Jesus," Ken murmured. "How much security do you have?"

Epsilon showed that unusual Stell^r smile. "Plenty. Don't worry, Ken."

Once they were in the dune vehicle, Nomad sat happily in the back with Rose on one side of him and Whitley and Ken on the other. Mitchum occupied the passenger seat, Epsilon drove. "We're putting you all in our most secure area in Dome 3, and breakfast will be served in an hour."

"Sofiya and Aaron, our curator and expert on Stell^r art, will be there, too," Rose said.

"How did Aaron become an expert so quickly on Stell^r art?" Whitley asked.

"Sofiya and I went through all the info on the artists and their art and put it together for him, then delivered it telepathically. And since he's a Viewer himself, he learned the information really fast."

"It's helpful having a Viewer as our curator," Epsilon added.

"Aaron is a terrific Viewer and a good friend," Mitchum said.

Epsilon pulled up in front of Dome 3, illuminated by outside lighting, and they all unloaded their bags and went inside. This was the dog's first time here and his first time inside something as massive as this dome. Nomad stopped just inside the door; stopped, and looked around, slowly, taking in everything. He looked up at Mitchum, who stroked the dog's head. "Yeah, I know. The place is immense."

"I'll show you around, Nomad," Rose said.

She wrapped her arms around him in a way that prompted Mitchum to believe she could communicate telepathically with him. Why not? If she wanted to, Rose could probably communicate with a colony of ants. The dog licked her face and started sniffing around, wandering a bit but finally following them to their rooms.

"Did he eat and sleep on the flight, Jim?" Rose asked.

"Yes."

"Then I'd like to take him to the greenhouse, if that's okay with you." Her eyes darted to Epsilon. "For rejuvenation."

"I'll go with you," Epsilon said. "But first, the dining room."

A rejuvenated Nomad? Mitchum suddenly understood the meaning of the phrase, *My heart sings.* Corny, perhaps, but true.

+++

The greenhouse occupied one of the largest structures, Dome 11, and every time Rose walked in here the explosion of varied scents nearly overpowered her. The smells of her earlier life on Xanthe, the fragrances of the contained world of Area 51, and the distinctive odors of Earth. This dome would become home to their agricultural wizard, Dax, and his family.

She, Epsilon, and Nomad made their way up one long row of plants, some already producing fruit, and at the far end reached long rows of dark soil awaiting Dax's transplants, his magic.

In the middle of all that soil was a single row of odd plants. Rose thought they resembled this planet's cacti in shape—but without thorns. They were a bluish green, only about four-feet tall, and their various offshoots—arms—seemed infinitely graceful. She remembered seeing a field of these when she was a kid and had asked her mother what they were.

Epsilon shared that *when he was just a youngster, centuries ago, we called them Joys.* "*My mother gave me a piece of one to savor when I was ill and it added several years to my life, triggered my body's healing ability, and increased my physical energy to the point where I could run twenty miles without tiring.*"

"I hope he likes the taste," she said.

Epsilon sliced off the upper tip of the longest arm and passed it to her. "I think he will. Especially if we join him." He cut off two more pieces, handed her one, kept the other for himself. Then they both sat down next to the dog, whose tail thumped the ground in anticipation.

Rose held out a piece for Nomad and spoke to him mind to mind. *We're going to join you in this feast, Nomad. I don't know if you and Jim ever watched Star Trek, but if you did, you'll remember Spock.*

To her complete shock, Nomad replied telepathically, *Spock. Sure. Live long and prosper.*

Epsilon heard it, too, and laughed with delight. Then he bit into his Joy and Rose bit into her piece and held out the chunk for Nomad. He sniffed at it, took it delicately between his teeth. He dropped to the ground, paws crossed in front of him, and set the piece of Joy on the top paw. He licked it, nibbled at it, and glanced at each of them. Both Epsilon and Rose chewed their pieces of Joy, then Nomad gobbled the remaining piece, emitted a sigh, and shut his eyes.

Is he okay? Rose mouthed to Epsilon.

And after a minute or two, the Stell^r leader did a very human thing: he flashed a thumbs up. He gestured at the dog's snout, where the gray had already begun receding. As they stared in wonder, the fading continued over his entire face and back across the top of his head. Even the few areas of gray in his coat now faded.

"So fast," Rose whispered.

"First dog ever to eat a piece of Joy."

Nomad suddenly rolled onto his side, then onto his back and wiggled around, as if the warmth felt good. Then he suddenly leaped up, barked at them both, and took off up the long row.

Rose and Epsilon glanced at each other, laughed, and hurried after him. "I don't remember it working this fast on me," she said.

"You aren't a dog!"

"Humans would be killing each other to get their hands on Joy, Epsilon. "

"Nearly nine billion people on this planet before the Stell^rs get here. They don't need decades added to their lives. This is strictly among the three of us—you, me, Nomad."

+++

Katherine and Dmitri arrived in the Sahara compound in a private jet they shared with 25 renowned art critics, curators, collectors. They landed at precisely 8:10 a.m. local time. Through the window, Katherine saw two large solar-powered vans waiting to pick them up and transport them to wherever the auction would be held. She suspected their first stop would be security.

No tactical missiles this time, no poison. Their weapons were simple. Cigarettes and a gold cigarette lighter with just enough flammable liquid in it to turn this entire disgusting alien compound to ashes. They had passed successfully through two airport security systems. That didn't mean they would get past the Stell^r technology or psychic power or whatever the hell these aliens possessed. If it came to the worst scenario, were they willing to die for this mission?

Nope, no way.

And that was why they would win.

As they rode down the escalator from the plane, she struggled to not look awed and absolutely gobsmacked. But my G-d, the incredible wonder of these magnificent geodesic domes, the deeply verdant green where once not so long ago there was only white, blowing sand. The wind still blew, hurling sand from an untouched Sahara desert landscape.

When they reached the vans, Dmitri touched the small of her back, nudging her toward the second van. She wasn't sure why until she saw that passengers boarding the first van were scanned with some sort of light and those getting on the second van were not. Why?

Then she saw why. The Stell^r in charge outside of the second van was distracted by something going on inside of it. He was leaning inside and looked like he was speaking to several people.

What kind of light were they using? What could it detect? See? Sense? Was the light conscious? It wouldn't surprise her. At this point, not much would.

She wondered what Colleen McCullough, her favorite Australian author, might have said about all this. Her book *The Thorn Birds,* published in 1977, more than half a century ago, referred to an Australian legend about a bird that sang only once in its entire life. She remembered reading about it in the front of the book when her grandmother had given it to her on one of her teen birthdays. She had memorized those words then and still recalled them now, even though she couldn't remember her exact age when she'd first read it.

From the moment this bird left its nest, it searched for a thorn tree, and didn't rest until it found one. "Then, singing among the savage branches, it impales itself upon the longest, sharpest spine. And, dying, it rises above its own agony to out-carol the lark and the nightingale. One superlative song, existence the price. But the whole world stills to listen, and the lord in heaven smiles. For the best is only bought at the cost of great pain.... Or so says the legend."

If she and Dmitri were successful, would the Stell^rs sing like the thorn bird?

They settled in the second van without having been scanned by any light. A current of excitement ran through the van as the critics, collectors, and the very rich speculated about the art they would see. The art that might be auctioned. Who might buy it.

She watched two more planes heading in for landing and wondered how many from the Sindikat would show up. She'd alerted everyone, of course, and offered suggestions for disguises and so on, but that didn't mean any of them had committed to this whole thing. After all, even though some of the world's billionaires still had nine zeros in their net worth, several of them—including her—had lost a zero.

But even that group remained enormously wealthy compared to the rest of the population on the planet, at least for now. And that wealth enabled them to remain in hiding, on the lam, and still enjoy their lives. Yet, these people were the very ones who would be most likely to hunger for a piece of Stell^r art. They would be here somewhere, she felt certain of that much.

The van, self-propelled, took a circuitous route around the compound, as if to emphasize their accomplishments here, then finally pulled up in front of a structure labeled Dome 4.

A woman stood guard at the entrance, her head and face hidden by a scarf that protected her against the blowing sand, and as each traveler approached, she touched some part of their bodies. Head, shoulder, arm, hand, it varied. And if they passed the muster of whatever this told her, she gestured for the individual to enter.

Katherine passed the muster.

Dmitri did not.

A gaping hole opened in the pit of her stomach. She glanced back and saw him step to one side, out of the line and next to the woman. Then he was approached by two human men and a Stell^r. *Damn.* They knew.

But how?

Dmitri carried only the cigarettes, the real thing, an old pack of Marlboros that were probably 30 years old. She had lit one of them weeks back just to make sure the tobacco and paper would burn. They did. Brightly. Fast with the paper, slower with the tobacco. Her grandmother, the same one who had gifted her with *Thorn Birds,* had been a smoker well into her eighties. It hadn't killed her. The changing climate in Australia had.

Katherine moved along with the others into the belly of this mammoth beast and found a chair among the 500 that were set up. A chair within six rows of the front, where the curator would unveil the great Stell^r piece of art—or several pieces, they didn't really know—that would be auctioned. She placed her bag on the chair next to her, saving Dmitri's seat just in case he was released for lack of evidence. Well, that and it also kept people out of her personal space.

For a while, visitors kept filing in, taking seats. And then she saw Dmitri and waved him over, grateful that she wasn't the only human in the group who was waving. He looked scared, bewildered, but saw her and hurried over. He sank into the chair she'd saved for him, pressed his hands between his knees.

"That was...weird."

"A Stell^r?"

He nodded.

"She...found...the Marlboros and...and whipped one out and held it between her long fingers and...pretended to smoke it and...and...in that moment, she looked like Greta Garbo. Or something." He turned his head toward Katherine. "Garbo smoked, right?"

How the hell would she know? She watched mostly old TV shows from the Sixties and Seventies, not movies from the 1930s. "Beats me. All I know is she had a husky, sexy voice. Look, we can get outta here. The jet is still outside, we can go back there."

"No. We need to do this. It's why we risked it. Why we're here."

He spoke as if she had a short-term memory problem. "I have zero desire to end up on their f-ing moon base." She glanced at him. "Did they confiscate the cigs?"

"Just the one she took. Got eighteen of them left. Enough to reduce this atrocity to an ashen memory."

"Hey, that's kinda poetic, Dmitri."

"Very funny."

They whispered back and forth like this for the next ten or fifteen minutes, as more art connoisseurs arrived and seated. Then a middle-aged man wearing round spectacles and casual clothes and holding a gavel stood in front of them. He tapped the gavel three times.

"Good morning. I'm Aaron, your curator. This auction is for a philanthropic cause. The money will be used to help the Earth's poverty-stricken countries and people. I'm honored to conduct the bidding on one or more of the most mind-blowing pieces of art I've ever had the pleasure of seeing. Stell^r art. Alien art. The Artist, Zee, will be on one of the starships that land next month."

Then, with great fanfare, he uncovered one of the paintings. Exclamations of awe and astonishment hummed through the crowd. "This beauty is called 'A Scene from Xanthe,' and is holographically rendered."

Katherine, like many others in the room, found she couldn't look at it too long; the explosion of lights and colors hurt her eyes. "spectacular," Dmitri whispered. "Earth has *nothing* like this. *Anywhere*. We need to bid on this, Katherine. And once we have it in our possession, we burn down this entire place."

"Zee's identical twin, Zelda, specializes in animals found on Xanthe, like this magnificent Glitterwing," Aaron went on, and removed the covering from a second, smaller painting. "The Glitterwing is one of the most unusual birds on Xanthe."

Unusual, magnificent, no adjective adequately described this piece of art. It literally was out of this world, art so stunning it didn't belong in any museum. It belonged in her living room, where she could feast her eyes on this at any minute of the day or night and instantly be transported. Apparently everyone else in the room experienced the same awe that she did.

"We will start with the Glitterwing," curator Aaron said.

Hands shot into the air. Someone—a man she couldn't see but whose voice she recognized as that of an Asian member of the Sindikat—called out, "What're the opening bids?"

"A billion US each or 200 Bitcoin," Aaron replied.

"A billion one," said the Asian man. "For the Glitterwing."

Bo Wang, that was his name, she remembered. A billionaire real estate developer.

"Should we go in on it together?" Dmitri asked.

"Yes."

"Any other offers?" Aaron asked.

Dmitri raised his hand. "A billion one five."

It went on like this for several minutes, with people in the audience watching her and Dmitri, bidding against Bo Wang and then against an American member of the Sindikat, Carl Peters. He had made his fortune developing, buying, and selling tech companies and had attended only one conference at her place in Amsterdam. She suspected his net worth still boasted nine zeros with double numbers in front of it. She was sure of it when he bid a billion and a half.

"How high can we go?" Dmitri whispered.

"I'm barely a billionaire these days. But let's go up one more notch."

"A billion five," Aaron announced. "Going, going..."

Dmitri shouted, "A billion six!"

"Pass me the cigarettes," she whispered.

He did so, discreetly, and she slipped them into her handbag.

"A billion six," Aaron announced. "...going...going...Anyone topping that bid for the magnificent Glitterwing?" He glanced around, but no more bids came from either Wang or Peters. "Sold to the gentleman in the fifth row. A billion six US dollars or 320 Bitcoin. We'll take a break before the bidding on Scenes from Xanthe and you, sir..." He gestured at Dmitri. "...you will come up after the auction with your information and payment."

"I'm going to the restroom," Katherine whispered. "When they evacuate the building because of smoke, Dmitri, you need to run up and grab that painting. I'll make sure I'm out front in a vehicle, and that the pilot knows we'll need to take off immediately. I'll go set the fire and...you have to do your part."

He gave her a dirty look. "You owe me, Katherine."

"I certainly do."

As other people got up, so did she, and headed for the door to the corridor, where she'd seen the sign earlier for the restrooms.

+++

Epsilon, Rose, Sofiya, Mitchum, Ken, and two of the Council members had watched the proceedings on the security cams. Nomad watched and nibbled at the bowl of food Mitchum had put down for him. His appetite hadn't been this voracious for months. Joy was working.

When the auction took a break, Rose nodded at Sofiya. "Jim, we're going to keep an eye on the redhead. She's planning something."

"She probably is always planning something," Mitchum remarked.

"Epsilon?" Rose looked at him.

"You two go, we'll watch things from here."

"Epsilon, I think it's time to beam the Asian and the American Sindikat members out of here," said Mitchum.

Epsilon nodded. "I was thinking the same thing. What about the redhead's buddy?"

"Not yet. Let's see what he'll do. But be ready."

Epsilon said, "Gamma, as soon as the men are out of their seats and walking to the door, give the signal. And keep her partner in sight."

"The Stell^rs on the closest craft hovering above us are on alert. Moon base with Zhukov and Shin and the rest of the group?"

"Yes. A private accommodation initially. Stay in contact, ladies."

She and Sofiya took the back escalator to the first floor. It brought them close to the hall where restrooms were located. Rose glanced at her phone, bringing up the security cam images from the hallway. She spotted Katherine the redhead fourth in line to enter. Perfect. "I'll cut in line behind her," Rose said. "Get in the back of the line and start telling the women to clear out. You're in a security uniform, so I don't think they'll ignore you."

"Excellent. I'm going to enjoy this."

She hurried into the hall. Rose followed her moments later. By then, Katherine was third in line.

+++

Mitchum felt a deep, undeniable satisfaction as Wang, pushing his way to get to the front door, suddenly vanished. No column of light this time, no hoopla, no demonstration. One moment he was there, the next moment he was gone. The American apparently realized something had happened and started elbowing his way toward the front door, looking around desperately, his expression increasingly more panicked.

Once Carl Peters made it into the corridor with everyone else, the crowd thinned out as people went in different directions. Peters spotted someone he knew and hurried over to the man. Mitchum recognized him: Henri Leveque, a European member of Zhukov's Sindikat. The two men spoke urgently, with multiple hand gestures, then Leveque slipped his hand into the pocket of his windbreaker and brought out an object that he pressed into the American 's hand. Mitchum couldn't see what it was.

On his handheld device, he rewound the scene and slowed it to a snail's crawl. At the moment Leveque gave Peters the object, Mitchum paused the image, enlarged it. "Hey, Epsilon, look at this."

Epsilon hurried over and stood behind Mitchum's chair. "Cigarettes and a lighter," Epsilon said. "Katherine's sidekick also had cigarettes. Didn't realize humans were still such avid smokers."

No, it wasn't that, Mitchum realized. Cigarettes burned. Years back, people would smoke in bed, fall asleep and the lit cigarette would set the bed sheets on fire. Then the room. And, ultimately, the house. "Uh, Epsilon, do you have any kind of sprinkler system in these domes?"

For the first time since they'd met, Epsilon looked mystified. "Why would that be necessary? We have a type of sprinkler in the sands that helped the desert turn green, we have a river, streams, ponds... We have alarms for any trouble, of course, but..."

"Damn. I think they're planning on setting this dome on fire. And maybe the others, too."

"But these domes aren't flammable."

"Everything inside them is."

And for the first time that he'd ever witnessed, Epsilon looked horrified, and Mitchum understood that fire in this sense had never occurred to him. But why should it? He wasn't human and his intimate knowledge of humanity was relatively brief. Mitchum leapt to his feet.

"Epsilon, can you get those two in here now? With us? No, all three of them. Yeah, take all three of them? Wang, Peters, Leveque."

"Done," Gamma said, and suddenly the three men appeared in the control room with them—Wang on his knees, Peters on his ass, Leveque standing shakily, then crumbling to the floor.

"What the..." muttered Carl Peters, turning slow on his butt, struggling to take in everything.

Wang let loose with a string of Chinese that roughly translated as, *We're screwed...*

Leveque rolled over, sat up and spun around to face Mitchum and Epsilon. He had a French accent. "We're lackeys. Go after Katherine Martin. She's here, a redhead who has had plenty of plastic surgery so you may not recognize her. She has been directing this Sindikat since Zhukov was taken away. *She* planned this. Her and Dmitri, that short, shrimpy Russian guy she was with. *Go. After. Them.*"

Ken had snapped to full attention the instant the three men landed in the room, and now he stepped out in front of Mitchum. "You don't speak to the President of the United States like that." His voice was tight, commanding, and his weapon was pointed in their direction.

Mitchum got up and, to Ken's obvious horror, approached the three men. "Sir, President Mitchum..." Ken moved so that he stood between Mitchum and the men.

"It's fine, Ken."

"Wait, sir, please." Ken marched over to them and demanded, "Turn over the lighter and the cigarettes. Now."

Peters reluctantly raised his arms. "In my pocket."

"Remove it," Mitchum snapped, stepping alongside Ken, whose weapon was an inch from the man's forehead. "And if he tries to pull anything, Ken, shoot him."

Peters visibly trembled now. "Okay, okay. I'm reaching into my pocket for the lighter and cigarettes."

He did so slowly, then extended his palm. Mitchum scooped the items out of his hand and looked at Epsilon. "Get these bastards out of my sight."

"Wait..." shrieked Wang. "You can't..."

Then all three men were gone.

+++

Rose followed Katherine into the restroom. One stall. One sink. That was it.

She turned the lock on the door.

Katherine didn't realize yet that she wasn't alone so when Rose saw her reach inside her handbag, she lunged and snapped it away from her. Katherine spun around. "What do you think you're..."

"Hello, Katherine," said Rose, then unceremoniously turned her purse upside down and shook it. The contents rained to the floor and among them was a lighter and a pack of cigarettes. "My, my, look here." She flung her long, bony arm towards the floor.

Katherine's frightened eyes darted to Rose's face, then she threw herself on the floor and grabbed the lighter. Rose spun, her right leg darting out, her foot connecting hard with Katherine's hand. The lighter flew across the bathroom and the pack of cigarettes slid across the floor.

"My hand, damn you, you broke my fingers, my wrist, you..."

"Silence," Rose snapped and strode over to the lighter and cigarettes and scooped them up. Then she returned to Katherine, still groaning on the floor. Rose crouched in front of her, brought her hand within inches of Katherine's face, and flicked the lighter on. The flame danced in front of her, and she scooted back, away from it. "So what is it with this lighter, Katherine? Huh?" She popped off the bottom of the gold lighter, held it up slightly. "Ah, This switch. Interesting. What happens if I turn this switch, Katherine?"

"Don't...please do-don't...d-do th-that."

Using just her long index finger, Rose flicked the switch as she held the lighter over Katherine's legs, and a seemingly endless stream of liquid poured over the fabric of her pants. Her shoes. "Smells stinky, as you humans say. Like something flammable, Katherine."

The flame went out. Rose brought the lighter close to her pants. Katherine scooted back again, tears coursing down her cheeks. "No," she whispered. "I'll burn."

Rose flicked the lighter on. "Burn like the witches at Salem, right? You know about that period in history?"

"I...I..."

Rose brought the flame to within an inch of the hem of her khaki pants. "How fast will you burn, Katherine? Seconds? Minutes? What about that magnificent painting you and Dmitri bid on? You going to let that burn, too?"

"I...I...You aliens invade our planet, our lives and...and we're just supposed to bow and kiss your blue behinds and welcome you to Earth? Ha. You...you...don't understand anything about how stuff works here. We, the powerful rich, are the rulers. We call the shots. We..."

Rose suddenly grabbed the hem of her pants and tore off a piece. Then she held the fabric to the lighter's flame, and fire erupted instantly, burning fast and furiously, and she dropped it to the floor. Katherine screamed, "Help me, someone help me! She's a crazy alien bitch!"

Pounding on the door now. Shouting out there. Rose unlocked the door. Epsilon, Mitchum, Ken, Whitley, Gamma, even Nomad stood there. Rose held up the lighter, pack of cigarettes, and gestured at the ashes of the burned fabric. "That's her plan."

Katherine scrambled to her feet and launched herself at Rose. Nomad moved before any of the humans or Stell^rs and slammed into Katherine's chest with such force that she stumbled back, arms pinwheeling for balance, and crashed into the wall. Rose rushed toward the snarling dog, threw her arms around him, and pulled him back. "It's okay, Nomad, it's okay. She gets the message. Thank you."

She felt his body relax, then he turned his head and covered her face in warm, wet, sloppy kisses.

Rose sat down on the floor, one arm still around Nomad. A myriad of emotions rushed through her—anger, disbelief, relief—and shock that she had been so deeply tempted to set fire to that fabric while it was still part of the clothing Katherine wore. She needed to take a closer look at what she had almost done but not right this second.

"It's time for Katherine to join her buddy Zhukov on the moon," Mitchum said.

"Agreed, Jim." Epsilon glanced at Gamma.

Rose kept her arm around Nomad, holding him tightly against her so the light beam didn't touch either of them. And just that fast, Katherine Martin was gone and transported to the shuttle craft hovering above, and very soon Zhukov and his Sindikat on the far side of the moon would realize they weren't going to win.

It was finally over.

Chapter 24

June 6, 2036

As soon as Zhukov saw all the people who had been walking into the dining room of the lunar base, he knew that he and his Sindikat were here for good. Even if some members remained hidden for now, the Stell^rs would find them eventually. The base would become a prison for the rebellious leaders of certain nuclear countries and for those delusional human billionaires who had sought to annihilate them.

He went to Katherine Martin first, Katherine in her torn khaki pants, weeping on the floor of the dining room, rubbing her fists against her eyes like a small, confused child. He wasn't sure how to comfort her, or if he should even try. But he realized he had to do something; everyone in the area—Stell^rs, humans—watched them. He dropped to his knees and put an arm around her shoulders.

"You did your best, Katherine."

She raised her head, stared at him as if he were a stranger, then blinked. "My *best?*" She exploded with laughter and pushed him away from her. "These blue aliens *won,* Alexander. Our planet is now theirs. You acted like a big fool and put the entire Sindikat at risk and now..." She threw open her arms. "Here we are. On the moon, the actual moon!" Then she punched him in the mouth with her fist and did it with so much hatred that the blow slammed him back and they both hit the floor.

No one intervened.

No one jerked her to her feet.

No one hurried over to him.

Presidents Shin and Khan just sat there and watched.

The other members of the Sindikat said nothing.

Zhukov knew he was stuck here for the rest of his miserable life and got up from the floor. His nose and mouth bled from the blow as he made his way back to the table where he'd been sitting. Carl Peters marched over to him and leaned in so closely Zhukov could smell the stink of his breath. "Katherine did more for the cause than you did, Alexander. Some of us hoped to implement real change. But you were interested only in power." Then he spat at Zhukov and shuffled away.

"Oh well," Khan said. "It could be worse."

"Yeah?" Zhukov snapped. "How? What could possibly be worse than all this?"

"They could have beamed us just to the lunar surface and right now, our bodies would be out there, frozen like next week's meals. Instead, we can try to thrive here."

"You're delusional."

"No, *you* are the one who is delusional," Khan told him and also walked away, back to the serving line for more vegan food.

A Stell^ar, a woman, came over to him and handed him a wet cloth. "Press against your nose and mouth, sir, to stop the bleeding and heal the injury."

He did what she suggested, then asked, "I'd like to see the landing when it happens."

"Of course. It will be projected throughout the base."

"When?"

"On June 6."

"Just one spacecraft?"

She smiled in that Stell^r way, her mouth barely moving, but her eyes lighting up. "Several hundred over the next month, that's my understanding."

"In the Sahara compound?"

"Yes, sir."

Several hundred.

And in that arrival, he and his Sindikat, the world's wealthiest most powerful people, would be relegated to history as mere collateral damage.

+++

At dawn on June 6, 2036, the skies across Earth filled with enormous spaceships.

Mitchum watched from the outside roof balcony of Dome 11. He watched with Laurie, Helen and her husband, Whitley, Ken, Nomad, Rose, Epsilon, and all the other Council members. Screens were on in the background as the ubiquitous press captured every second, every possible emotion of people from every country, in cities and towns, in rural villages, on back roads to nowhere across the entire planet.

Pockets of unrest still prevailed, but not like it had in the beginning. Humanity was already greatly benefiting from these aliens—technology, longevity, power sources, and housing. Even the climate had begun to respond with a slower glacial melt, a correction in the salinity of the oceans, a shift in the Gulf Stream that took hurricanes out into the Atlantic to churn harmlessly until they died, and of course, the flourishing of farmlands and orchards that kept the world fed. Prosperity now seemed to be nearly universal, war was now only a dark history, and disputes were usually settled amicably. And all of this, Mitchum thought, had been taking place, slowly and progressively since that worldwide announcement at the UN five years ago. And the first group out of the 100 million Stell^rs was only now arriving.

Mitchum shaded his eyes with his hands and watched these amazing starships above him slowly descending from high above. Laurie, standing to his right, reached for his hand and squeezed it. "If anyone else had been President these last years, it would have been *Independence Day* all over again, Jim. You opened the door to a new era of prosperity and peace on Earth."

Had he? Mitchum really didn't know. In retrospect, Area 51 and meeting Rose had changed everything he thought he'd known about what was true and real. And that was the foundation from which he'd made his decisions, and on which he'd based his hopes. And that was still true.

When his term was officially up at the end of the year, Helen would run and was likely to win in November. He would help make sure of that reality. He had no idea what he would do or pursue once he was out of office. Epsilon had offered him a seat on what would become a Human/Stell^r Council and although it interested him, so did traveling and just catching up on normal life, whatever that might be now.

Not long after the spaceships had appeared in the skies across Earth worldwide, the first one landed in the Sahara. Mitchum could barely absorb and make sense of what he saw. The ship looked to be 100 times the size of the largest ocean liners. Epsilon had told him each starship held 10,000 Stell^rs, and he'd seen the images, of course, of the pods in the sleeping area. He'd seen the images of lonely Dax, the agricultural whiz kid, sitting among the pods that held his partner and daughters.

Then the massive door of the Celestial Dawn opened and that Stell^r Dax came down the ramp with a woman Mitchum assumed was his partner and two young girls he believed were their two daughters. Mitchum's heart seemed to stop. The girls were little Stell^r beauties, bopping along with enthusiasm, pointing at everything, laughing, joyful. The family's love for one another was so apparent it deepened his awe. He felt so overwhelmed by the reality of the moment, he wasn't sure of much of anything else.

Moments after the Celestial Dawn landed and Dax and his family exited, other starships started to land. Mitchum and Epsilon, with Rose between them and Nomad trotting alongside, headed out to greet Dax and his partner and daughters. Mitchum felt a deep satisfaction that the US Government, and for that matter anyone else, could no longer deny that the aliens had landed. That they were here.

And oh, guess what?

The aliens were friendly.

They were truly good beings.

And already they were transforming Earth and providing the human race with a brighter future for generations to come. In his heart, Mitchum believed this had been the plan all along. Perhaps it had been written somewhere in the stars or in some secret book of destiny that humanity would be saved from its own self-destruction by ancient, cosmic beings.

The Stell^rs had done all that and much more.

The End

Epilogue

2045

The Zorgons realized that Xanthe was now fully evacuated, and they desperately needed to know where the Stell^r ships were headed.

Nucleaus, as head of the formidable Zorgon military fleet, ordered that their focus would be an initial attack on the Stell^rs' remote space stations. The plan was to capture the commanders of those stations and learn where the rest of the population had relocated. And they would do whatever it took to make them talk.

It would take them about a year to get to those stations, and throughout that journey, they would be monitoring the galaxies with their newest long-range eavesdropping technology. They would be listening...for changes. For hints. For new voices.

One way or another, the Zorgons, he thought, would eventually find them. It was the heart of his personal destiny to eradicate the Stell^r existence. However long it would take, nothing would stand in their way.

UFO quotes by U.S. Presidents since 1961

"In the councils of government, we must guard against the acquisition of unwarranted influence, whether sought or unsought, by the military-industrial complex. The potential for the disastrous rise of misplaced power exists and will persist."

Dwight D. Eisenhower (34th President of the United States)

***

"The U.S. Air Force assures me that UFO's pose no threat to national security."

John F. Kennedy (35th President of the United States)

***

"I am not at liberty to discuss the governments knowledge of extraterrestrial UFO's at this time. I am personally still being briefed on the subject."

Richard Nixon (37th President of the United States)

***

"I believe the American people are entitled to a more thorough explanation than has been given them by the Air Force. I think we owe it to the people to establish credibility regarding UFO's, and to produce the greatest possible enlightenment on the subject."

Gerald Ford (38th President of the United States)

***

"One things for sure, I'll never make fun of people who say they've seen unidentified objects in the sky. I've seen one myself."

Jimmy Carter (39th President of the United States)

***

"I was in a plane last week when I looked out the window and saw this white light. It was zigzagging around. I went up to the pilot and said, 'Have you ever seen anything like that?' He was shocked and said, 'Nope.' And I said to him:

'Let's follow it!' We followed it for several minutes. It was a bright white light. We followed it to Bakersfield, and all of a sudden to our utter amazement, it went straight up into the heavens."

Ronald Reagan (40th President of the United States)

***

"I know some. I know a fair amount."

George H.W. Bush (41st President of the United States)

***

"If we were visited someday, I wouldn't be surprised. I just hope that it's not like 'Independence Day', that is a conflict."

Bill Clinton (42nd President of the United States)

***

Jimmy Kimmel in 2017 asked George W. Bush if he looked into UFO's or if he would share that information with the public. Bush replied: "I'm not telling you nothing."

George W. Bush (43rd President of the United States)

***

"What is true, and I'm actually being serious here, is that there are...there's footage and records of objects in the skies that we don't know exactly what they are. We can't explain how they moved, their trajectory. They did not have an easily explainable pattern."

Barack Obama (44th President of the United States)

The Stell^rs story will be continuing in Earth Year 2025

About the Author

Early career background on the Author

In the summer of 1982, Jeff was selected as a Presidential Management Intern and was recruited by the U.S. Air Force where he held a top secret clearance. He worked on special projects at several military installations across the country. In 1983, he was appointed to an assignment in the Reagan White House. After that, he accepted a position in the Pentagon for the U.S. Department of Defense. He left government service in 1988 and went to work in the private sector.

Jeff has always been interested in the subjects of Ufology, extraterrestrials, space exploration, time travel, and the muti-dimensional universe as it impacts the human experience and consciousness.

The Stell^rs is his first science fiction book that is meant to open the eyes of people who have not delved too deeply into the idea of extraterrestrials and their interactions with humans. It is also for those who strongly believe this to be true and contemplate when this eventual big reveal will take place and how it actually may happen.

Jeff resides in Florida, the home of the Kennedy Space Center (KSC). The combined total number of launches from Cape Kennedy and KSC exceeds 4000 since 1950.

Jeff watched his first launch on February 20,1962 with John Glenn aboard the Friendship 7 spacecraft.

He has been looking up at the stars ever since.

www.ingramcontent.com/pod-product-compliance
Lightning Source LLC
Chambersburg PA
CBHW020908200626
46814CB00001BA/239